Praise for Leslie Kirby DeVooght

An interior designer. A swoony romance writer. A fun list of challenges. DeVooght has mixed all the key ingredients of this story into a tasty southern charmer sure to keep readers smiling and coming back for more.

Becca Kinzer, Author of First Love, Second Draft

Leslie DeVooght's captivating characters fill Stealing Magnolias with humor, loving relationships, faith, and even grief. Gentle southern charm and unpredictable twists had me gasping one minute and laughing out loud the next. And then there were secrets. The true to life setting and relationship struggles kept me reading to the breathtaking epilogue. It's an unputdownable book.

Angel Moore, Author of Their Family Arrangement

A charming southern romance filled with heart, surprises, and lots of sweet tea. I absolutely loved Stealing Magnolias! I thought I had the plot figured out in the beginning, but by Chapter 4, Leslie took me in a completely new—and delightfully unexpected—direction. The story is fresh and fun, with a unique plot that kept me turning pages late into the night.The setting in the Georgia Low Country is beautifully drawn, and the characters—especially the swoon-worthy leading men—were both realistic and unforgettable. But what really stood out to me was how Leslie wove her faith into the story in such a meaningful, authentic way. It was impactful without ever feeling preachy.

Heather Tabers, Author of *Their Burden to Bear*

Stealing Magnolias is a sweet story that reminds us of our unique gifts and different calls to service. It was a refreshing and fun read that made me grateful for talented writers and a home in the South!

Lara C. Patangan, Author of *Simple Mercies*

A sweet southern romance perfect for summer reading!

Lindsey P. Brackett, Award winning author of *Still Waters*

Dripping with southern charm, Stealing Magnolias is a fun romance with a good message about finding and using your gifts for God, and not trying to mold yourself to others' expectations.

Pamela Baker, Author of *Message Sent through Time*

A Girl's Guide to Having it All

Also by Leslie

<u>Magnolia Bluff Series</u>
Stealing Magnolias
How To Sparkle

<u>Love Inspired</u>
Taking a Second Shot

A Girl's Guide to Having it All

Leslie Kirby DeVooght

Lanier Price
PUBLISHING

Dedication

For Libby. When I started this story, I knew I wanted Carleigh to be an ENTJ like you, but goodness, that is where the similarities end. I love that you know Jesus so well and love God's word. You are an inspiration to me and so many others. Being your mom fills me with an almost sinful amount of pride. Never stop being who you are for anyone. You are an absolutely beautiful child of God.

Prologue

Spencer

Sharing a secret with your best friend should be second nature . . . unless that secret is that you want to kiss her. Even the chilly mountain air that had settled overnight in the Shenandoah Valley couldn't stop me from sweating. At least I could blame it on the hike that Carleigh insisted we take to the gazebo at the top of a hill behind Washington and Lee University. Of course I didn't complain when she clasped my hand and tugged me along the trail. Nope, I loved the warmth of her palm pressed to mine. Besides our dance lessons and an occasional hug, physical contact wasn't a part of our relationship, but surprises were.

Although until this moment, I'd never considered how the recipient dictated whether a surprise was a positive revelation or a blitzkrieg.

My strategy had been to confess my feelings after our law school graduation ceremony. I'd chosen the lawn of the colonnade under a starry sky as the perfect romantic battlefield. But Carleigh diverted my advance, insisting we partake in the all-night class party, and instead of merely making an appearance, we stayed until the end.

Carleigh squeezed my hand as we crossed the dew-covered field. "What a night! Thanks for indulging me. I know crowds aren't your thing." She beamed, her dark brown eyes connecting with mine for a moment before she returned her focus to our destination.

But it was long enough to make my senses buzz and my brain loopy with anticipation. While my liquid courage had worn off, the gaze of a beautiful woman combined with sleep deprivation led to the same result. I might be ready to take a risk, throw caution to the wind, take a leap of faith, but I couldn't just plant a kiss on her lips. Especially since she'd almost lost her friend Lawson after they'd kissed. I needed to approach with caution.

Clamping my mouth shut, I inhaled through my nose and held my breath until my pulse regulated. "It wasn't a bad time, but I'm glad you suggested a sunrise hike. I want to talk to you about something." At least I'd have the backdrop of the sun rising over the mountains for my confession that I'd fallen for her and maybe our first kiss.

"Really? Me too!" She grabbed my other hand. "I have some amazing news!"

Then, in a very un-Carleigh way, she bounced on her toes, releasing my hands and lifting her arms in the air as she twirled to the gazebo.

Taken aback, I stared after her. What was her news?

"Spencer, come on." She patted the spot beside her.

"Right." I crossed the distance. "Sorry, you're just very—" Maybe this wasn't the best time to tease her.

Carleigh narrowed her eyes. "What's that grin for? What am I very?"

"Bubbly." I laughed as I sat beside her, bumping my elbow against hers.

"That's the meanest thing you've ever said to me." She crossed her arms over her chest in mock offense, but after a second, she turned and smiled. "Normally, I'd make you pay with at least an hour of silence, but not today." The first rays of the sun made the copper highlights glimmer amongst the waves of her dark auburn hair.

My fingers itched to thread their way through her long locks and draw her closer. "You go first." As all the moisture in my mouth evaporated, I clasped my hands in my lap and observed how the flesh around my knuckles whitened.

"You're the best. After college, I didn't think I'd find another friend like Lawson. I don't know how I scored two amazing guy friends. It's too bad Lawson insists on living all the way in Georgia. I'm so glad I'll be working in the same city as you, aanndd . . ." Carleigh drew out the one-syllable word.

We'd both taken jobs in DC and found the perfect apartments, but we'd been waiting to see if we got the units. I shot my gaze to her. "No way."

Nodding wildly, her smile stretched across her face. "Yes, we got the apartments on the hill. We'll be living across the hall from each other. Just like on *Friends*."

Friends . . . friends . . . friends.

Carleigh was so happy, and to see her smile was worth the detour in our relationship.

I gathered her into a hug. "Fantastic."

I just hoped we'd be more on the timeline of Monica and Chandler and not Ross and Rachel. But at least they all ended up together in the end.

Chapter 1

Ten years later . . .

Carleigh

Queen Esther stayed one step ahead of me as we hurried down the hall, my brain filtering through the most efficient way to execute the morning routine with far less time than I'd allotted. After I slipped on my glasses and spit out what I could only assume was cat hair, I reached for the doorknob, but the diva kitty blocked my path with a formidable glare. She shifted her gaze to the kitchen, making it clear she expected her breakfast before I got the fuel I needed to start the day.

"Yes ma'am." I curtsied quickly before I hustled into the kitchen. To be fair, I should've thanked her for swatting my face to wake me.

I snatched the gourmet cat food from the refrigerator, measured her breakfast into a bowl, and shoved it into the microwave. Once the hum of the machine filled the room, Queenie nuzzled my ankles, beckoning for a scratch. I relented because I always did. Maybe I spoiled her, but I loved giving her the royal treatment, and she loved me. She tolerated my best friend Spencer and rebuffed everyone else. Not even the meanest of the mean girls could scowl like Queenie. During high school, I'd suffered plenty of withering glares. But unlike entitled teen girls, my cat behaved the way she did for good reason.

After being abandoned during a winter storm, I rescued her and named her after my favorite Bible character. Queen Esther was smart, courageous, physically fit, and a deal closer. Seriously, she had it all, notwithstanding the whole harem thing. As a lobbyist myself, Esther's astute dealings in King Xerxes' court on behalf of her people inspired me.

Similarly, Queenie represented all the cats at the rescue where I volunteered. If my schedule allowed it, I would've adopted more. Some might describe my life as hectic, but I thrived on the pace. The tortoise may have won the race in the fable, but in real life, the hare's chance to win was ninety-nine point nine percent—basically a sure thing.

When the microwave chimed, Queenie sashayed to her feeding station. After I placed the bowl before her majesty, I grabbed Spencer's surprise package and tore off the morning motivation from the calendar. The messages were my little way of thanking my best friend for how he supported and encouraged me.

As I dashed across the hall and let myself into Spencer's apartment, I skimmed the quote. *A good plan violently executed now is better than a perfect plan executed next week. George Patton.* Hmmm, we'd have to discuss the mathematical accuracy of the sentiment when we had more time.

As a responsible adult with a successful career, I should've learned to brew a pot of coffee, but our routine had succeeded for nearly a decade. Every morning, Spencer left his apartment unlocked when he returned from his run—yes, he's one of *those* people. Not that I didn't exercise, I just preferred more competitive activities because winning is fun. Running always seemed pointless unless there was a race, but since the training was boring, I rarely won. So following the rules of logic and my personal life philosophy—if I couldn't win, I wasn't taking part and running was out.

The surprise game Spencer and I played was the only one where I didn't keep score, and only because he said he'd quit if I made it a competition. We'd been *not* keeping score since law school, but his surprises were always fantastic, so it still felt like winning.

He one hundred percent would love this gift.

As I crossed to the kitchen, Spencer's morning playlist seeped through the wall along with the sound of the shower. I filled my oversized mug with the elixir of life while I read a note attached to the top of a to-go box.

C– Food truck on the mall. Bacon, egg, and cheese burrito. Have a great day! –S

Spencer ran along the National Mall. He said it inspired his day, and I was happy to enjoy the fruits of his labor when a food truck pulled up. As I lifted the box, I heard the shower stop. "Good morning. I didn't get home until after midnight, and now I'm running late."

"Set your alarm for PM instead of AM again?" He asked, his voice muffled.

"You got it, and I don't have time to chat. Thanks for breakfast. You're the best."

"You're welcome. Dinner reservations are for eight at Rose's," Spencer called.

Breakfast in hand, I hurried to the open door. "I'll text if I'm running late."

"Carleigh, take the afternoon off," he shouted.

"Not a chance. Bye." Why would he think I could take an afternoon off? It's not like it was a national holiday, and if Congress was in session, I was on the job.

With no time to spare, I munched on the burrito and gulped my coffee while I dressed and listened to the news. Forty-five minutes later, wearing a cropped jacket over a light gray belted sheath dress with my hair in an elegant chignon, I waited for the barista to complete my order while I switched my sneakers for a pair of classic pumps. Obviously it wasn't a contest, but there was nothing like the charge of adrenaline from a win. I didn't need the second cup of coffee, but I'd earned the prize—a cinnamon latte. Not to mention, I'd ordered my associate, Jordan Gray, her favorite iced dirty chai as a surprise.

Once I had the drinks, I strode into the crowded elevator and confirmed the legislative schedule. One of our clients had an interest in a bill that was to be debated in committee, so we couldn't miss the opportunity to help the congressmen see the benefits of voting our way.

"Good morning." Jordan joined me as I stepped off the elevator.

I held out the cup carrier. "For you."

"Thanks. You're the best boss."

"I try. Now, do you have an update on the port funding?" I asked as we proceeded down the hall. We represented the Georgia Ports Authority and were advocating for harbor improvements at the Brunswick location.

"They might delay part of the funding." She held open my office door.

"That won't work. Let me know if you need me to step in." I lowered my bag beside my chair as my phone vibrated with an incoming text from my other best friend.

Lawson: Call me when you have a minute. I have big news on this big day.

With no time to ponder his odd message, I liked it and dropped my phone on the desk. When I had more time to talk, I'd call him. He never complained when I didn't respond immediately. We'd been friends too long to hold grudges. Plus, he wasn't the easiest to track down. As the manager of a country club, he was often on call twenty-four seven. Even if we didn't communicate for weeks, we simply picked up where we left off.

When my phone buzzed again, I gave it a quick glance.

> Spencer: Thanks for the massage gun. I've been thinking about ordering one.

When I'd spotted the tab for the company open on his phone, I immediately ordered the device. The discovery made me feel sort of like a WWII spy finding the secret code to save the world.

> Me: You're welcome. I may need to borrow it.

> Spencer: Anytime. It's supposed to rain Saturday. Do you want to reschedule tennis?

> Me: Sure. There's a new exhibit at the National Gallery.

> Spencer: If I agree to go, I get to pick the movie this weekend.

> Me: We'll discuss terms over dinner.

> Spencer: No fair. You'll use your powers on me.

I chuckled but didn't respond because Jordan shifted in her chair, catching my attention and making me very aware of my lack of professionalism. Regaining my composure, I pressed my lips into a polite smile and centered the yellow legal pad in front of me before lifting my pen.

Call it old-fashioned, but when we strategized, we left no electronic trace of our plans. Hey, this was DC, home of political operatives and scandals. Sometimes we tossed out wild ideas that may or may not be totally above board, but of course, we toned them down before we executed the plans.

Jordan tapped her pen on her notebook. "Before we get started, I hope it's okay if I take a longer lunch on Friday. We're closing on our condo."

"Are you really moving to Virginia?" I sipped my coffee.

"You make it sound like we're headed to the sticks."

"Well . . ."

"Carleigh, Courthouse is on the orange line. It's named after the metro stop."

"But you do have to take the metro."

"Not always." She shook her head. "We can bike or walk to Georgetown."

"Nice try, but don't forget who taught you the elements of a persuasive argument. Won't you miss the Hill?"

"Like I said, we can visit, but we don't have to. The neighborhood has great restaurants and shops. We found a historic condo in Colonial Village."

"Sounds like *your* dream home."

Jordan stared off wistfully. "Now, don't report me to the feminist police because I can barely admit it to myself, but I'd live anywhere with Cooper, and he loves the running and biking trails. None of this was in my ten-year plan. I'd planned to establish my career before getting involved in a serious relationship. But it just happened . . ."

I dropped my focus to the page, doodling a spiral as the rest of her words, which I'm sure were about falling in love and finding your soulmate, failed to register. Instead, my brain did something I rarely let it do. It started wandering, which always led to doubts.

Marriage was something I'd always believed would be part of my life. I would have it all. A successful career, a loving husband, two children—one boy and one girl—a chef's kitchen even though I don't cook, and of course a library with a rolling ladder. But what if it didn't happen? What if—

No, I don't do doubts. I do decisions based on facts and probabilities.

"Your secret is safe with me," I interrupted her confession because, really, we'd already spent enough time talking about neighborhoods.

"Sorry, we have so much to get to. I shouldn't be rambling on about my fiancé's hobbies."

Unfortunately, although my brain had agreed to drop the subject, a pebble of concern still landed in my stomach, rippling out with one last question. If I didn't make room in my schedule for dating, how was I going to find a husband?

But there was no reason for angst. The answer was simple—I had plenty of time.

With a couple of firm nods, I refocused my attention on Jordan. She studied me like she was trying to decipher why my head had bobbed, so I smoothed on a calm expression and said, "Buying your first home is exciting, and a long lunch Friday is fine. Now, we need to find enough votes to ensure Marsh Hammock Developers can continue work on the base housing project."

"I'm on it. The donation they made to the local rep's campaign should get his support. Also, Ashton and I are identifying more allies that'll need similar legislation."

"The representative from Marsh Hammock will know companies to contact."

Jordan jotted a note. "I'll reach out today."

"See who we can get up here for a dinner. With the right legislators, we might wrap this up before it goes to committee."

"Got it, and I'll share everything with Ashton so she'll be ready to step in while I'm on my honeymoon."

"Right. Is it really in just a couple of weeks?" I had the perfect gift for her. While it hadn't been on her registry, they'd appreciate the custom night sky print I'd ordered. The canvas was imprinted with the way the stars appeared on the night of their first date.

"Yes." A line of concern crossed her forehead. "Two weeks from Saturday."

"Don't worry. Your wedding is on my calendar, and more importantly, on Spencer's. I'd forget my own birthday if he didn't remind me." If it weren't for my best friend, I'd be a cat-obsessed workaholic.

"I totally get it. Until I caught bride brain, I didn't believe in it, but I'm staying on top of things and will be better than ever after a week on a tropical island."

"Great, now let's discuss the details for your meeting with Congressman Morales."

Once Jordan and I finished reviewing the base realignment plans and outlining our strategy to secure the current subs at Kings Bay, we headed to the legislative buildings. While she met with the Congressman, I did the rounds with a list of staffers. Legislators relied heavily on their staffers' advice, so I spent a fair amount of time learning the distinct personalities and how best to work with them.

After finishing my appointments, I stepped outside into the hot, humid June afternoon as my phone buzzed.

Lawson: Just being sure you didn't forget your best friend left you a message.

Me: <thumbs up emoji>

Shaking my head, I pocketed my phone. With tourists and government employees crowding the sidewalks, I made it a rule to never text and walk, and Lawson's calls were never brief. I'd call him when I could give him my undivided attention. Right now, I needed to focus on my lunch with the chief of staff for the junior senator from Georgia. She'd been elected by a slim margin and would be vulnerable in the next election, so I wanted to confirm her staff knew who to turn to for help. In politics, everyone understood that returning a favor was always part of the deal. If we helped Congresswoman Yates get reelected, she'd be one of our new friends and ready to help our clients.

As I strode down the sidewalk, my phone vibrated. If it was Lawson, I'd have to let it go to voicemail, and I hated to do that to him.

But it was Spencer, so I tapped the screen. "Hey, running to lunch at the Monocle."

"Okay. Will you still make it home before dinner?"

"So far, so good."

"Great. Come over when you're ready. I may have a surprise for you."

"Now, I'll definitely hurry. Bye."

"Bye." He ended the call as I reached for the restaurant door. Perfect timing as usual. A comfortable warmth filled me, as it often did when Spencer checked on me. Our relationship nestled in a consistency that I could rely on like the cherry blossoms in the spring.

However, during lunch, concern niggled in my belly like I'd forgotten something, but I couldn't check my schedule while discussing how we could align our clients' needs with the senator's goals. Instead, I attempted to freeze the sensation with a long drink of ice water.

Surprisingly, the feelings subsided until we left the restaurant, but then my stomach quivered. Surely it was just guilt over not calling Lawson. I didn't want to cut our conversation short, and I needed to hurry to the Capitol for the committee vote. It was best to wait.

But my declaration didn't stop the prickling along my skin, raising my heart rate. I rarely ignored my instincts because their accuracy was unsurpassed. But crashing on the marble stairs was not on my agenda, so I couldn't scroll my phone for the cause of my anxiety. Instead, I squared my shoulders and hoped whatever my gut was trying to communicate wasn't important. Blessedly, as I entered the committee room, the complexities of the process filled my mind and eased my nerves.

As soon as the vote concluded, I stepped into the hall and saw a missed call and a voicemail from Lawson. What was going on?

Chapter 2

With guilt, and now worry, motivating me, I switched my pumps for my running shoes and power-walked home. But as I closed my apartment door and pulled out my phone to call Lawson, it vibrated. Without bothering to identify the caller, I answered.

"Happy birthday, my firstborn and most amazing daughter!" Mom gushed.

So, not Lawson, and apparently, I *had* forgotten something. Smacking my phone against my forehead, I laughed in relief. Queenie awoke and leveled me with her most haughty glare.

"Sorry," I whispered, and I swear her shoulders heaved with angst before she rose and stretched.

"Carleigh? Are you okay?"

"Yes, Mom." I followed my incensed cat into the kitchen and started preparing her dinner.

"Have you had a nice day? Do you have any plans with that sweet Spencer?"

"My day's been fine, pretty normal, and Spencer and I are going to dinner at Rose's. Remember, we went there when y'all visited." I placed the bowl of cat food in the microwave.

"Yes, I remember. It was very romantic. Have you and Spencer finally decided to drop the charade and admit you're in love?"

Wow, that was fast even for her, but at least we could get through this part of our nearly scripted dialogue. I delivered my line, "Mom, I promise we're just friends. Spencer went on a date a couple of weeks ago." It'd been more like a couple of months, but details seemed unimportant at this juncture.

"Hmm. I hope you're not making a mistake."

After rolling my eyes to the heavens for a divine intervention, but receiving nothing, I changed the subject. "How are things down south?" I removed Queenie's dish from the microwave and set it on the floor.

"Excellent. Zoe and I tried on vintage engagement rings while we were antiquing the other day. She's such a breath of fresh air. It's so nice to have a girl around. I wish you'd find some time to visit. You'd love Zoe."

"I'm sure." But from the sparkly, blonde, bubbly appearance of my brother's girlfriend, it seemed highly unlikely that we'd be planning sleepovers. Actually, from what I'd gleaned about Zoe, she probably would plan a sleepover, complete with cookie dough eating and nail painting. I, on the other hand, cringed at the idea.

"Well, I'll let you get ready for your date."

"Mom, it's not a date."

"Whatever you say, honey. I hope it's wonderful. I still can't believe it's been thirty-five years since you made me a mom. It was one of the best days of my life. Dad and I love you and are so proud of the successful woman you've become. I tell everyone how you're changing the world."

Mom might've pressed all my buttons with her antics, but she also knew what to say to warm my heart and almost make me miss home. I hugged one arm around my middle. "Thanks Mom. I love y'all too."

"Carleigh . . ."

"Yes."

"Be sweet to Spencer and tell him we said hello, and we'd love for y'all to visit."

I dropped my arm to my side. "Mom, I told you—"

"Y'all can visit even if you're just friends."

"Fine. Love you."

"Good night, honey."

Once she'd disconnected, I crouched to pet Queenie. "It's mine and Lawson's birthday, and we're thirty-five." My heart seized. *Thirty-five. We're thirty-five!* "I'm thirty-five. Lawson's thirty-five. I'm not married. He's not married." I sprang to my feet and screeched, sending Queenie dashing under the couch as I raced out of my apartment.

When I threw open Spencer's door, he met me, holding out an oversized cupcake covered in sprinkles with a three and a five candle pressed into the top. "Happy Birthday!"

"It's my birthday! My thirty-fifth birthday!" I waved my phone, adrenaline pumping through my veins like it was preparing my body for battle.

With his brows tugging together, Spencer retreated a few steps. "I know. Generally that's why people light candles and put them in cupcakes." He said the words haltingly, as if he was speaking a different language and I needed time to interpret each word.

Normally, his patronizing pace would've frustrated me, but in this moment, time needed to slow down and not just in the metaphorical sense. Actually, time needed to stop and reverse. If anyone still had a clock with hands, I'd have grabbed them and slung them in a counterclockwise direction. Instead, I zeroed in on the candles' taunting flames and puffed them out.

"I'm surprised you're this upset about being a year older. You seemed fine earlier." Spencer reached out slowly and clasped my arm. "Let's sit down." He guided me to the couch and placed the offending cupcake with its accursed candles on the coffee table. "I know thirty-five is sort of a milestone birthday, but what about it—"

"It's not the age thing." I collapsed against the couch, covering my face with my hands.

"Ohh-kaay," he drew out the syllables, adding an extra one to the end.

"Sorry, you don't understand."

"I'm really trying to."

"I have to marry my best friend." My hands slapped my bouncing legs as I glanced in his direction.

He stared at me with wide eyes, nodding as if he were grasping the concept. "All right, but it seems a little sudden. We haven't even kissed. I mean, we could have a long engagement. Give me time to catch up—"

I screwed up my face, shaking my head. "I'm not marrying you."

"Wow! I didn't realize I repulsed you that much." He drew a frame in the air around my face. "Since I'm way behind on whatever's going on, please confirm that I am your best friend, or have you acquired a new one in your spare time?"

"I'm sorry. Of course you aren't repulsive." I caught his hand and relaxed my expression, but my insides churned. "And you are my best friend. But I didn't mean you; I meant the best friend I share a birthday with."

"Lawson? Your birthday buddy." He shot me a look, not hiding an ounce of annoyance, which normally I'd be proud of him for exhibiting, but not tonight. Tonight, I needed him to be less like me and more like the caring guy he was.

I nodded. "Now you're catching on."

"But you haven't seen him in a couple of years. Do you talk to him more than I know?"

"No, I'm not having secret midnight conversations with Lawson."

"Hold on." He slipped his hand from mine and held up a finger. "Did he call you and propose over the phone? I mean, I've only met the guy a couple of times, but it doesn't sound like his style. He seems more like a well-planned, romantic, Instagram-reel-worthy type of proposal guy."

"He is." My gaze shifted to my phone, still clenched in my hand.

"So he didn't propose?"

"I don't know?"

"Is that a question? Because I definitely don't have the answer." Demonstrating his supernatural patience, Spencer's expression had softened to mere confusion. With pinched brows, he studied me as if I'd been possessed, which basically described my current state.

"No. I don't know."

"How do you not know? Didn't you talk to him?"

"Not exactly." I swallowed, trying to ease the thickening in my throat. "But he texted twice and asked me to call him, and then he left a voicemail. What else could he want?"

"It *is* your birthdays."

"Fair point." I aimed a shaky finger at my phone. "Will you listen with me?"

"Are you kidding? There's no way I would not be here for whatever he has to say. I mean, if you're getting married, I'll need to prepare for the big day. Will it be a destination wedding or a full-on ballgown and black-tie affair?"

"Ha ha." But before I could tap the screen, Spencer caught my hand. "Wait, why did you think he was calling to propose? Oh no, don't tell me you made one of those ridiculous marriage pacts like if you weren't married by—"

"—our thirty-fifth birthdays, we'd marry each other." I finished his sentence. "We struck the deal after college graduation." At the time, the odds were less than five percent that neither of us would marry by our deadline. It seemed so far away.

Spencer's lips twitched, his eyes brightening to my favorite shade of cerulean, the one that came when he was amused but not now.

Where was the stormy gray that his irises turned when he was concerned or worried? *Brilliant. Two words that meant the exact same thing?* Fantastic, now my vocabulary was failing me too.

"Do not laugh," I advised.

But he burst into what I could only describe as guffaws. Seriously, he was guffawing so hard that the ridiculousness of the situation triggered a giggle that worked its way through all the knots inside me and escaped before I could slap my hand over my mouth to stop it.

Even though the laughter settled my nerves somewhat, I wouldn't give Spencer the satisfaction. "Never mind. I'll listen by myself." I started to stand, but Spencer caught my hand and pulled me back to the couch.

"No, don't go. I'm sorry." He squeezed my hand. "I won't laugh anymore."

"Fine," I said because I truly was afraid to listen to the message without him. And after all, he had apologized and his warm hand around mine always comforted me. "But if I even sense a snicker, I'm out of here." I tapped the voicemail icon.

"Hey, birthday girl. I'm sorry we haven't been able to talk today. Normally, I wouldn't leave this kind of news in a voicemail, but I've got to tell someone, or I guess, something. I'm going to propose to Willa tonight, but I haven't told her about our pact. What were we thinking? I guess we weren't. Anyway, assuming she isn't put off by the whole thing and says yes, you'll officially be off the hook. If you get this before seven, give me a call. Willa is surprising me with a romantic dinner, but I found out about it, so I'm going to pop the question and surprise her. There's a gazebo overlooking the river on the property with great views of the sunset. It's so romantic and the perfect setting. Wow, I hope you get this and tell me I'm not jumping the gun. I mean, we've only officially dated for a few weeks, but I love her so much and want to spend the rest of my life with her. Okay, I guess that's it. If I don't hear from you before seven, I'll call later tonight. Bye."

I checked the time. Seven fifteen. "Too late."

"Man, I hope she says yes. That guy sounded so nervous." Spencer pointed at my phone. "Is he usually like that?"

"Not at all."

"But I guess that means you don't have to marry him." He snapped his fingers. "Too bad."

"Yeah, I'm not so sure about that."

"So you didn't know he was in a serious relationship?"

"I don't even know who Willa is." I stood. "What kind of name is that, anyway?"

"Isn't there an acclaimed American writer with the same name?"

"Don't take her side." I crossed the room to the window, turned, and started back. "How are you so calm?" I ranted. He wouldn't feel the same way if I'd neglected our relationship like I had with Lawson.

"Whoa." Spencer held up his hands in surrender. "I thought you'd be relieved, and I don't know, happy for your friend."

"Why would you think that?" I tossed my hands in the air. Why hadn't I kept up better with Lawson?

"Are you serious?" He squinted, studying me.

I glared at him. Of course, I wasn't relieved. Worried, concerned, troubled, yes, but not giddy with hope. Lawson couldn't get married yet, but it wasn't too late for me to help him. Surely, he was just bending under the pressure of our childish pact. I could set his mind at ease. It wasn't too late.

Spencer approached me. "Car, I get that Lawson's news came as a shock to you, but—"

"It's not just that it came without warning. He's making a huge mistake. I feel terrible I didn't answer his messages and haven't done a great job of keeping in touch. I don't know who this *woman* is or how she ensnared him, but I should've been there to talk some sense into him."

"He sounded pretty certain. I'm not sure even you could've persuaded him to wait, much less abandon his intentions altogether." Spencer tossed an arm around my shoulders. "But if it makes you feel better, there's still a chance she'll say no." He gave me a squeeze. "And since there's very little you can do right now and Rose's charges a rather hefty fee for no-shows, let's go and enjoy ourselves."

"I guess you're right." I dropped my head to his shoulder, spying the giant cupcake. "Was that supposed to be dessert or an appetizer?"

"Whichever you wanted, but now we're out of time, so I'll just put it in the fridge while you change your shoes."

I glanced down at my running shoes. "Sorry I messed up your surprise. It was really sweet. Thank you."

"You're welcome. I wanted to make your day special." He lifted the plate with the cupcake. "It's not every day you turn thirty-five."

Anxiety tightened around my heart. "Do you ever worry about finding the right person and getting married?"

"Not really. I figure when the time is right, everything will fall into place." He lifted his brows as he gestured to the door. "If you want to discuss this more over dinner, we can, but we need to get going."

"Right," I agreed even as the hairs on my neck jumped to attention.

Chapter 3

When Lawson and I made the marriage pact, I doubt either of us thought we'd go through with walking down the aisle and saying our vows. But for me, it'd been a safety net of sorts, so I didn't have to worry about ending up alone. Between Spencer and my co-workers, I was rarely alone, and that's the way I liked life. Even if all of them failed to show up, I had Queenie. I stroked her soft gray hair while I waited for Lawson's call.

As soon as I'd returned home from my birthday celebration, I'd texted him for an update on his proposal. Dinner with Spencer had been lovely, and although he'd offered to discuss marriage, he didn't bring up the subject, probably afraid I'd cause a scene at the mention of anything wedding related. Instead we'd settled for reminiscing over our past birthday celebrations, letting go of pretenses and enjoying our time together. This was one of the best parts of our relationship—the way we knew how to be with each other. He understood I needed to keep the conversation light and the emotions warm and fuzzy.

Regrettably, I'd learned in high school the importance of choosing friends wisely. Not doing so back then had led to me adopting the motto *Success is the best revenge* and nothing improved your chances of success like the right team. Lucky for me, Lawson and I'd joined forces in high school and remained close through college. Then I'd bonded with Spencer in law school. They were the best friends and would always be members of Team Carleigh.

After Spencer and I graduated from law school, we'd moved into a historic house. The second floor had been converted into two one-bedroom apartments and the rent was just a little over our budgets. During the early years, there'd been few dinners out, no vacations, and the bare minimum clothing purchases, but we'd had each other and the entire Smithsonian for free entertainment. Over the years, the rent hadn't increased at the same rate as our salaries, so now we could enjoy more luxuries and save for larger places, maybe even houses. Although I couldn't imagine leaving the Capitol Hill neighborhood, I'd caught Spencer checking out homes in Virginia and Maryland. But nights like tonight must have reminded him how great our neighborhood was.

After Spencer and I'd returned from dinner, we'd shared the cupcake, which I might've skipped, but it was my favorite—lemon blueberry with cream cheese frosting. Then Spencer sent me home to text Lawson. Once I'd changed into my pajamas and curled up on the couch, I'd put on the news, but I couldn't focus as an unsettling quiver of energy buzzed through me.

Trying to see what I'd missed, I replayed my last conversation with Lawson. It hadn't been that long ago. Okay, it'd been a few months, but we'd texted and kept up on social media, and I hadn't seen a new woman in any of his pictures. After dumping his cheating girlfriend, Lawson had reconnected with my brother Brad, who'd served as the general contractor for the new Magnolia Bluff country club. Brad suggested Lawson to the owners for the general manager position, and they'd hired him. Lawson explained that the neighborhood, which was located an hour west of Savannah, wouldn't have very many houses and was being developed for busy executives to have a relaxing place to get away—thus the name, the Retreat at Magnolia Bluff. He was relieved to have a new job away from his ex, and he'd vowed to never date another co-worker.

"Call me." I swiped a finger over the display, for the hundredth time making sure that I hadn't lost the signal. To my surprise and relief, it vibrated, and Lawson's picture filled the screen. In my excitement, I fumbled the phone, ending the call when the button collided with the floor. As I grabbed for the phone, Queenie screeched and leaped to the far end of the couch, cowering in the corner.

"Sorry, sweetie." I tossed her an apologetic look as I jabbed at the screen.

"Hey, Carleigh." Lawson answered before the first ring. "I hope I didn't wake you."

"Nope, I just got home from dinner, but I guess you've had a more exciting night?" I resisted the urge to launch into a cross-examination, a skill I'd perfected in my trial practice class.

"Not that you set the bar real high, but my night was beyond amazing. Even if you'd had dinner at the White House and waltzed with the president, not the current president but a much younger, attractive JFK-inspired one, like in that scene from that movie that you love with Annette Bening—"

"*The American President.*"

"Right. *The American President.* If you'd lived that whole scene with the man of your dreams, my night still would've been better. Not that it's a competition. I'm just trying to express how great it was."

"Thanks for clearing that up, and I'm guessing from your enthusiasm that Willa said yes."

"Even better, she doesn't want a long engagement."

What did that mean? I pressed my palm into my stomach, my abdominal muscles tensing. *Carleigh, get a hold of yourself.* With a whoosh, I exhaled, shaking my head.

"Carleigh? Are you there? Did you accidentally mute? Carleigh."

"Hey, sorry. I'm here. Wow, congratulations, I guess."

"You guess? That's not exactly the response I expected."

"Forgive me. Until a few hours ago, I was unaware you were dating someone. Then I find out you're planning to propose, and now, I hear that the wedding's next weekend." As selfish as it was, I was still fixated on how I no longer had a plan B, and what if I had waited too long to find a plan A? I hadn't put as much time into finding a spouse as I should've, but until today, I'd thought I had time, and if I didn't, I had Lawson. Not that I wanted to marry him, but what was going on? Clearly, he'd decided he needed to hurry and find a wife, so he'd settled for this Willa woman. I just needed to assure him that he had plenty of time, just like me. We all had plenty of time.

"The wedding isn't next weekend. We haven't set a date, but we're looking at the first weekend in September because people have Monday off for Labor Day. I hoped that would work for you because I want you to be my best woman."

"Oh. Well, of course I want to be your best woman. I'm glad you still want me even though we haven't been as close lately."

"Are you kidding? We've been friends so long, I can't imagine getting married without you by my side. And I'm sorry about not keeping you updated on everything with Willa. It's been a whirlwind."

"I gathered. Who exactly is Willa and where did she appear from? I thought you were living out in the woods."

"You actually know her."

"I do?"

"Yes, she said you were her favorite babysitter."

Hoping I'd misunderstood him, and he wasn't robbing the cradle, I said, "Come again?"

"I sense you freaking out. Do you need to take a minute? Maybe get Spencer for support."

"I'm fine. Please tell me you aren't marrying a teenager."

"Willa isn't a teenager, and news flash, we're thirty-five. If my math is right, you haven't had a babysitting job in nearly twenty years. She's twenty-six and a successful event planner, not to mention brilliant and beautiful and so thoughtful. She just took a position as the Social Director for the country club."

"Hold on. What happened to your policy about not dating co-workers?"

"I decided I loved Willa too much to let that stand in the way, and my boss told me it was ridiculous. Linda's the one who suggested we get married so we wouldn't be dating anyway."

"Linda's your boss?"

"We haven't talked in a while. Let me back up a little. I forgot to tell you about Wyatt."

"Wyatt Ramsay, Brad's wild friend." I rubbed my temples. I should start a flowchart to keep up with all these people and the goings on at Magnolia Bluff.

"Yep."

"I thought that guy would be in prison or dead by now."

"He's been close to both. He's been arrested a couple of times but only for minor stuff. Anyway, he's turned his life around, and Brad hired him for one of his crews, but he wanted to work in the kitchen, so I got him a job."

"That's great. It was super nice of you and Brad to help him out, but what does this have to do with Willa?"

"Willa is Wyatt's little sister. Do you really not remember babysitting her?"

I gagged, bile scratching the back of my throat. "I think she puked on me."

He chuckled. "Seriously? That's hilarious."

"You wouldn't say that if you'd been the one covered in regurgitated tuna noodle casserole. I smelled like the dumpster at a seafood restaurant."

"Oh, well, I doubt she remembers that incident. She adored you and can't wait to reconnect. I promise she won't throw up on you again. She's grown into a remarkable woman who I love with my whole heart. Please give her a chance."

"I'll do my best. It just would've been nice to have met her as an adult before your wedding." Because anyone related to Wyatt couldn't be good news. He'd nearly ruined Brad and Lawson's lives with his antics.

"Me too, and trust me, it took me some time to look past her age, but I'm so glad I did."

So it wasn't love at first sight. A shiver of expectation slipped up my spine. Willa wasn't so perfect, but I needed to do more research before I made any moves. My intuition wasn't alarming me for no reason, but I wouldn't put Lawson on the defensive with wild speculations. Until I had firm evidence, I'd be the supportive friend I'd always been.

"I'm happy for you, but I need to get to bed. Keep me in the loop with the plans. Love you."

"Love you, Carleigh, and thanks for not freaking out too much."

As soon as the call ended, I swiped my screen, opening the search engine. When you worked in politics, the best strategies always came from understanding all the parties and how they could best be persuaded to reach the conclusion you wanted. Lawson might think he wanted this child-bride, but he was looking through the haze of new love. This wouldn't be the first time he'd thought he'd found the perfect woman. Just look at his ex. She was having an affair right under his nose. No, when it came to women, I'd always helped Lawson keep the right perspective. This was no different, but the stakes were higher, and time was of the essence. If he was about to make a huge, and rather permanent mistake,

I'd help him see the light before it was too late. It's what good friends did. They spoke the truth even when it was hard.

Chapter 4

While I shared almost everything with Spencer, he didn't need to know about the sleuthing I'd undertaken all week to ascertain whether Willa was right for Lawson. Spencer tended to see the best in people, which was a great trait—until it left you vulnerable. I preferred to understand the battlefield and properly strategize my offense and defense. My research was the best way for me to help Lawson.

After staying up way too late reading through my intel, I apparently turned off my alarm without fully waking. Then, with storm clouds blocking out the sun and the sound of a steady rain massaging my exhausted brain, I continued to enjoy a lovely dream of waterfalls and rainbows until Spencer's ringtone broke through the enchanting scene.

Still in the warm embrace of something that felt like nostalgia, I tugged my robe over my silk tank and sleep shorts and hurried to the door without bothering to put on my glasses. Even through the fog, I'd registered Spencer's promise of a cinnamon latte and a rosemary, fig, and Camembert Danish from my favorite café. He pampered me, but I sacrificed for him too, enduring his obsession with country music and the concerts that went along with it.

After unlocking the deadbolt, I opened the door. "Good morning."

"You sure, princess?" Spencer said, and even with my blurry vision I caught his smirk as he passed me the coffee. "Late night?"

"I just slept a little too well." Which was surprising given the angst that had simmered inside me as I'd sorted Willa's life in pictures and posts. She'd been quite the overachiever and goody-two-shoes, not at all Lawson's type. I closed the door and sipped my drink as I started for my room. "Be back in a sec. I need to get my glasses."

"I haven't seen you in days. Thanks for that quote from Abraham Lincoln. *I have an irrepressible desire to live till I can be assured that the world is a little better for my having lived in it.* It's really given me something to ponder."

I hurried to the bedside table. "You're welcome."

"Oh, and my parents said to thank you for the peaches you had delivered to their house. My office devoured our box before I could get more than two," he called from the kitchen.

"I'm glad everyone loved them. Nothing better in the summer than a ripe peach." I slipped on my glasses.

"For sure. What's been happening at work all week?"

"Not much. I've been busy with a special project." I froze in the doorway, smacking my palm to my head.

"Carleigh, tell me this isn't what I think it is." Spencer's voice thundered down the hall like a father scolding a toddler. *Fantastic.* He'd found my research. Now, I'd have to convince my friend who knew me way too well that my research was harmless, which it was, of course. But while I knew I was helping Lawson, Spencer might not see it the same way.

For days, I'd spent my spare time collecting information on Willa Ramsay. While I'm aware that it's not great for the environment, I'd printed most of the data because it helped me organize my thoughts to hold something tangible. My plan had been to get up early and compile it in a binder before my art museum outing with Spencer.

I hurried to the kitchen. "It's nothing. I'm just trying to get to know Willa." After setting my cup down, I reached around the table, gathering the papers.

"Is this what you've been doing all week?" He tapped the stack I'd made. "I shouldn't have believed you were fine with Lawson's engagement."

"It's no big deal." I carried the papers into the kitchen and placed them on the far counter. "I just conducted a little online research." Maintaining my composure, I opened the fridge and retrieved Queenie's food.

"By online research, you mean cyberstalking, correct?"

"Don't try to cross-examine me." I placed the bowl of food in the microwave.

"Carleigh." His voice rose as he drew out my name.

"Trust me, with what I've discovered, I'm fine because there's no way he'll marry Willa Ramsay." I ruffled Queenie's hair as she nuzzled my ankle. "Willa was a cheerleader in high school." The microwave chimed as if to underscore my statement, and I removed the bowl and placed it on the floor.

"Nice red herring, and I can't wait to hear how that part of Willa's past disqualifies her from becoming Lawson's wife." He settled into one of the chairs at the table and began removing our breakfast from the paper bag. "But first, I want to make sure you haven't broken any privacy laws." He gestured to the chair opposite him like he was a police detective and I was the suspect who'd been brought in for questioning.

"Don't be so dramatic." With an indifferent one-shoulder shrug, I joined him at the table. "My investigation was totally above board. You know I don't break rules."

"But you don't mind skirting them if it helps you get what you want."

"Not what I want. It's all part of the business, and everything I do is for my clients' best interests."

"Who exactly is your client in this scenario?"

"Lawson, of course." I unwrapped my Danish, my mouth watering.

"Is he aware of your *business* relationship?"

"You know, I'm not sure this breakfast is worth all this antipathy when I'm just helping a friend. I'd do the same for you."

"Please don't." Spencer massaged his neck, a sure sign that he was reaching the end of his patience.

This reaction is why I hadn't mentioned any of this to him. But now, I needed to put his mind at ease. It's not like I'd hired a private investigator. Although that might not be a bad idea. *Focus Carleigh.*

"Stop worrying. All I did was check out her social media accounts. It's not like I invaded her privacy. She sent me a friend request on Facebook, I accepted it, followed her back on Instagram, and read her LinkedIn profile." And maybe I'd used some other tools I had at my disposal for learning about people's pasts, but nothing was illegal. Lawson deserved my best work. He must be unaware of who he was planning to marry—a cheerleader.

Never letting his focus waver from me, Spencer lifted his cup to his mouth and sipped his coffee.

Not one to back down from a challenge, I trained my eyes on his, and energy zipped between us, powering me with confidence. We rarely disagreed, but when we did, these moments were our silent path to resolution.

I swallowed, ending the stalemate. "They aren't right for each other."

"Because she was a cheerleader." He lowered his cup and lifted his sandwich to his mouth.

"Partly." I broke off a piece of pastry and ate it. Even to me, it sounded juvenile, but in high school, Lawson and I'd made fun of the cheerleaders while we played varsity tennis.

"Is she still a cheerleader?"

"What?"

Instead of responding, he took another bite and arched his brows, questioningly.

"No, of course not. She's an event planner."

"So how long ago did she take part in that wretched activity of supporting her school teams?"

"You know my view on cheerleaders. They pretend to be real athletes, but they smile too much. There's all the jumping, and don't forget the yelling and clapping."

"How long?"

"High school, but there's no way he'd be with one." People didn't change that much, especially not Lawson. After he watched Wyatt tank his life, Lawson was steady and serious about his life choices. A pang of guilt struck my gut. I should've been there for him then, and I should've been more available now. If I'd only known Wyatt and his sister were creeping around Magnolia Bluff.

"It seems he *is* with Willa, and she's packed away her pom-poms." Spencer continued eating.

"Fine, but—"

My phone vibrated, and I snatched it from the pocket of my robe, gripping it to stop my fingers from quivering. I stared at the phone screen as a not so unpleasant, but definitely unwanted, rush of tingles zipped up my arms.

It was a text from an unknown number. Normally, I'd ignore it, assuming it was spam, but right now, Spencer needed a few seconds to calm down. He rarely got so upset. On the occasions when I let worry get the best of me, he was always my anchor—steady and sure. A wave of warmth rolled through me. If only I could give him the same measure of comfort.

Oh, well. I tapped on the message and at once regretted my choice.

Unknown number: Hi, Carleigh! This is Willa! Lawson gave me your number. I'm so excited about the wedding and can't wait to hang out with you!! It's going to be amazing! Since the timeline is short, I wanted to let you know about the bridesmaids' dresses so we could coordinate your ensemble. Unless you want to wear a tux, which is totally fine. I just noticed from your social media that you seemed more like a dress girl!

"Ha, just so you know—" Reenergized, I held up the phone so Spencer could see the screen. "The innocent Willa has also been inspecting my social media profiles."

His eyes skimmed the words. "And she thinks you're a *dress girl*. How nice."

"What?" I turned the phone around and reread the beginning of the message. "Oh, yeah."

"And she's not wrong." He smiled, his gaze looking somewhat dreamy, which made goosebumps scatter over my skin. But I couldn't let down my guard. First, Lawson and now Spencer were falling under her charms.

"About what?" I rubbed my arms.

"Emerald green."

"Hold on. I didn't get that far." I continued reading.

Unknown number: The bridesmaids are wearing floor-length gowns in cranberry, so you might want to get something in an emerald green. It would look lovely with your auburn hair! <3 I'll send a picture of the bridesmaids' dresses and the link to the wedding website so you can stay up-to-date! <3

After I liked the message, I set my phone on the table, pinched off a bite of my Danish, and popped it in my mouth. This wedding might have been voted out of committee, but there was ample time for Lawson to come to his senses and vote no on the floor.

"Carleigh, what do you think?" Spencer drank his coffee.

"About what?"

"The dress color."

"I don't know." I focused on the perfect harmony of flavors on my tongue as the Camembert tamed the peppery rosemary and tart fig.

"You do look beautiful in emerald green."

"You think so?" I rolled a stray rosemary needle under my finger. "I always feel like a Christmas tree with a red bow on top."

He chuckled, shaking his head. "Not at all." His eyes brightened with realization. "Remember our first Thanksgiving in DC? We only had a couple of days off, so you couldn't go home."

"We could barely afford rent, so a plane ticket wasn't in the budget."

"Right, so we went to my grandparents, and you wore an emerald green dress that looked like a long-sleeved collared shirt on top but had a matching belt and longer skirt."

"My mom bought me that dress." A comforting warmth settled inside me.

"Well, I just remember you looking pretty. You wore your boots with it, and the gold link necklace with the monogrammed charm that I'd given you for your birthday."

Our budgets had been so tight in those early days, Spencer's gift probably cost him a month of peanut butter and jelly sandwiches for lunch. I rubbed the spot just below my throat where the charm sat when I wore the necklace, which was almost every day. And he still wore the vintage cufflinks I'd given him after I sold my collection of decorative trinket boxes on eBay.

"That was nearly a decade ago. I can't believe you remember what I wore with such detail."

"Um, right. It was a great day. I guess it just stuck with me." He rocked backward, rubbing his palms along the tops of his legs. "Anyway, why don't we postpone our trip to the gallery and hit some shops to find your dress?"

"I don't know." Did agreement equal defeat? I ate another bite.

"Come on. You don't have to agree with Willa, but you know you don't want to wear a pantsuit."

"I've seen some pretty stylish tuxedos for women with mother-of-pearl buttons on white satin shirts. I could pull it off."

"Of course you could, but you know you don't want to, and you'd never wear it again." With a smug grin, he took a large bite of his breakfast sandwich like he'd won the debate.

"Low blow, hitting me with the economics of the purchase."

"What are friends for?" Spencer mumbled the question with his mouth still full.

I rolled my eyes. "Still, it seems premature to buy a dress to a wedding I don't think will happen."

Spencer swallowed a swig of his coffee. "Why don't you check out the website Willa sent?"

"Yeah. I'm not interested in reviewing that today."

"Carleigh, give the woman a chance." He tapped my phone as he stood. "At least respond to her text." He walked to the kitchen and filled a glass with water.

"Ugh. I already liked it. Isn't that enough?"

"I'd say there's a better than ninety percent chance that she'll be Lawson's wife in about three months, so you might want to play nice." Gulping the water, he walked back to the table.

"Fine." I opened the message chain, but surely, the probability was much lower.

As I selected the thumbs-up emoji and sent it to Willa, Spencer watched over my shoulder. "Not exactly the friendliest of responses."

"I'm not looking to make a new friend. I just don't want to lose the one I currently have. And I give the wedding a thirty percent chance of happening." Finished with my breakfast, I rose and gave Spencer's chest a firm pat. Gracious, he'd certainly been doing his pushups. My brain glitched for a moment, but then I found my point and held up a finger. "I forgot to mention that she's planning this wedding for the opening weekend of college football season. Lawson never misses a Dawgs game, and they'll start the season in the top five."

"He did agree to the date." Spencer brushed my hand away. "Maybe he loves her more than the Georgia Bulldogs."

"He's probably just trying to find a way to do both."

"This may come as a huge shock to you, but when people fall in love and decide to get married, there isn't much that can keep them apart." Spencer stuffed the wrappers from our breakfast sandwiches into the bag.

"I'm not saying that he doesn't *feel* like he's in love, but they barely know each other. If they did, she'd never have planned the wedding for that weekend."

After he put the trash in the bin under the kitchen sink, Spencer turned to face me. "Maybe try to be happy that Lawson has found his person."

"I'm more worried that he's found the wrong person. Maybe if this hadn't happened so fast, I'd be on board, but seriously, what's the rush?"

"Every relationship is different. Some people don't need years with someone before they're ready to take the next step." His gaze settled on me.

For a second, I couldn't read his expression, but the flutters in my belly set off an alarm, telling me to abort this conversation, and I didn't ignore my instincts. "Because I don't want to ruin our Saturday going round and round about it, I'll agree to shop for a dress if we can table wedding talk."

"Deal." Stepping in front of me, he extended his hand, his expression back to normal, eyes a peaceful blue-gray with an easy smile.

Resisting the urge to exhale a sigh of relief, I clasped his hand and gave it a firm shake. "And I'm only acquiescing because I need something to wear to Jordan's weddi—event, so it won't go to waste." Determined not to utter the dreaded *W word*, I escaped to my room. "I'll be ready in fifteen minutes."

"I'll be here."

Chapter 5

Because I have an exceptional ability to create worst-case scenarios in rapid succession that increase in intensity until I'm panicking, I rarely wallow in my worries. Instead, I manage my anxieties by safeguarding my life with systems that provide guide rails to keep me on track and chugging forward. I'm kind of like the Little Engine That Could—if that little blue train was a high-speed bullet train.

Two weeks later, as Spencer entered my apartment to escort me to Jordan's wedding, his eyes grew wide. "Wow, um, you look gorgeous."

"Thanks, but it's not like you haven't seen me in the dress." Although after seeing my reflection, I had done a few twirls through my living room.

"But not with your hair fixed and the high heels instead of bare feet." He blinked rapidly. "You just, wow. You're going to need to apologize to the bride for taking the attention off her." His gaze shifted around, never quite meeting my eyes.

While my heartbeat clicked up a notch from his compliments, I waved off his attention. "I doubt that. Still, thank you for being impressed."

"Of-of course, but you rarely disappoint." Spencer shot his focus to his watch, a blush dusting his cheeks. "I mean, we better get going. Don't want to be late."

"Hold on. I have a little surprise for you." I grabbed the Brackish bow tie he'd been eyeing for months from its pine box and dangled it in front of him.

"Is that what I think it is?" His brow knitted.

"Do you like it? Is it the wrong one?"

"Yes. No." He shook his head. "Yes, I love it, and no, it's the right one. But Carleigh, they're so expensive."

"I wanted to get you something nice that you really wanted, so just say thank you, and take off that boring black bowtie." The Charleston artisan had handcrafted parts of navy and green pheasant feathers and dotted guinea feathers into a bow tie. It was more like a piece of art than an accessory.

He tugged off his bowtie. "Thank you."

As I reached around his neck with the band, my fingers grazed his skin and my heart did a sort of flippy thing. I secured the hook under Spencer's chin and smiled up at him.

He inhaled a shaky breath, almost like he was startled. Then he lunged for the door. "Um, thanks again, but we better get going."

"Right. We don't want to be late."

"Cab's here." Spencer jerked open the door.

"Right behind you." My heart tripped and fell as he hurried down the stairs like he was running from a gator. Meanwhile, I focused on securing the lock instead of whatever was going on with my cardiac organ. Maybe I needed a pacemaker.

Once in the cab, we fell into what can only be described as the least companionable silence of our relationship. Whatever was going on between us needed to stop, but nothing had happened, so why wasn't Spencer talking to me? He definitely wasn't mad. He seemed more agitated, switching his focus out the window and at his phone, while fidgeting with his cufflinks. His behavior left me in a state I rarely found myself—speechless.

When we finally arrived at Jordan's church, we slid onto a pew, and Spencer leaned close, whispering, "In case you didn't notice everyone staring, you are stunning in that dress. Not a Christmas tree in sight." His joke eased the tension between us, even if chills scattered over my arms.

I brushed off the goosebumps. "Thank you for making me go shopping."

"You're welcome."

I had to admit that I loved the way I looked in the emerald green dress from the moment I tried it on. Pleated chiffon created texture on the halter top, cinched at my waist, and then fluttered over the floor-length A-line skirt. Not to be forgotten, the back of the dress was almost as impressive as the front. Six covered buttons accented the tailored waistband, creating the base of a triangle with the bow at my neck.

His smile eased the last of my concerns, and I poked my elbow playfully to his side. "By the way, you don't look half-bad yourself." With his dark hair combed back and his well-fitted tuxedo, he'd be the one garnering all the attention. I opened my bulletin. "Surely there's a single bridesmaid?"

"Or groomsman for you." Spencer cocked a brow.

"I'm good."

After our last discussion about Willa and Lawson, I'd tried not to think of them, much less bring them up in conversation, and no wedding updates had arrived from Magnolia Bluff. I'd been perfecting the whole ignorance is bliss thing by concentrating on work, keeping busy with my commitment to the shelter, and spending every spare hour I had enjoying the summer sunshine on the tennis courts. Hey, don't judge. Worrying about marriage would've only interrupted my perfectly happy balance.

Unfortunately, Spencer was fine with the interruption, regularly gauging my thoughts on the future. Usually, it was some marriage-adjacent subject, like having kids, neighborhoods, family traditions, or some other topic we'd rarely discussed.

"How do you expect to find a husband if you don't date?" Spencer asked. Until now, he'd stopped short of bringing up my love life or his.

"I date."

"When was your last date?"

It'd been a minute, not that I didn't know every detail of my last date, but since it'd been less than a memorable experience, and Spencer thought I'd been at a work event, I searched the embellished wooden beams of the vaulted ceiling for a believable answer.

"Wow, that long?" Spencer teased.

Rather than lie, I lowered my gaze to him and said, "I'd rather focus on the present than the past and enjoy this magnificent space. If you want to dredge up failed romances, we could examine the trail of broken hearts you've left, like Jordan for starters."

"Nice try, but Jordan ended things with me because—" He stopped, switching his attention to the front of the church.

I followed his line of sight, but it was the same as when we entered. The string quartet sat off to the side and played that kind of classical music that made my heart full. Spencer continued to stare straight ahead, but his jaw twitched like he was clenching it.

"Are you okay?"

"Yep. Fine."

"Oh, no. You don't still have feelings for Jordan?" I grabbed his hand. "Why didn't you say something? I could've found another date. Is that why you've been so obsessed with the future? Are you worried that you haven't found your person?"

"Shh." He glanced around before he turned to me, his brows tugging together. "Calm down. Half the people in here are now watching for my answer."

"Sorry. I feel terrible that Jordan broke your heart," I whispered.

"Jordan didn't break my heart." Spencer pulled his hand free and clasped the back of his neck. "We only dated for a few months, and while she technically ended the relationship, I wasn't into it either. We mutually decided that we're better as friends. Besides, I like Cooper. He's great to talk baseball with. I might even join his softball team."

"Then why are you acting so weird?"

Spencer folded his program in half and then in half again.

Patience not being one of my gifts, I snatched the paper from him. "What aren't you saying?"

Sighing, he slanted his body toward me. "When we decided to stop dating, Jordan mentioned that our friendship"—he gestured between us—"was an issue for her."

"Why didn't you say something?"

"Because you work together, and I didn't want things to be any more awkward than they were already going to be."

"Oh." Guilt knotted my stomach. Was that the whole truth? What if this was the case with his other short-lived relationships? I hated that he'd kept this problem from me.

But before I could ask any follow-up questions, the music grew louder and the people around us adjusted in their pews for the processional. As each bridesmaid passed, I wondered if she might be a good match for Spencer. Their dresses were all the same deep rose color but in different styles—one strapless, one with an asymmetrical top, one with cap sleeves, and one with a sweetheart neckline. What did the style each chose say about her personality?

When they'd all lined up along the altar rail, we stood and watched Jordan and her father travel down the aisle where a beaming Cooper waited for his bride.

I glanced at Spencer. The corners of his lips lifted in a slight smile. Of course he was happy for Jordan and Cooper, and so was I. Marriage had always been part of my plans, and it still was. I hadn't prioritized it, but what about Spencer? He'd dated several women over the years. Surely our friendship wasn't the reason they'd all failed.

Spencer was an amazing man—intelligent, hardworking, and always found time for his friends and family. If it hadn't been for him, I'd never have decorated for holidays or celebrated my birthday. Spencer was the kind of person who made moments special, even if it was just breakfast. Not to mention, he made an excellent tennis partner. He liked to win almost as much as I did, and he was in great shape with all that running and weight training. It made no sense that none of the women he'd dated had stuck around to marry this near-perfect man. It couldn't be my fault that my best friend wasn't married.

Without warning, Spencer flipped his gaze to me, and I gave him a quick smile before focusing my attention on Cooper and Jordan. Heat scampered up my neck at being caught staring at him like he was a prize colt. Maybe he hadn't noticed.

The minister stood between the couple holding hands as Cooper repeated the traditional wedding vows. Before he could finish, he paused, cleared his throat, and wiped away tears. My heart trembled. Would a man ever look at me like that?

I'd made a very intentional decision to establish my career before marriage and a potential family. But what if I never found the right man to share my life with? As the doubts and questions piled up, I couldn't concentrate on the ceremony.

Then there was applause, followed by a triumphant march from the organist. Tears pooled in my eyes, and I sniffled, willing them to halt.

This is why I stuck with activities I understood and knew how to accomplish. I hated uncertainty, but more than that, I hated how I became emotional when I felt anxious, so I made sure I didn't.

"Well, this is a first." Spencer wrapped an arm around my shoulders and gathered me into his side. Thankfully, I could trust him with my unfortunate display of emotions, and I appreciated the warmth of his support even if it included a sarcastic jab.

I swiped away the moisture under my lower lashes. "What are we doing?"

"Hmm." He rubbed his warm palm over my arm. "I'm not sure how to answer that or if this is the place and time to discuss it."

"I just want you to have everything you've always wanted, and I know that means a wife and family. If I've been an issue in your relationships, I'm sorry."

"If any of the women I'd dated had been the right one, she'd have accepted our friendship as part of the deal."

Shifting out of his embrace, I turned to face him. "Are you sure?"

"Absolutely."

"Fine, but I'm going to make it my personal mission tonight to ascertain which women are single and help you meet them." I stood.

He rose. "Carleigh, that's not necessary. Let's just enjoy ourselves."

"This'll be fun. I love a good challenge."

"That's what I'm worried about."

"What? That I'll find your fiancée before you can?"

"Has it occurred to you that I might want to choose my future spouse and have my own ideas of what she'd be like?" He stepped into the aisle and waited for me to exit the pew.

I clasped my hands around his arm. "Of course, but it doesn't mean I can't help."

"Carleigh, I appreciate your concern, but I'm not in a hurry to get married. Unlike you, I can be very patient, and I have faith that when the time is right with the right woman, everything will fall into place."

As Spencer escorted me out of the sanctuary, I replayed his words. While they should have filled me with hope, instead I had a sinking sensation. What would happen to *us* when Spencer fell in love with the right woman at the right time and everything fell into place?

In the walled garden of the reception venue, the scent of jasmine and roses perfumed the warm night air as we chatted with other guests during the cocktail hour. After enjoying our fair share of savory puffed pastries and stuffed mushrooms, I decided that the emptiness I'd been experiencing was hunger, which also explained my emotional state at the church. But with my blood sugar regulated, I happily strolled with Spencer to our assigned table and joined my co-workers and their dates. With no small amount of relief, I observed that only one couple was married.

As Ashton took her seat beside me, she introduced her boyfriend Brock, and I introduced Spencer to them. Then she asked if I'd seen the pictures of Jordan and Cooper's new condo.

"Not yet. I can't imagine moving all the way out there, but she seems excited about it." I gave Spencer a knowing glance.

"Where is it?" Spencer asked, avoiding my eyes and instead focusing on Ashton.

"Colonial Village in Courthouse." Ashton leaned forward, showing us her phone display. "I didn't want to go that far either, but the neighborhood is so charming." She swiped the screen, changing the picture from a red brick building with a white columned entry to an interior picture. "And they got a newly renovated two-bedroom condo. Look at this kitchen."

The floors were hardwood with white cabinets and stainless-steel appliances. The lighting and fixtures were brass. I liked the clean lines and timelessness of the décor, but that didn't mean I wanted to move.

I nodded. "It's nice."

"They were lucky to get a renovated two-bedroom unit in Colonial Village." Spencer's shoulder touched mine as he peered closer at the phone screen. "When I checked the other day, there were only a few on the market."

I shot my attention to him, nearly bumping his nose with mine. "Are you planning on moving?"

"I was just seeing what's out there." Holding up a hand, he shifted away from me. "Courthouse has a lot going for it, and even though it's in Arlington, it's still close to work."

"Of course, and Jordan mentioned running trails." I lowered his hand and gave it a reassuring pat. "You should check those out." *But then get on the metro and come home.*

"I might." Spencer eyed me skeptically. "Did you know Colonial Village is one of the earliest garden-style apartment communities in the country? Eleanor Roosevelt planted some of the trees in the neighborhood." Of course, he threw in the history tidbit for my benefit.

"That's interesting." I gulped my water, trying to settle the nerves clashing in my stomach. Every year since we'd both made partner, we rehashed the same dreaded conversation about renewing our leases. Spencer wanted to move somewhere out of the city center, but I loved the energy and the convenience of the Hill. So far, I'd won the debate, but he seemed more serious this time. He'd definitely done more research than normal.

"So, Spencer, you're a runner. Brock and I are training for the Marine Corps Marathon." Ashton passed her phone to her date.

Brock stored it inside his jacket. "It's our first. Have you done one?"

"I'm more of a 5K guy. I don't have time to train for that kind of distance." Spencer gestured to me. "We play tennis most Saturdays."

"That's cool." Brock rested his arm on the back of Ashton's chair. "We play some."

Ashton glanced between us. "We should set up a game."

"Sure." I smiled. I'd have to buy her a coffee to thank her for changing the topic, but my brain was steadily drafting a list of follow-up questions for Spencer. *What other neighborhoods had he checked? Was he also looking for me? Had he hired a realtor? Was he going to buy or keep renting?*

When a dramatic drum roll echoed through the room, I startled, fumbling my water glass, but only a few drops sloshed out.

As the bride and groom started their first dance, Spencer removed the glass from my grasp. "Relax. I promise I haven't been house hunting without you."

I nodded, rolling my shoulders to alleviate the tension. If anything was certain, it was Spencer, and he would not leave me anytime soon. But wariness prickled my skin, warning that *soon* was coming increasingly faster. Ever since my birthday, I kept hearing the proverbial clock. Tick-tock, tick-tock.

I wrapped my arms around my middle and grasped my elbows, so my hands wouldn't cover my ears of their own volition. Was I having a very early midlife crisis? Thankfully everyone's attention was on the dance floor, and by the end of the mother-son dance, I'd re-gained my composure. As dinner was served, I shoved my worries to the back of my brain, hoping Ashton would present another benign conversation topic.

"Have you heard where they're going on their honeymoon?" She lifted her goblet.

Hallelujah! This girl was getting her favorite pastry with that coffee.

"A resort somewhere in the Caribbean." I smoothed my napkin in my lap. "Maybe St. Lucia."

"That sounds so relaxing and romantic. Blue waters, palm trees, and ocean breezes." Ashton took a sip of her chardonnay. "Now, I'm ready for a vacation."

"Not yet. You're helping me while Jordan's away, and we have a lot to complete before the August recess."

"Of course, and I'm all in, but I'm planning a long weekend as soon as we get a break. Lucky for me, Brock's favorite hobby is planning trips. He takes care of everything—hotels, restaurants, travel arrangements, excursions." She nudged her boyfriend. "I'm going to need a spa day."

"What's your favorite destination?" Spencer asked.

Brock rested his fork and knife on his plate. "In the states or internationally?"

"Wow." I buttered a bite of roll. "Sounds like you've traveled a lot."

"My parents both became airline pilots after they served in the Air Force, so travel was always part of our lives."

"That's incredible. What an interesting way to grow up," Spencer said.

"For sure, and I'm still curious, what's your favorite destination?" I probed.

"In the states, I'd have to say it's a toss-up between Sedona, Arizona and Kennebunkport, Maine."

"Those are pretty different locations."

"Yeah, it depends on the time of year and my mood, and it probably makes me a poor judge, but I love almost every place in between too."

"What about internationally?" Ashton grinned. Clearly she already knew the answer and liked it.

"Ecuador. The rainforest, the Galapagos Islands, hiking, scuba diving, and Old Quito is so charming. Not to mention the delicious food."

"He keeps promising me a trip there, but with our schedules, we haven't been able to find the time."

"We will." Brock kissed Ashton's forehead.

"How about you?" Ashton looked between Spencer and me. "Where would you go for your honeymoon?"

"Kokomo," Spencer said without hesitation.

"Like that song by the Beach Boys." I shook my head. "It's not a real place. Is it?"

"Oh, it's real, and from what I've seen online, it's amazing." Brock nodded. "Good call, man." He raised his hand over Ashton and my heads for a high-five. "That's a good one."

Spencer smacked Brock's hand. "Thanks."

"What's so great about it?" I moved the food around on my plate.

"First, it's not in the Caribbean. Not that I have anything against any of those islands, but for my honeymoon, I want to go somewhere unique and more off the grid." Spencer's blue eyes brightened like this might be one of his favorite topics, and he couldn't wait to share his discovery. But why hadn't he mentioned it before?

"Kokomo is a private island in Fiji. This Australian property developer rescued an abandoned resort there and made it into a tropical paradise. It's located at the world's fourth-largest barrier reef, the Great Astrolabe Reef, so the diving is some of the best, especially because it's so remote." Spencer lifted his fingers as he counted off Kokomo's assets. "There are waterfalls, white sand beaches, interesting culture, friendly people, farm-to-table meals."

"Are you sure you aren't on their marketing team?" I laughed.

Chuckling, Spencer lowered his hand. "I guess I may have spent a little too much time exploring the website."

"When did you make this discovery?"

"A couple of weeks ago, but I can't imagine going anywhere else now." His gaze met mine, his sudden seriousness sending a shiver though me.

"You should totally book it," Brock said.

Spencer glanced to Brock. "I hope I get the chance."

I rubbed away the goosebumps on my arms as the guys continued to discuss travel plans and past vacations. Once we finished our meals, the servers cleared our plates as the father of the bride gave a toast. After the cake was cut, the band opened the dance floor.

When I passed the bride on my way to the ladies' room, I complimented her on the wedding. Jordan asked if Spencer was seeing anyone because her cousin had recently moved to the area, and I assured her he would like to meet her.

When I returned to our table, Ashton informed me that the guys had gone for cake. But a few minutes later, Brock returned without Spencer. He explained Spencer was talking to the bride, and he didn't want to interrupt. They ate a few bites of cake, but when the band began a slow song, Brock led Ashton to the dance floor.

As I watched the couples swaying, my concerns about marriage mounted again. I retrieved my phone and began searching the internet to ease my marriage woes. What can I say? Research did for me what others got from yoga.

A while later, Spencer arrived at the table with two plates of wedding cake. "Sorry it took me a while. Jordan insisted on introducing me to her cousin Mary Katherine."

"No problem. While you were gone, I did a little research, and I have some good news."

He forked a bite of cake. "What's that?"

"We aren't behind on the whole getting married thing, especially in DC."

"Carleigh, I told you I wasn't in a rush. Are you?"

"I'm not going to lie, I was getting a little anxious earlier, but not anymore. You do know Emerson said *knowledge is the antidote to fear.*"

"You've mentioned it before."

"Because it's true. Anyway, don't you want to hear the results?"

"As if I have a choice."

"Fantastic. In the States, the median age for people to marry is the highest in Washington DC. For women it's thirty-one and for men it's thirty-two and a half, but I'm going with the statistics from Sweden instead. Guess how old the average age is there?"

"Please just tell me."

"Thirty-seven for men and thirty-five for women, and that's the average, so some people are older."

"I understand the dynamics of an average, but thanks for the math lesson. Now, can we enjoy our cake since we don't need to worry about finding someone to marry tonight?"

"What about Mary Katherine?"

"Who?"

"Jordan's cousin. The woman you just met."

"Did you have something to do with that introduction?"

"Maybe?"

"Carleigh . . ."

"Fine, yes, but I merely mentioned to Jordan that you were single and interested in meeting someone."

"At the moment, I'm not sure that's entirely true." His shoulders rounded. "What about you?"

"What about me?"

"Are you going to start dating? Am I supposed to set you up?" He clasped the back of his neck. "Or are you hoping that Lawson will change his mind?"

As my mouth gaped, I stared back at him without words, a very weird sensation for me and twice in one night.

Spencer chuckled, shaking his head. "Do not take my amusement to mean that we won't return to those questions, but I didn't realize you could be rendered speechless." He patted himself on the back. "I should get some kind of award."

"You're terrible." I shoved away my plate of cake. "You've ruined my appetite even for dessert."

"I doubt your ailment will last very long with your sweet tooth." He tilted his ear toward the band. "How about I apologize by dancing with you to your favorite song?"

As I heard the familiar intro notes for *Brown-Eyed Girl*, warmth radiated from my center all the way to my fingers and toes that yearned to dance. But I didn't like admitting defeat.

"No thank you." I averted my gaze from Spencer to a droplet of condensation sliding down my glass.

"Come on. I'm sorry. I love how you are always there for me." Spencer slid his hand over mine. "We do need to discuss some things, but this isn't the time." He tugged. "If it makes you feel better, I'll give you the win, and this can be your victory dance. You know you want to, and there's honestly not much I love doing more than dancing with you."

While I was ready to forgive him, I waited an extra beat before I shifted my attention to him. "Can we do all the twirls?"

"Of course." Without missing another beat, Spencer spun me onto the parquet floor. During our first year of law school, one of our professors taught ballroom dancing, and we signed up, hoping it might help our grades. Turned out, Spencer was a gifted dancer, and I loved when we got the chance to use the moves we'd learned.

Singing and laughing, we moved to the floor. Under the twinkling chandeliers of the ballroom with the music reverberating through us, we found our rhythm, the one we knew so well, and my anxieties about the future and any lingering awkwardness that'd crept into our relationship spun away with each turn.

If only that song could have gone on forever, but it couldn't, and before I knew it, Ashton had linked her arm with mine, and we were joining the other single women for the bouquet toss. Usually, I stood in the back and let the other girls fight it out because if I wanted the flowers,

I'd win the game. But Ashton wanted to be in the middle of the melee, so I obliged her. Okay, maybe I was considering snagging the good luck charm, but I didn't even have a boyfriend, so it seemed a little greedy for me to catch it.

Then before I could give it another thought, the white and pink rose blossoms arched overhead, and in one of the strangest moments of my life, I froze, my arms pinned at my sides. The bouquet skimmed a pair of manicured nails in front of me and then bounced off my forehead and into Ashton's hands.

"Oh my gosh." She lifted the flowers in front of my face. "I caught it! I caught it!"

"You did." My pulse raced, and my fingers buzzed. Where had all this adrenaline been when I'd needed to act? I rubbed a circle where the flowers had grazed my forehead.

"It was headed straight for you, and I thought you'd want it, but then it literally fell in my hands." Ashton bounced.

I forced a smile but couldn't bring myself to join her in the bouncing. "I'm glad it all worked out. You and Brock seem serious. Maybe you'll get your Ecuadorian honeymoon sooner than you thought."

"But what about Spencer and Kokomo?"

"Oh, Spencer and I are just good friends."

Ashton tilted her head, examining me. "Are you sure? Because the way he looks at you, well, it looks like a lot more than friendship."

Before I could respond to her allegation, Brock slipped between us and lifted Ashton off the ground, spinning her around. She waved the bouquet in the air like a trophy and then it was the guys' turn to line up and catch the garter.

At once, the room was too loud, and the air seemed hot and thick. Instead of watching the spectacle, I escaped to the garden, where I breathed in the heady scents of the roses and jasmine. The cool breeze that skated over my skin settled my nerves, so I could think rationally.

Had Spencer looked at me differently than any other time? Not really. He'd admired my appearance, but since we'd arrived at the reception, his expressions had seemed typical. Ashton was simply projecting her romantic feelings with Brock onto us. Nothing had changed between Spencer and me. Our friendship was too important to consider romantic thoughts.

Before I could ponder it further, Spencer tapped me on the shoulder. "May I have this dance?" He raised his arms for a waltz.

"Of course." I joined him as a wave of comforting warmth flowed through me. Our relationship might look like something else to others, but this is who we were—best friends and nothing more.

Chapter 6

I thrived on routine, and my routine was fine-tuned for success. A week after the wedding, any lingering concerns over what I needed in life had been settled, and I was a hundred percent sure that I could have it all. According to my calculations, I did need to get the ball rolling, even if I wasn't quite ready to take the plunge, so I set up an online dating profile.

But on Saturday morning, finding my match was the last thing I was thinking about while I played with the shelter kittens. Nothing brought me more joy than matching a child with a purring fluff ball. Not as keen on receiving inadvertent scratches from the cats—okay some were intentional—Spencer oversaw the paperwork part of the adoption process.

Currently, happiness filled me as a little girl brushed the head of the ginger tabby that I held over the enclosure rail.

"Mommy, I want this one. She has green eyes like me." The girl studied the face of her new friend.

The girl's mother scratched the cat's chin, eliciting a purr. "She is sweet."

"What will you name her?" I asked. Over the years, I'd found that once a potential owner named a pet, they rarely changed their minds about adoption.

"Apricot." She looked to her mother for approval. "Because she's the same color, and they're my favorite snack."

"Excellent choice."

"Wonderful. It's a perfect name, and while you take care of the paperwork, I'll give Lucy a lesson on taking care of Apricot." I gestured to the front desk, where Spencer held up a clipboard. He smiled at me, his gaze perfectly normal. Ashton's words had needled me all week, leaving me analyzing all Spencer's expressions. So far, I'd observed nothing out of the ordinary.

"Perfect. I'll be right back," Lucy's mom said.

Once the paperwork was completed and I'd finished explaining the basics of pet care with Lucy, I placed Apricot in a cardboard carrier and brought him to the front of the building with Lucy whispering assurances through the holes of the box to the now unhappy and loudly meowing cat. I passed the box to Lucy's mom, and she hurried Lucy out the door.

"Another successful adoption day." Geanine, the director of the shelter, flipped the sign in the window to closed. "I don't know what we'd do without you two."

"We love it." I brushed orange cat hair from my navy shorts. "The cat food I ordered should be delivered by the middle of the week."

"Thank you, Carleigh."

"We'll see you in a couple of weeks." Spencer held open the door.

As we started our trek home, contentment rolled through me like a calm sea. I needed to plan a day on the water. As a child, I loved our family outings to the beach. Everything seemed so simple when the most important part of my day was seeing how high I could build a drippy castle. I loved lying at the shore's edge and letting the warm waters of the Atlantic Ocean tickle my skin as the tide came in and out.

"What're you thinking about?" Spencer nudged my side.

"How much I could use a lazy beach day."

"We should plan one."

"I wish. After today, I'm going to be working most weekends until Congress takes the August recess. Ever since the container ship's collision with the bridge, things are speeding up on the port issues. We need to make sure that any regulations or laws that are enacted actually help and don't just seem like a good idea in the DC bubble." As we approached Mama's Italian Restaurant, the scents of oregano, basil, and garlic drifted out, making my stomach mutter.

Our routine on the Saturdays we volunteered ended with pizza, a movie, and large bowls of ice cream. If it were up to me, I'd get the same pizza every time, but Spencer liked to mix it up, and his creations were usually delish.

As we arrived at the restaurant, I reached for the door. "What kind of pizza do you want?"

"I love that you trust me implicitly with your pizza order."

"I trust you implicitly with most things. You have great taste."

"You're just saying that because I usually choose what you like." He smirked.

"Not true. Okay, maybe a little true. But isn't that what's so great about our relationship? How well we know each other." A ribbon of contentment wrapped around my heart.

"I do love that, but I guess I forgot to mention my date with Mary Katherine. I'm sorry."

"The Mary Katherine? As in Jordan's cousin?" I tugged my brows together in mock confusion, joking with him in our usual way, but then out of nowhere, something like loneliness opened within me like an empty room. A room with bare walls, no windows or art, no furniture, just blank space that wanted, needed, to be filled.

"She invited me to a gallery opening for one of her friends." He rocked onto his heels, his teasing grin gone.

I rubbed my stomach, trying to ease my discomfort. "Oh, that's nice."

"Are you okay?" With a tilt of his head, concern tightened Spencer's features, his eyes turning smoky as he studied me. "I thought this was what you wanted, but I can cancel."

"No, it's fine. I'm just tired. Have fun. I know how much you love art galleries." I bobbed my brows, hoping my sarcasm would mask my weird angst. This is what I wanted—or at least it was what I thought I wanted.

"Okay, if you're sure." Spencer glanced at his watch. "I need to hurry and get a shower before I meet her." He began backing away but with a careful eye on me, like he might detect something if he kept watching. "Church and lunch tomorrow?"

"Sounds like a plan." I waved. "Have fun. I want a full report." *Ugh.* That was absolutely the last thing I wanted, but it sounded like something I'd normally say.

Spencer's expression relaxed into a smile. "All right. See you in the morning." With a quick wave, he turned and jogged down the sidewalk.

Drained of energy, I sank onto the bench in front of the restaurant. After a few deep breaths, I shook off my sullenness. A change in the routine could be fun or at least interesting. I pulled out my phone and placed an order for sweet and sour pork with fried rice and steamed dumplings. Still needing a boost, I texted Lawson, who as far as I knew hadn't come to his senses about marrying Willa, and my schedule hadn't left me with much free time to work on his case.

Me: Hey. Can you chat? We haven't talked in forever.

Lawson: Sorry. It's crazy here with summer activities and all the new residents and the wedding plans.

Me: No worries. Busy here too.

Lawson: Have you talked to your brother?

I stared at his words as ropes of uncertainty wrapped around what had been an empty hole inside me. This is why I didn't go home for visits. I hated all the ways past hurts still affected me. No matter how much success I achieved, when I was home, I was still that awkward high school version of myself who never fit in. Unlike my brother, Mr. Popularity.

Swallowing, I typed the appropriate adult reply and not the petty one I wanted to, reminding Lawson that he was my friend first and Brad's second.

Me: Not recently, but mom says he's doing great.

Mom never failed to provide an update on Brad's life. Until recently the reports weren't impressive, but when the pendulum started swinging the other way for Brad, it'd been with astonishing speed and luster. My parents always touted my achievements, but what if I failed to get married? On our last call, Mom gushed about Brad and Zoe's fantastic relationship and hinted, in a not-so-subtle way, that they'd be getting engaged—

Me: Does this have to do with Zoe?

Please no. Please. I'm supposed to be the successful one. I was supposed to have it all together, so why did it seem like everything was slipping through my hands?

Lawson: Can't say.

Me: Not nice.

Lawson: Sorry.

What? Was he really not going to tell me what was going on with my brother? *Fine.* I stood, shoved the phone in my pocket, and strode to the Chinese restaurant.

At home, I arranged my takeout containers on the coffee table and searched for a movie. But with the impeccable timing of a little brother—although at six foot four inches, no one would describe him that way—Brad invited me to accept a FaceTime request.

Seriously? He couldn't just call or send a text? Better yet, a DM on Instagram would've been adequate, and bonus, I wouldn't have seen it until I checked my feed, which I rarely did.

I could ghost him, but then I'd have to deal with it later, and since my night had already been derailed by Mary Katherine, I might as well get it over with. I tapped the accept button.

My Greek god of a brother and his sparkly blonde girlfriend appeared on the screen. While I hated to admit it, it was obvious why the producers from the Living Well Network had given them their own show.

"Hi." I glanced at my face on the screen, making sure I wore a pleasant expression. Instinctively my jaw clenched at my disheveled appearance, but I pressed the corners of my lips up and crinkled my eyes. Next to these two, I didn't just look a mess with my frizzy hair and fading makeup. No, I more resembled Cinderella before the fairy godmother works her magic, and I don't mean that pretty Disney cartoon version. I mean the one Drew Barrymore portrays in *Ever After*, minus the soot.

But it didn't matter because they were too wrapped up in each other to give me more than a glance.

"Hi, Car. We have some big news." Brad's accent was as thick and syrupy as ever. He gazed at Zoe and she at him for what seemed like an eternity. When his bright blue eyes shifted to meet mine, jealousy scratched at my pleasant resolve. Sure, I put on a good show of loving my eye color when I heard the song dedicated to the nostalgia-inducing brown-eyed girls of the world and their fun-loving ways. And I'd never turn down Spencer's invitation to dance to the song that was more ours than mine. But it didn't change the fact that Brad had managed to get all the best genes in the looks department. It wasn't fair, but since God hadn't listened to my complaints and granted me a miracle, I'd accepted my auburn hair, pale skin, and brown eyes as being a payoff for being the most successful sibling. Of course, now Brad was giving me a lot of competition for that title.

"We're engaged!" they said in unison, and Zoe held up her hand, revealing a diamond ring.

"Congratulations. I'm so happy for y'all." Or at least, I knew I should be and hated that unwanted jealousy invaded my conscience.

"Thank you. Please say that you'll be a bridesmaid. We're keeping everything small, but I want all my sisters to be bridesmaids, and soon you'll be my sister too." Zoe crinkled her nose, her focus once again drifting to Brad.

"Of course. I'd love to be a bridesmaid." And I didn't even roll my eyes at the whole sister thing. It wasn't Zoe's fault that I was in such a funk, and she deserved to be happy. Brad, on the other hand, I was still reserving judgment on.

"Wonderful. We can do some dress shopping when you're down here for Willa and Lawson's wedding!"

"We'll see." I caught my eyelashes fluttering and stopped them. Apparently, they were trying to overcompensate for my lack of enthusiasm.

Brad angled the phone toward himself as Zoe disappeared from view. "Hey, it was great to talk to you. We need to go. You can stay on, but Mom just poured champagne for a toast, and I'm warning you, there will likely be lots of tears." He cringed in a way that was supposed to indicate that we were somehow on the same team and Mom was our adversary, but we hadn't been on the same team in a lot of years. Brad had made sure of that, and I didn't trust him not to sabotage me again. He'd done nothing to earn my trust. Just because my parents were buying his act, didn't mean he'd changed.

"Oh, no, that's okay. Congratulations again." I ended the call before Mom could intervene and use her magical powers of guilt to keep me on for the toasts. Besides, my food was getting cold, and I was starving. I was just doing what I needed to do to stay alive.

I pinched my chopsticks together and surveyed my surroundings. My life was objectively pretty great, but *having it all* meant a husband and a family. Logically, I knew I had time. If only Lawson hadn't gotten engaged, I could've handled Brad and Zoe's news better. I'd been expecting it for months. But every time I thought of Lawson with Willa, my skin crawled. He might deny it, but that stupid marriage pact had prompted his rushed proposal, and if they didn't call off the wedding soon, I'd have to step in and save my friend, or at least make sure he wasn't making a massive mistake.

Chapter 7

I'm sure all those people putting together capsule wardrobes and eliminating hurry from their lives found value in a slower pace with less clutter, but I wasn't one of them. I was best at my busiest. My hectic schedule didn't leave room for worry, and without my notice, a month skipped by without anyone mentioning weddings. It'd been pure bliss.

But it all ended when I checked my mail after a late night at the office. Jordan, Ashton, and I hadn't left for dinner. Instead, we'd ordered power salads to keep us going a few extra hours. As I entered my apartment, the heavenly scents of sweet peas and peonies greeted me. During my busiest days, when I only responded to texts with emojis and left for the office before Spencer made the coffee, he often surprised me with something lovely at the end of the day. On this occasion, I found a vase of flowers and a note on the kitchen table.

C– I hope you're eating and sleeping. Queenie and I tried to wait for you for dinner. Well, I did anyway. By the way, I fed her. Hope to see you soon. – S

With warm fuzzies floating inside me like dandelion seeds on a breeze, I pressed my face into the bouquet and inhaled. My eyes fluttered closed and for a moment, peace embraced me.

Unfortunately, as I opened my eyes and spotted the large ecru envelope with my name scrolled in elegant calligraphy across the front and one of those heart stamps in the corner, the peace evaporated. I moved it to the back of the stack, and for once appreciated the solicitations for a dozen services I had no use for as a single woman living in an apartment in the city. But the final piece of mail only made things worse. It didn't have a stamp because my landlord had slipped it in my box, and I didn't need to open it to know what the envelope held. It was the dreaded notice that we needed to renew our leases in six weeks, the week after Labor Day and the dreaded wedding.

Lately, Spencer and I hadn't spent a lot of time together. He'd been hanging more with Cooper out in Arlington, watching baseball games and practicing with the softball team. But when we did get together, Spencer brought up our future. Although he wasn't pressuring me to make any decisions about renewing our leases, he clearly thought I needed to give more consideration to my long-term plans. He usually included how much he loved our life. Actually, he was using the *L*-word to describe almost everything we did together, and it made my nerves skitter. Luckily, I'd been too swamped at work to linger on his insinuations. Fine, I clearly had pondered his limited vocabulary and was considering buying him a thesaurus.

I dropped the mail on the table except for the wedding invitation. After I traced my name, I ran my finger along the edge of the thick envelope. The tangible evidence made it clear the wedding was happening even if I pretended it wasn't. I glanced at the clock on the microwave. It was only slightly after midnight. Lots of nights, Spencer stayed up reading a novel or watching what he swore were educational documentaries on YouTube. I didn't quite see how watching a guy prepare steaks with ten different methods or a guy experimenting with explosives from World War Two qualified as educational, but if it meant he might still be awake, I didn't care.

After I checked on Queenie, who was peacefully sleeping on her bed, I crossed the hall and knocked on Spencer's door. When he didn't answer, I should've gone back to my apartment, but adrenaline was pumping through me, so I sent him a text.

Me: Hey. Are you awake?

Me: Spencer?

Me: ????

Spencer: Do you need to go to the hospital?

I chuckled.

Me: Maybe . . .

Spencer: I'm coming.

Within seconds, Spencer opened the door as he tugged a t-shirt over his head, covering what I'd forgotten was a very toned abdomen. Hey, he might be my best friend, but that didn't stop me from noticing that the man didn't miss too many days at the gym.

"Thank you for the flowers. They're beautiful and smell fantastic." I closed the door behind me.

He combed his fingers through his hair, leaving it sticking up in several places. "You're welcome, but if this is the thanks I get, don't expect more surprises."

"Sorry. I got the wedding invitation today." My fingertips grazed the doorknob. "But we can talk about it tomorrow. I didn't mean to interrupt your sleep."

"Carleigh, what *did* you intend? It's the middle of the night."

"Go back to bed. I'm sorry."

"No, I won't be able to sleep now." He gestured to the couch. "What's the matter?" He sat, rubbing his face.

I dropped on the cushion beside him and held up the invitation. "They're getting married."

"Yeah. We've already covered this."

"But I didn't think it'd happen."

"You've also made that abundantly clear." He smacked his hands to his thighs.

"O-okay." I gripped the invitation to stop my fingers from trembling, but the lump in my throat prevented me from saying more. I stared at the rows of black letters, willing my nerves to settle enough for me to calmly exit Spencer's apartment. He clearly wasn't going to comfort me.

But then, as he wrapped one arm around my back, he gently slipped the invitation free and placed it on the table. "Carleigh, I'm sorry. I shouldn't have snapped at you. You're shaking." He settled his hand around mine. "You came here for support, and all I ever want is to make you happy, but instead I was a complete jerk. What can I do to make it better? I don't even have any sweets unless you want a chocolate protein bar."

I sniffle-laughed as I turned to face him, our noses a breath apart, and suddenly the air around us grew heavy. As he searched my expression, his pupils dilated, and I rolled my lips together. What was happening?

I needed to get control of myself before I made the same mistake I'd made with Lawson. Everyone had kept insisting we date, and I abandoned my intuition and kissed him. It'd almost ended our friendship, but this felt somehow different.

Sighing, Spencer averted his gaze and drew me closer, holding me firmly against his chest. "It's late. We should table this conversation. Our future is too important to discuss when we're exhausted and emotional."

As his thundering heartbeat drowned out his words, heat flooded my face. Sure, I was upset about Lawson getting married, but Spencer wasn't the solution. "That stupid marriage pact caused all this angst."

"Maybe it wasn't the worst thing." He rubbed my back, sending a wave of delight fluttering through me.

I pushed out of his embrace. "What are you talking about?"

"Whoa. I wasn't trying to start anything. I just feel—" He shook his head. "

And before he could continue talking about his feelings, I said. "This really isn't the best time for us to dive into our emotions. We can talk when we get back from Georgia."

"What?"

"I need to go to Magnolia Bluff and talk to Lawson, and with Congress going on recess at the end of next week, I have more flexibility in my schedule. Not to mention all the vacation time I've banked. This is perfect."

"Why don't you use that time for an actual vacation? It'll give us a chance to really talk. We could ask Brock for a recommendation. I'd love to go . . . well, I guess anywhere with you, so you can choose."

"You can't be serious. I can't go on a vacation when one of my best friends needs my help." I shot him a look. "Have I mentioned that this time last year Lawson was in a serious relationship with another woman who cheated on him?"

"Yes, but Willa didn't cheat on him."

"Willa is his rebound. Not exactly the best start for a relationship, forget a marriage. I just don't want to see him make a mistake."

"Carleigh, I get that you're concerned for your friend, but Lawson is a grown man. You should trust him to know his own feelings." Spencer grabbed at the back of his head.

While I could see his frustration mounting, I also knew how the pressure of the marriage pact was affecting me. But I wasn't going to confess those misplaced impulses.

"I couldn't forgive myself if I didn't do everything in my power to make sure this is right for him." I snatched up the invitation. "And I can only do that in person. You could go with me. You said anywhere."

"Anywhere for a vacation. Not an ambush." He flexed his fist. "I'm fine with being your date for the wedding, but there's no way I'm flying to Georgia to help you break up a wedding."

"I just said I needed to talk to Lawson. If he decides not to get married, I'll be there to support him." I stood. "I shouldn't have bothered you."

"If you'd listen to me and consider what I'm saying, what I've been saying for weeks, you'd see how messed up this is." He slung his hand wide.

"I have no idea what you're talking about." I pulled open the door. "All I'm doing is trying to stop a friend from making a terrible decision."

"How do you know it's a terrible decision?" Spencer jumped to his feet. "At the very least, you should give Lawson the benefit of the doubt before you swoop in and convince him that the woman he loves is wrong for him."

"I tried your method, and he hasn't figured it out. If she's the right woman for him, I won't be able to convince him otherwise."

"We both know how talented you are at persuasion."

"Thanks for the compliment, but I wish you'd support my decision."

"I can't comprehend why you don't want Lawson to get married, but at least he's had the chance to have a relationship without your interference."

"What's that supposed to mean?"

"Nothing."

"Are you really blaming me for all of your failed relationships?"

Spencer pressed his lips into a line, glaring at me.

"Fantastic. Believe what you want." I marched across the hall to my apartment, and without giving it a second thought, booked a one-way flight for Savannah and reserved a room at the only hotel close to Magnolia Bluff. Then I did the thing I'd been avoiding for weeks. I opened the wedding website and tried, unsuccessfully, to hold back the tears.

The next thing I knew, Queenie was nudging my hand. I tried to open my eyes, but they were caked closed with makeup and dried out contacts. Both were a result of the insufferable tears I'd been unable to thwart while reading the details of the wedding events and reliving my fight with Spencer.

I scratched Queenie's head. "Just give me a minute, and I'll get your breakfast." After shuffling to the bathroom, I washed my face, removed my contacts, and put on my glasses. Still exhausted, I made Queenie's breakfast.

I needed coffee, but when I tried to turn Spencer's doorknob, it didn't budge. We'd had disagreements before, but he'd never locked me out. Maybe after our late night, he wasn't out of bed. I lifted my fist to knock, but when his words hit me again, I lowered my hand, pivoted, and returned to my apartment. If he didn't want to see me this morning, I needed to give him space.

Chapter 8

To my dismay, Spencer needed exactly sixty-three hours, forty-two minutes, and twenty-one seconds to respond to the self-deprecating text I'd sent him when I'd realized my coffee maker was no longer operational. I'd thought if I made light of my coffee woes, we could just move on without a round of apologies—just agree to disagree.

But Spencer wasn't that type of guy. Rejection was hard for him, and I didn't realize he'd been using me as an excuse for his relationship issues. While the women he'd dated hadn't been right for him, I'd kept my opinion to myself . . . mostly. Besides, it seemed like every one of his relationships ended amicably, so no one ever got hurt, and if my memory was correct, Spencer was still friends with every woman he'd ever dated.

When he finally did return my text, it was only to ask if I needed a ride to the airport. I think he'd hoped I'd say that I'd decided not to follow through on my plans. Or alternatively, he'd have one last chance to talk me out of going. I also thought that once I responded to his obvious olive branch, we'd be back to our normal messaging. But I was wrong. He only asked for my flight details, and after he had them, he texted what time we needed to leave.

To my relief, his frustrations with me didn't extend to Queenie. In a particularly low moment, I'd given myself bonus points for coming up with a reason to text him. Although I did need someone to take care of my cat while I was in Georgia, so it wasn't all that calculating.

But the line of communication I'd planned for didn't happen. Spencer merely responded with a thumbs-up emoji. He didn't even ask for directions, not that he needed them. He knew the drill. I considered texting him to see if he'd collect my mail, but it felt too desperate, and he always did it when I was out of town, so I didn't bother. Truthfully, I couldn't bear another emoji response. I was almost looking forward to him launching into his arguments against my plans on our ride to the airport.

But once we were in the car, Spencer proved me wrong again. If his texts had been cold, he was downright frigid in the flesh. Not only did he not argue with me about my plans, he didn't say much of anything. In fact, he responded to my questions with as few syllables as possible until I gave up. Normally, I'd have confronted him about his immature behavior and insisted that an important part of friendship is talking about life, but I didn't want to fight with him when I was leaving. Not to mention, the way he was gripping the steering wheel and grinding his molars made his sentiments fairly clear.

When we finally arrived at the airport, Spencer parked at the curb and though he was angry, he couldn't stop being a gentleman. He lifted my suitcase from the trunk. "I hope you have an uneventful flight." He said his customary line as he passed me the handle of my roller bag.

My heart shivered at leaving him with things between us in such a weird place, but what could I do or say to improve our circumstances? We'd reached an impasse, but once I returned, surely everything would reset to normal.

"Thanks for driving me." I moved the bag to my side. Spencer always hugged me goodbye when he brought me to the airport. It was part of our routine like his line, but would he initiate the gesture? I stared at the buttons on his shirt, my chest tightening with every breath as I waited, willing him to reach for me.

"You should go." He stepped backward.

But I buried my pride and wrapped my arms around him. "Not without a hug."

He stiffened at first, but as I pressed tighter and held on longer, he sighed heavily and returned the embrace, his muscles relaxing with the move.

The tension that'd been weighing on me since I'd found Spencer's door locked slipped away as his hand slowly rubbed my back. It wasn't our usual quick hug between old friends. It was the embrace of two people who'd been through years together with all the ups and downs, and still needed the assurance that even if life changed, they'd always have each other to lean on. And I didn't want it to end.

With every rotation of his palm on my back, I reconsidered my mission, but I just couldn't shake the certainty that I needed to get on the plane. My gut was telling me to go, and it never failed me.

"I'm sorry you don't agree with my decision. I don't want this to come between us."

His hand stopped moving. "I know."

As he lowered his arms, releasing me, I shifted away, but his fingers caught my wrist.

"Don't go." He slid his hand around mine.

"I'm sorry." I squeezed his hand. "I have to. When I get there, I'll text." This was usually the last thing I said to him before I walked into the terminal, but he didn't let go. I lifted my gaze to his and offered him a slight smile, trying to be encouraging while also being sensitive to the fragile state of our relationship. "I'll be back in less than a week. Remember, this is what I do. I close deals."

He nodded, letting my hand drop away from his. "Just be sure your *client* is happy with your progress on the project and gets the results he wants."

"Of course."

"Have a great trip." He pivoted and hurried to the car.

As he pulled away from the curb, hollowness opened inside me, like I'd just lost something. But I hadn't. Our friendship could survive this disagreement. Everything would be fine. I grabbed the handle of my bag, squared my shoulders, and strode into the airport.

Like Spencer said, I just needed to make sure my client was satisfied, and Lawson would be. He just didn't know what he wanted. He'd been blinded by all that blonde hair, long legs, and big smile. After I opened his eyes to all the reasons he should press pause on this wedding, he'd thank me for helping him see reality and he could move on with his life. I hated that his failed engagement would likely result in him having to find a new job, but isn't that why he'd instated his no-dating-coworkers policy? If only I'd done a better job keeping in touch with him, I could've reminded him of it before we'd arrived at this unfortunate intersection.

I pressed my palm to my stomach, trying to fill the pit in my gut with something besides guilt over the way I'd neglected Lawson and hurt Spencer. At least Lawson would be happy I was coming to see him. As soon as I got through security and located my gate, I found an empty seat and texted him that I was otw.

> Lawson: When you say you're otw, you do mean on the way, right?

> Me: Yes

> Lawson: Are you driving? What about work? What about Queenie? Is Spencer with you?

> Me: Flying

My phone vibrated, with a call from Lawson.

"Hey, I was typing a response."

"Yeah, but I had too many questions. I can't believe you're on the way."

"Me either, but with Congress on recess, I had some time, and it seemed like a good idea. It might be our last chance to hang out before you're a married man." I cringed.

"We can still hang out after I'm married. You're going to love Willa. Everyone does. She's such a beautiful person and I don't just mean her looks. She's also beautiful on the inside, like really good to her core. You know what I mean? Like she can't stand to upset anyone and tries to help everyone. She's always optimistic and full of joy."

I tapped my foot on the floor as he concluded his description of a person that I doubted existed. There was no way the woman he'd described could be Wyatt Ramsay's sister. Since my brother and I shared virtually nothing in common, I wouldn't normally judge a person based on her sibling, but Wyatt was a different kind of trouble.

"I'm looking forward to meeting her, but I hope we can schedule some time for just the two of us."

"When will you get here?" He asked.

"My flight lands in Savannah at two thirty, and then I've got to rent a car. It's about an hour to Magnolia Bluff, right?"

"Yeah, but aren't you going to see your parents?"

"Not right away. I want to see you. To be honest, I haven't told them I'm coming." And I didn't plan to. Not at the risk of being forced to go shopping for bridesmaids' dresses with Zoe and Mom.

"Oh, okay. I take it Spencer isn't with you?"

"No, he couldn't come on such short notice, and I needed someone to take care of Queenie. I don't like boarding her. I think she worries that she's back at the shelter. The last time I had to leave her there, she hid under my bed for a week when we got home."

"You sound like a crazy cat lady."

"I don't have to get on this flight."

"I'm just messing with you. Besides you have to come now because you need to throw me a bachelor party."

"Oh, well, when you put it like that, I'll definitely be canceling my flight."

"Ha ha. But seriously, if you aren't going to your parents, where are you staying?" Lawson asked.

"The B&B in Haslemere. Is it nice?" I glanced at the gate agent who'd started sending passengers to the plane.

"Yeah and the owners are great. It's a friendly town. I would've moved there, but I wanted to be closer to work. Still it's only a short drive to my house and Magnolia Bluff."

"Even better." I stood. "Gotta go, but I'll text when I land, and by the way, keep my visit on the down-low for now. After I get settled, I'll check in with my family."

"Not a problem. I can't wait to see you."

"Me too. Bye." I loved that he knew my family dynamics well enough to know that I wasn't being mean; I just needed some time on my own. Warmth gathered inside me, covering the pit of guilt, worry, and loss. I'd made the right decision, and I couldn't wait to spend some quality time with Lawson. With a lot more hope, I felt lighter as I boarded the plane.

As I stored my suitcase in the overhead compartment, my phone vibrated and I checked the message on my smartwatch.

> **Spencer: Do you want to marry Lawson?**

What the what? I squinted at the tiny print, then dropped into my seat, retrieved my phone, and re-read the message from Spencer—same words, larger print. Why would he even ask that question? All I wanted was to help Lawson.

> **Me: That's irrelevant.**

Spencer: It's very relevant.

Me: I have to put my phone in airplane mode.

Spencer: Just think about it.

I tapped the little airplane on the screen, but unfortunately, it didn't make the message go away. I checked my seatmate, hoping for a distraction, but she'd inserted her earbuds and was playing a game on her phone. Fantastic, alone with my thoughts for two hours, and I doubted I'd think about anything but his ridiculous question and why he thought this was the best time to ask it. This wasn't the kind of thing I wanted to discuss on the phone, but with all this time to *think*, the first thing I'd do when I was in the privacy of that rental car was call Spencer.

I glanced at the conversation, why didn't I just say no? Shivers slipped up my arms, but I brushed down the hairs trying to warn me. What did they know?

Chapter 9

Take this as fair warning: when the hairs on your arms rise up and wave their tiny caution flags, you should pay attention. And I normally do, but I let my guard down as I waited in the rental car line, texting Spencer and Lawson that I'd arrived. Hopefully, Spencer wouldn't respond right away because I didn't want to have this conversation with an audience of weary travelers.

I'd assumed the physical reaction I'd experienced before takeoff had been the result of Spencer's probing question, but I didn't need to be warned about him, at least not yet.

Then when I felt a tap on my shoulder and turned only to be wrapped in Lawson's arms and spun in a circle, surely his surprise was the cause of my gut telling me to prepare for the unexpected. But Lawson's sudden appearance wasn't what the warnings were for either.

Nope. The alert became evident, however, when Lawson put me down in front of a beaming blonde woman I recognized from my computer screen as Willa Ramsay. Then those signals to be on guard for a sneak attack made sense, and my initial happiness at seeing Lawson fled like the British at the Battle of New Orleans.

"I'm so glad you're here, so Lawson can spin you around instead of me. I'd be turning green from motion sickness." Willa stepped in for her own hug because that's how things are done in the south between old friends and apparently friends of old friends.

"Me too." I quickly patted her back and shifted out of her embrace, not convinced she might not puke on me. Hey, it'd happened before, and I found people rarely changed what came naturally.

"When I told Willa you were flying down today and planning to rent a car, she insisted that we pick you up. So here we are." He put an arm around Willa and drew her to his side.

"Here you are." I smiled, shaking my head.

Lawson's brow knitted. "Is that okay?"

"Of course." I clenched my jaw.

"Are you sure? Because you're making that face you make when you're not sure whether to be happy or mad."

This was the problem with close friends. It was hard to fake it around them. I relaxed my expression. "I'm fine, and it was so thoughtful of you to come, but I'm going to need a car, especially since I'm staying in Haslemere."

"Willa has a perfect solution for that too." He gazed down at her like she'd found the cure for cancer while also achieving world peace. Yep, she'd used all her assets to cast a spell over my best friend. Lawson was too trusting. Of course, after he'd had his heart broken by that terrible woman who'd been cheating on him, Willa's purported sweetness and innocence made her seem like an angel sent straight from heaven.

"Really?" My pulse raced. If I knew one thing, whatever Willa's solution was, it would not be perfect.

"Yes." She smiled wider, which hadn't seemed possible. "You can stay with me at Magnolia Bluff. I'm living in the Retreat owners' guest cottage until the wedding, and I have a spare bedroom. It's just been renovated, so it's super nice with a small kitchen and living area. You'll be right in the middle of all the fun and not all the way over in Haslemere."

"Oh, wow." I strived to control my expression. "That's so generous of you, but I wouldn't want to impose."

"I promise it's not an imposition," Willa said.

"And it'll give y'all a chance to get to know each other better." Lawson nodded.

"That's true." And it also would give me a chance to uncover her weak spots. No one was as good as she appeared to be or as Lawson thought she was. If anyone fully appreciated that truth, it was me, and I would've thought Lawson.

But sadly he failed to recall how broken I'd been in high school after my childhood friend, Bree Flanders, dropped me without a care. Everyone believed she was a sweetheart too. Thankfully, Lawson had been there to catch me, and I'd figured out that I didn't need a lot of girlfriends with all their drama. Instead I focused my energies on being the best at everything I did, and in the end, the payoff had been a lot better than being a part of Bree's circle of Peach Puffs. It sounded so stupid now to think I'd ever wanted to be a Puff, but even though I'd come a long way since their rejection, my chest still tensed at the memory. If Peach Puffs were still a thing when Willa made it to high school, she was the kind of girl they'd have invited to join them, and while Lawson might not see the similarities, I sensed them to my core.

"Wonderful." Willa turned her attention to the baggage claim. "Let's get your luggage."

I twirled my roller bag in a circle. "This is all I have." Because the visit would hopefully be brief.

"For three weeks?" Her brows creased before she blinked away her concerns. "You must be one of those expert packers. I've watched some of their videos, but I haven't mastered the skill. You'll have to show me your secret techniques."

"Yeah. You'll have to give us a demonstration." Lawson eyed me skeptically as he took my suitcase handle and led us toward the sliding doors.

"Oh, it's nothing." I sidled up beside my new girlfriend as we made our way outside where I almost lost my manners when the oppressive heat and humidity attacked me. As we walked to the parking garage, I removed my cardigan. "Enough about my packing prowess. Willa, tell me about the wedding plans."

"Actually, your timing is perfect. Since you're here, you'll be able to come to my bridal shower. With our short engagement and the opening of the club, I'm only having one party, but it's going to be amazing. My friends are going all out with the theme." She raised her brows at me, grinning like she really wanted me to ask about the details.

While I'd rather take a class on mindfulness—what a complete waste of time—I needed to play along.

"What's the theme?" I wrinkled my nose, channeling my best version of a teenage Peach Puff. I may not have donned the title, but I'd observed those girls enough to pretend to be one.

"Blush and Bashful."

"Like from *Steel Magnolias*?"

"Yes. So you know how Lawson and I met while planning a wedding at the Retreat at Magnolia Bluff last spring?"

I nodded along. While I still hadn't gotten all the details of their whirlwind romance, I had skimmed the story of how they met on the wedding website.

"Well, the bride, Wren, was obsessed with all things southern even though she's from Chicago, so she suggested the theme to Zoe and Linda, and they latched onto the idea."

I wasn't at all surprised my future sister-in-law was an accomplice to these shenanigans. Were there seriously four grown women planning a party around this pink theme? It sounded more like the theme for a child's birthday party, but Willa was very young.

"Who's Linda?" I asked as we approached Lawson's Jeep Cherokee.

Lawson lifted the rear door and stowed my suitcase. "Remember, she's one of the owners and developers of the Retreat."

"She and her husband own the cottage where we're staying. Linda loves to entertain and insisted on hosting the shower," Willa said.

"Linda takes all the credit for getting us together." Lawson opened the front and back passenger doors at one time.

Willa and I both made for the backseat. I'd never let her beat me at being more generous, but like an expert martyr, she slipped in first. "I'll take the back."

"Are you sure?" Lawson asked. "What about your motion sickness?"

Yeah. The last thing I needed was having her projectile vomit on me from the backseat. At least if I sat back there, I'd be out of the splash zone.

"I'll be fine as long as I sip my ginger ale." Willa lifted a green bottle from the cup holder. "And I can see out of the windows, and there isn't a detour through the mountains." She winked. "Besides, I'm sure y'all want to catch up."

"You're the best. Thank you." Lawson patted her knee.

If they kept this mushy stuff up, I'd be the one gagging, but I simply said, "Thank you," and climbed in the front seat.

"Tell Carleigh about how Linda set us up." Lawson closed our doors.

"First, she invited me to stay at the cottage the week of Wren and Nathaniel's wedding because I was still living in Savannah, and once you meet Linda, you'll understand that it's a waste of energy trying to decline her hospitality. It's easier just to give in and let her pamper you."

"Got it." I clicked my seatbelt.

"Anyway, she told Lawson and me that she was going to host a casual dinner for us with her husband, Fred, in their gazebo that overlooks the river, but when I arrived at the cottage, she'd left a note, saying she'd forgotten that they'd made plans to pick up her godson at the airport and wouldn't be back for dinner."

Lawson joined us. "She sent me a text to meet Willa, but I didn't find out they weren't coming until Willa told me." With a glance at his fiancée in the rearview mirror, Lawson started the engine. "Chef had prepared the meal, and while I was hesitant to give into Linda's scheming, I wasn't about to pass up Chef's food."

"It turned out to be a magical night."

Looking out the back window, he reversed the jeep. "Not that we got together right away."

"That was your fault." Willa playfully smacked his shoulder.

"Sorry it took me so long to catch up."

"I've had a crush on Lawson since the sixth grade."

"Really?" I shifted sideways in my seat to see them both. "If my math is right, Lawson and I were twenty when you were eleven."

"I didn't reciprocate." Lawson laughed.

"No, he told me to find a guy my own age."

Lawson steered out of the parking garage. "Um, I didn't want to get arrested."

"Details, details." Willa flipped her hand dismissively, and for a moment, I appreciated her sass.

But just because she wasn't the worst didn't mean they should be rushing into marriage, especially since it sounded like this Linda person and Willa were likely conspiring against Lawson.

"Speaking of details. Tell me more about this *Steel Magnolias*-themed shower. I've never heard of such a thing."

Lawson veered onto the highway. "No one's ever heard of something as bizarre as what Wren, Zoe, and Linda have concocted, trust me, and I only know a fraction of what's going on."

"He's so right, they've gone way beyond *Steel Magnolias*. It's more like if Sydney, Julia Roberts' character, was planning the shower. Everything will be a shade of pink. I saw Zoe carrying in stacks of material the other day. They've tried to keep the details a secret, but I *am* the event coordinator at the Retreat, so I still hear things."

"Like what?"

"For starters, not only will there be the famed red velvet armadillo cake, but there'll be hot pink, sparkling rosé and azalea garden punch, pale pink chocolate-covered strawberries, framed quotes from the movie, and all the guests are to wear pink. They may be making pink sunhats as party favors."

"Unfortunately, nothing I brought fits the dress code." I resisted the urge to offer a fist bump up to Lawson.

"You could borrow something from one of the ladies." He smirked, getting way too much pleasure at what he knew would be just short of torture for me.

"Absolutely, we're about the same size."

"Thanks, Willa." I shot Lawson a side-eye, but he was focused on the road. "Did you already tell everyone that I was coming early?"

"No, but I don't know how you'll keep it a secret for long with your brother and Zoe at the Retreat almost every day," he said.

"You're right, but can y'all please give me a couple of days?" If I worked fast, I could still avoid this pink party and my family.

"Our lips are sealed," Willa said.

"Thanks." My phone vibrated, and I slipped it out of my pocket to read the message.

> Spencer: Glad you made it. Sorry about my last text. Can you talk?

> Me: Lawson and Willa surprised me at the airport. Currently, I'm in the car with them, so I'll call if I ever get some privacy. <prayer hands emoji>

Spencer: Yikes!

Me: That's only half of it. I can't wait to talk to you. You won't believe what's going down.

Spencer: On the edge of my seat.

I laughed under my breath, releasing a little of my pent-up angst over the state of Spencer's and my relationship. If he was apologizing and making jokes, we were on the way back to our comfortable place, and I couldn't wait to be there.

Chapter 10

Willa was a more skilled adversary than I'd expected. Her incessant and practiced hospitality was a tactic I hadn't accounted for, requiring me to adjust my plans.

Practically glued to Lawson's side, the wannabe-bride kept him under her powers. It was like he was hypnotized by her blue eyes. To break the spell, I needed to get Lawson alone so I could have an uninterrupted adult conversation with him. After the drive to Magnolia Bluff, dinner at the clubhouse with Willa, and then a tour of the Retreat grounds with the inseparable couple, I didn't know how I'd accomplish a tête-à-tête with Lawson.

However, I did appreciate the lovely setting, and the breeze off the river helped temper the heat and humidity. There were tennis courts, a vegetable garden for farm-to-table dining, a dock with kayaks and canoes, and nature trails for strolling, biking, or even golf cart rides. Lawson pointed out a trail covered in crushed oyster shells that led to his house a couple of miles away. Willa said they planned to install more recreational areas over the coming year and complete the golf course. The Retreat at Magnolia Bluff was just the kind of place I could see many of my clients spending their holidays, but I wasn't here to scout a location for a corporate getaway.

When I finally claimed exhaustion, they miraculously agreed to part for the night. At the guest cottage, Willa showed me my room, and I told her I had some things I needed to take care of in DC. I did want to talk to Spencer, but more than that, I didn't want to end up sitting in our jammies trading ghost stories and eating cookie dough. I did enjoy both under the right circumstances, but any situation that involved Willa was not the right circumstances.

After I heard Willa's bedroom door click shut, I dug out my tablet and logged into the Wi-Fi. Lawson had explained that it'd been terrible before Linda had worked her magic with an internet provider to have fiber optic cables installed. This Linda person intrigued me. She could be a potential client, especially if she planned future development projects in the Low Country. This was one of my areas of expertise.

On the bedside table, I used a framed watercolor painting of twilight on the river to prop up my tablet before I sent a FaceTime request to Spencer. Hopefully, he'd still be in a forgiving mood.

When his smiling face filled the screen, I exhaled with relief. "Hey, it's good to see you."

"You too. How are things going?"

"Great question. I'm not sure. Somehow I've ended up sharing a cottage at Magnolia Bluff with Willa."

He chuckled. "Is she there?"

"Yes, but I have my own bedroom."

"So is she as bad as you thought she'd be?"

"Exactly as expected." But I didn't want to talk about the precious Willa. "More importantly, how are you? I'm sorry things have been weird between us. I take full responsibility."

"Really?" Spencer's eyebrows shot up.

"Sure. Lawson isn't your friend. Y'all barely know each other."

"Got it, and I guess that's part of what I need to talk with you about. Please be patient with me as I try to explain, because I'm sure it's not going to come out right. But just give me a chance to get it all out before you respond."

"Of course. I don't want us to be at odds either, and I'm sure whatever you have to say will be—"

"Car." Spencer held up his hand. "Maybe it'd help if you covered your mouth."

"Sure, whatever you want." I pressed my fingers over my sealed lips, the corners twitching to tip up into a smile.

"Nice try, but I can tell you're about to burst." He rolled his eyes. "Anyway, I've been ruminating over why I've been so unnerved by your reaction to Lawson's engagement. What I've come up with is that I care about you in the same way you care about Lawson, and I hope you care about me. I'm trying to be a good friend and help you see another perspective because I don't want you to get hurt or be disappointed. You've been friends with Lawson for so long, and I'd hate for your relationship to be damaged in a way that can't be fixed." He held up a finger, halting my potential response. "The problem is we're both sure of what's best for our friend, you for Lawson and me for you. At this point, we've both expressed our opinions and those don't need to be rehashed." Pausing, he tilted his head slightly. "What do you think?"

As I lowered my hand from my mouth, the tension rolled off my shoulders. I was thankful he hadn't brought up the marriage question. I wasn't ready to hash out whatever had motivated him to ask it—or my failure to respond in the negative. I'd never seriously considered marrying Lawson, but I also didn't want to end up alone. Was that the answer?

"Carleigh?" Spencer interrupted my thoughts, which were illogical and contradictory, and why I didn't need to discuss them with him at this juncture. Normally, I'd have continued the debate, but winning didn't feel important—an entirely different problem I'd need to analyze. For now, I just wanted to say something to reassure him. "You're the best, and I don't know why you put up with me."

"Yeah, me either." He grimaced dramatically.

"Nice." I waved a hand over the screen.

"Please don't go. I'm just kidding."

"Relax. I'm glad we can joke. I've missed it."

"Me too. If anything, this time apart has shown me I can't imagine a life without you."

Was he really considering giving up on me? My breath caught in my throat as tears pressed at the corners of my eyes, and I tried to make room for the right words. Being vulnerable, even with Spencer, was so hard for me, but he deserved a response, so I swallowed away my trepidation. "I've missed you so much."

"Don't cry. Please. It's contagious." He swiped under his eyes.

"Let's never do this again." I sniffled. "We should've had this conversation before I left, but I'm going to talk with Lawson ASAP, so I can come home."

"I can't wait for you to get back. I'm working on a surprise for you."

"Really?"

"Don't try to guess what it is, and if you don't like it, it's no big deal, but if you do, well—" Shaking his head, Spencer dropped his gaze. "I'm not saying anything else. You'll just have to wait and see."

Shivers skittered up my neck with anticipation. "Can't wait, and I'll keep you updated. My hope is still to be home before the blush and bashful bridal shower."

"I'm sorry, the what now?"

"The blush and bashful themed bridal shower. It's inspired by the wedding in *Steel Magnolias*. According to the *blushing* bride, everything and everyone will be shades of pink."

"I have no words."

I laughed. "This feels good."

"It does, and as much as I'd like to stay up and chat, I have an early meeting. By the way, Queenie misses you. I swear she glared at me the entire time I was making her dinner."

"She's such a diva. Thanks for taking care of her and me."

"Not a problem. Keep me updated. I'll pick you up at the airport."

"Have I mentioned that I can't wait to see you?" I asked.

"A few times, but I don't get tired of hearing it. Sleep well." He ended the call, and I fell back against the pillows. Spencer truly was the best guy, and talking to him renewed my determination to talk to Lawson sooner rather than later. I glanced at the clock. It was only ten o'clock. Energy buzzed through me as I cracked the door and peeked out. The coast was clear.

As I left the cottage, I switched on my phone flashlight. Willa had shown me the golf cart she used to get around the Retreat and mentioned that I was welcome to borrow it. Of course, she no doubt wouldn't be pleased to discover I'd snuck out of the cottage and was going to meet her fiancé to convince him she wasn't the girl for him. But when she found the right guy, she'd appreciate my sacrifice. Everyone would win.

I started the golf cart, grateful it was electric, emitting a soft whir. But when I put it in reverse, a loud, high-pitched tone echoed through the quiet night, alerting anyone with ears that I was on the move. I switched the lever back to neutral and held my breath as my body temperature skyrocketed. What a rookie mistake. Of course, I didn't drive golf carts as often as many of my colleagues who used days on the golf course to broker deals. Unfortunately, the few times I'd tried the tactic, it'd failed.

With my competitive nature, I couldn't focus on social niceties when there was a game to win.

I fanned my face, waiting for someone to discover and report me—to whom I'm not sure, since this wasn't exactly a high crime area. The only bandits were likely the furry, black-masked variety that enjoyed raiding dumpsters more than *borrowing* golf carts in the dark of night.

Since I couldn't depend on the engine to propel the golf cart backwards, I got out and pushed the cart as far as was necessary. Back in the driver's seat, I feathered my shirt from my body, trying to cool down, but it was useless in the balmy night. My best option was to start moving and hope I dried on the ride to Lawson's house. With the headlights off, I steered onto the road and followed the gas lanterns that looked lovely but didn't provide much light. Still, I could see where to turn onto the path. Finally, in the safety of the pine tree forest, I switched on the lights, which should've calmed my nerves. Instead, I shivered as shadows emerged.

With no time to lose, I slammed the pedal to the floor, and experienced little satisfaction since the increase in speed was hardly perceptible. Maybe this wasn't a good idea, but I continued. With the wheels crunching the shells along the path, I prayed that none of the wild animals I'd learned about on my second-grade field trip to the Okefenokee Swamp lived this far north. What had those teachers been thinking taking a bunch of children on a boat ride through alligator-infested waters? For weeks, the taxidermy black bear and panther from the nature center, along with the caged rattlesnakes, had haunted my dreams.

Finally, a light appeared and soon I stopped at a gate. After opening it, I returned to the driver's seat and steered onto a paved road. There were a few small houses further down the street, but I spotted Lawson's Jeep in the driveway of the closest one. After I parked the golf cart, I walked to the door, smoothing down my hair.

Nerves fluttered through my stomach as I knocked. This would not be easy, but Lawson and I'd been friends a long time. We'd figure it out together. What had happened to his dreams of managing a prestigious resort or a historic golf club? This compromise amounted to quitting, and he needed help to see around the bend in the river to the ocean that awaited. While Willa wasn't concerned with encouraging Lawson to achieve his dreams, he could still have it all.

When the door swung open, Lawson gave me a quizzical look and then surveyed the area behind me. "I wasn't expecting you. Is Willa hiding somewhere?"

Did she often play hide and seek with him?

I shook my head. "It's just me. I couldn't sleep, so I just popped over to see what you're up to."

"Just watching the Braves game." He held open the door, gesturing me inside. "I thought you were tired."

"I was, but when I tried to relax, I got a surge of energy."

He closed the door. "I'm impressed you found your way."

"It's pretty much a straight shot." I stood in the living room. The kitchen and dining area opened to the left and a hallway to the right led to the rest of the house.

"I'm aware. You weren't freaked out by the woods?"

"You know me. Always up for a challenge." I pointed at the darts cabinet hanging on the wall. "How about a game?"

"Sure. It'll be one of my last because this fine piece of craftsmanship doesn't fit with Willa's design aesthetic." He opened the doors and passed me three darts.

"What kinds of sports does she play?" I, of course, knew the answer, but letting people realize the truth of their situation usually proved more effective for convincing them.

We crossed the room, stopping at a piece of tape on the floor, just like in his college apartment. We'd had a lot of great talks over darts.

"She's more of a fan, but she does play tennis." He rotated a dart between his fingers. "When she lived in Savannah, she went to the gym and took some classes. We have a gym here, so she uses it, but we haven't started any classes. She and Wren go for long walks most mornings."

"That's nice. Wren is the newlywed neighbor and *Steel Magnolias* fan?"

"Right. I'm sure you could join them."

"We'll see." I lifted a dart, aimed, and sent it flying. It landed just outside the ring around the bullseye. Undoubtedly, I was out of practice. "What about a tennis match? Is there anyone who I could partner with?"

"Um, Willa's not exactly up to your level. We mostly just hit the ball back and forth for fun."

Wincing, I almost threw a dart at the window, but I managed to hit the target. *Play for fun?* The only fun was winning. What was the point otherwise? I waited for Lawson to take his turn. "Oh, well, I'm sure y'all have other things in common. I mean besides your jobs."

His dart landed in the bullseye. Clearly, he'd been training. "Actually, we have a lot of history, but also we're a good balance for each other. And we're looking forward to developing new interests together." With a shrug, he crossed to the board and pulled out the darts. "Are you really this bad?"

"You know I'd never let you win."

"True."

As Lawson turned around, my smartwatch vibrated with a message, but it indicated it was a picture from Spencer, so I tugged my phone from my pocket. Something like felicity fluttered around my heart. After days of little communication with him, seeing anything from him felt more like an unexpected gift. I wouldn't take my friendships with Spencer or Lawson for granted anymore. I didn't get to see Lawson every day, so when we connected, it usually felt special. But I'd grown too comfortable having Spencer always available, and I didn't like being separated from him.

Smiling, I opened the message and found the sweetest selfie of Spencer and Queenie. Well, Spencer looked sweet, bits of blue shimmering through his gray irises. Queenie, on the other hand, glared at Spencer's profile, her head cocked to the side like she was considering swatting his nose off his face.

Spencer: We miss you. Good night.

As I started to type a response, Lawson looked at the screen and nudged my rib. "Just as I thought."

"What?" I liked Spencer's message and shifted my focus to Lawson.

"You do this thing where you bite down on your smile like you're trying to stop your face from expressing your emotions. I've seen you do it for years, and usually it's a reaction to Spencer."

As he finished his accusation, I rolled my lips over my teeth.

Lawson chuckled. "Too late. What's the deal with y'all anyway?"

"We're best friends. Just like you and me."

"You keep telling yourself that." Lawson smirked.

"It's true. Besides maybe my smile was for Queenie."

"But you're not sure?"

"What?"

"You said *maybe*, so on a subconscious level you know the truth."

"When did you become a psychologist?"

"Interesting." He tapped a finger to his chin.

"What?"

"You keep dodging the question."

"I do not. Spencer and I are friends. That's it." I snapped my mouth shut. How had this conversation become about me? I needed to grab the ball and serve it back to his side of the court. "Speaking of friends, isn't it weird dating the much-younger sister of one of your friends?"

"It was at first. I couldn't see Willa as anything but a teenage girl, but she's always been mature for her age." He passed me three darts. "By the way, I know what you're doing."

"What do you mean?" I focused on the bullseye.

"You're trying to change the subject, and I'll let you win for now. But just so we're clear, I think Spencer is perfect for you, and you should give the guy a chance."

I flung the dart. "Because women and men can't be friends? You can't believe that adage."

"We did kiss that one time."

I cringed. "Don't remind me."

"Yeah, it wasn't our finest moment, but it did let us test the waters and make sure we didn't want to go for a swim. I'm assuming you haven't put a toe in Lake Spencer."

I fisted a dart. "No, and stick with managing clubs. Your metaphors are terrible."

"The point remains that he might be interested in more than friendship, but you haven't even stepped up to the edge of the dock." He laughed. "Sorry, I couldn't resist."

"First, not only do I remember our kiss, but I also remember how awkward things were afterward. I'm not looking for a repeat with Spencer. And second, since you're so concerned for his well-being, I'm happy to report that Spencer has dated plenty of women and just started seeing a new one."

"Yeah, that doesn't prove anything, but I'll drop it if you'll help me with something else."

"Anything to put me out of my misery."

"Great. We won't need these." Lawson took my remaining darts and put them in a pile on an end table. "Didn't you and Spencer take ballroom dance lessons in law school?"

"Yes, but the deal was that if I helped you, you'd drop your speculations about Spencer."

"They aren't speculations. I only mentioned it because I need to learn to dance as a surprise for Willa." He switched on a wireless speaker and tapped the screen of his phone. "Will you teach me the basics for the shag? Willa brought in a teacher for the club members, but I was touring a development similar to Magnolia Bluff with Linda and Fred, so I missed it. Willa wanted to teach me afterward, but we've been swamped with work, and we're running out of time before the wedding."

I resisted the urge to point out that they didn't need to be rushing to the altar and immediately put him on the defensive. Waiting for the right moment was always part of a winning strategy.

"You're lucky my teacher was from South Carolina. The shag isn't considered ballroom dancing, but he taught it to us anyway," I said.

"So you can teach me?"

I sighed. "Do you have a playlist with beach music?"

"Do you make a splash when you cannonball?"

"I assume that sad metaphor means yes."

"You'd be correct." Lawson tapped his phone and a familiar song filled the room.

After we shoved the couch out of the way, I instructed Lawson to stand beside me and demonstrated the basic steps for the man's part. Once he'd mastered it, I moved in front of him. "Hold out your hands." I lifted my arms to waist height and rested my hands in his.

"Okay, now we do the same steps, but I'll be mirroring you. Ready?"

"Yep." Lawson caught on quickly, and we were having fun even if I'd let him distract me from the purpose of my visit.

"Do you want to try a turn?" I asked.

"Am I ready?"

"Sure. We just keep counting one and two, three and four, five, six. The trick is to make the turn on the first four counts and come back to the basic rock-step for five, six."

"Let's try it."

We started with the basic steps, moving to the beat of the music.

"Whenever you're ready, release my hand and then I'll turn under your arm." I squeezed his hand.

"Okay." As we ended the next combo, he let go of my hand and I twirled, but as I came around, we bumped into each other, and I fell off-balance into Lawson's chest, laughing.

At the same moment, the front door swung open.

"Are we having a dance party?" Wyatt, Willa's brother, stopped in the doorway, taking us in. "Where's Willa?" He clenched his fist at his side.

Same old Wyatt with no impulse control.

Swallowing my laughter, I righted myself. "She's sleeping."

"Wyatt, you remember Carleigh Chastain, Brad's sister. We're old friends." Lawson gestured in my direction, seemingly unaware that Wyatt thought we were messing around behind Willa's back.

"Apparently." Wyatt jabbed a finger in my direction. "But what's she doing here?"

"Oh, man." Lawson threw up his hands in surrender. "This is perfectly innocent. Carleigh got in today and is staying with Willa at the cottage."

"Then why is she here?" Wyatt folded his arms over his chest, displaying a gallery of tattoos.

"Relax." I glared right at him. Not that we owed the neanderthal an explanation, but for the sake of Lawson's face, I continued. "I couldn't sleep, so I drove over and then Lawson wanted dance lessons to surprise your sister."

Lawson looked between us, but his gaze settled on me. "Carleigh, it's late. You should head back and get some sleep. I'll walk you out." He stepped toward Wyatt, who was still guarding the open door. "Wyatt, please keep this on the down low, so the surprise isn't ruined."

"Of course, man." He dropped his hands, retreating. "I'd do anything for Willa." He shot me a warning look, dripping with disapproval.

As if. Frustration pounded through my veins. How dare he, of all people, accuse me of doing something wrong? With the confidence of his past thrusting me forward, I crossed the room and stopped in front of the foolish man. "It's a relief to see you've finally decided your sister's well-being is important."

"You don't know anything about me or my sister."

"Not surprisingly, you don't remember what I know." I lifted my brows confidently. "But I've heard you've cleaned up your act, and I hope for Willa's sake, it's true." I strode onto the porch.

Lawson shut the door behind us. "Wow, that didn't go like I expected."

"Why is he here?" I started for the golf cart.

"He's been staying with me until he can get his own place which, turns out, will be next week. I didn't mention it?"

"No. I knew he was working with y'all, but I would've remembered if you'd said he was staying here because I don't trust that guy."

"Carleigh, he's changed, you'll see."

"I hope you're right." I sat and turned the key.

"Thanks for the lesson. See you tomorrow."

"Be careful." I reversed out of the drive.

"You don't always have to get the last word," he shouted.

"Neither do you!" I pressed the pedal down and again was disappointed in the lack of power, ruining my dramatic getaway.

Chapter 11

Within ten hours, I realized just how fast news travels in a small town. I awoke to the scent of something delicious—definitely in the cake category with cinnamon and butter. Not one to pass up breakfast goodies, even if Willa was doing the baking, I slipped on my glasses and strolled into the living space.

While I did find Willa perched on the couch, I also discovered my brother and his fiancée, Zoe, who was extracting a pan from the oven. She wore a sequin-trimmed apron over a shimmery turquoise tank and a ruffled hot pink skirt. Mom had described Zoe's outfits on several occasions, but nothing prepared me for her sparkle. She'd even sprayed her hair with something to make her blond curls shimmer. No wonder Dad often referred to her as a fairy.

Willa shook her head. "I told no one you were here."

"Good morning!" Zoe set the pan on the stove and spun around. "It's a long story, but when I found out you were staying with Willa, I insisted she let me make you breakfast. It's so good to finally meet you in person, Carleigh!"

"Hi, Car." Brad wrapped me in one of his signature hugs, and even if things were strained between us, I couldn't resist hugging him back.

"You're in for a treat. Because of Zoe, I've gained ten pounds and I'm having to add extra workouts."

"You still look wonderful to me, and I'm the only one that matters." Zoe patted his abs, which I'm sure were still rock hard regardless of Zoe's baked goods.

I think my brother was born with muscles everywhere, making the rest of us mortals feel inadequate. But he never did much with his athleticism. If I'd heard the phrase, *he's not living up to his potential* once from my parents, I'd heard it a million times. But while they bemoaned his lack of accomplishments, to the people who mattered most in high school, Brad reigned on the throne of popularity. With all my success since high school, I should've been over how my brother not only ignored me, but also how he'd guaranteed I lost the one thing I cared most about to the girl who'd hurt me the most.

Maybe it was just me, but there's something about being rejected, undervalued, and ignored by my classmates that stuck with me. Mostly, I used it for motivation to achieve, but the teenager inside still grew anxious at the memories, even with my stellar resume.

Brad pecked Zoe's head. "Now that Car is finally up, can we please have a piece of cake?"

"I'm sorry. Y'all shouldn't have waited for me. I ended up having a late night, and for the first time in weeks, I didn't set an alarm." Anxiety buzzed under my skin. I wasn't ready to face all of this without coffee.

"Don't worry about Brad. This is his second breakfast. He ate an egg sandwich on the way here." Zoe sliced pieces of cake and put them on plates. "I hope it lives up to your Nana's. This is her cinnamon cake, and it's a bit temperamental, but it looks like it rose perfectly."

"I'm sure it will be delicious." As I filled a mug with coffee, I swallowed the lump in my throat. Nana only made this cake on special occasions. To me, it tasted like love. If Zoe was trying to win me over, she was doing an excellent job. I took my coffee and cake to the table.

"It smells heavenly, but I can only have a taste." Willa rinsed her cup and placed it in the dishwasher. "The wedding diet doesn't allow for decadent cakes." This from the woman who'd make a Barbie doll jealous. Willa paired her navy pleated tennis skirt with a pale pink sleeveless collared shirt, displaying the Retreat at Magnolia Bluff logo, and a pair of white leather platform sneakers. While the skirt was a conservative length, it still made her long legs appear longer.

"Well, at least take some to Lawson and the staff." Zoe arranged several squares in a container.

"Of course. I'll get to be the hero of the day when I show up with treats, and I'll be sure to give you credit." Before snapping the lid on the container, Willa pinched off a tiny bite. "I'll savor this morsel on my way to the clubhouse." She lifted the box, grabbed a large bag, and headed for the door. "Carleigh, I'll check on you later, but if you need anything, text me."

"I'll be fine. I've got some research to do." *If I could show Lawson the career he was sacrificing, it might give him the perspective to realize the mistake he was making.*

"Don't work too hard," she said as she left.

Brad joined me at the table. "Actually, your timing is great. I was just finalizing plans for Lawson's bachelor party. I know you're his best woman, but we didn't think you'd be here early enough to celebrate."

"You've made plans?"

"Yeah. I'm sorry if I overstepped, but no one knew you were coming."

"No, it's fine. I'm just not used to this version of you." I popped a bite in my mouth, and when the warm, slightly sweet cake melted with the butter and cinnamon and brown sugar on my tongue, I closed my eyes but stopped short of moaning. After thoroughly savoring the flavors, I swallowed and opened my eyes. "Zoe, this is like eatable happiness. I shouldn't have let you send so much with Willa."

"I'm so glad you like it." She beamed at me. "I wish I could stick around, but y'all have lots to discuss, and I have a design meeting with Wren at the Walenskys' house."

"I'll meet you for lunch around one?" Brad stood.

"Sounds good." After a quick hug and kiss, Zoe backed toward the door. "Carleigh, I know Willa mentioned the shower to you, but we need a girls' night. If the guys are having a bachelor party, we should get a night too."

"But I'm going with the guys, so you don't need to include me."

"Of course we'll include you. Willa wouldn't have it any other way. We can discuss details later. Byeee." Zoe waved as she exited the cottage.

"Willa barely knows me." I ate a large bite, hoping for comfort from the food, but it merely mellowed my concerns. I needed to work faster or Zoe would be covering me in glitter.

"What's your deal?" Brad asked.

Lost in my thoughts, I startled and choked down my now ruined bite. Then to clear my throat, I took a few sips of coffee. "I don't have a deal."

"You obviously don't want to be here."

"Sure I do." I smiled.

"No, you don't, and it's written all over your smug face." He met my gaze. "You think you're better than all of us, and we're all so beneath you because we might not choose to live in the city and climb the corporate ladder. We might instead choose to fill our days with good friends, satisfying careers, and the beauty of God's creation. In the past, I'd have ignored your behavior, but I'm tired of it and I don't want you messing things up for Willa and Lawson. So I'll ask you again. What's your deal?"

I clenched my jaw as he finished. His betrayal and failure to apologize, or even acknowledge it, ripped through me, tearing down my restraints and bringing all the past hurts rushing to the surface. If he wanted to fight, I wasn't about to retreat.

I glared at him. "You, for one."

"What about me?" He pointed at his chest.

But this part of the apology was his responsibility. Shouldn't the person who'd wronged you have the decency to remember? If you had to ask for an apology, it didn't seem genuine, and he should be aware of what he'd done.

The all-too-familiar pit of loss opened within me. "I don't trust you, and while Zoe seems great and genuine, I can't understand what she sees in you."

"Have you considered that I may have changed in more ways than you know?"

"Not really. Mom's told me about your accomplishments, but they don't prove anything about your integrity or loyalty."

"Are you serious? I could've started my own construction business years ago. Instead I worked without complaining while Dad micromanaged me, because I wanted to continue the family business. Meanwhile, you don't even come home for holidays. Not to mention your failure to communicate. You've got Mom convinced your phone doesn't have service in half of the nation's capital."

Indignation rose in me at his accusations. "I get that you don't understand my life. Believe it or not, I am busy, and I can't always stop to field calls from Mom about her newest find at the antique shop. In fact, I should thank you for bringing Zoe into her life so she has someone to shop with."

"You really don't get it." He rubbed his temple. "It's not about the shopping or the purchases. It's about having a relationship with someone, learning about them, finding joy in the moments."

"I have relationships, and I find joy in them."

"How is Spencer? Or did you mess that up too?" He scowled.

Why was everyone so concerned about my relationship with Spencer? I was getting tired of defending our friendship. "Spencer is fine, and we are fine. My relationship with our parents is fine, and while I don't expect to be bosom buddies, Zoe and I will get along fine." My chest tightened.

"It's just me then. What did I do that's made you so bitter?"

"You really don't know?" I studied him, my anger rumbling just below the surface. Did he seriously not understand how badly he'd hurt me?

"Carleigh, if I had an inkling of what I did, I promise I'd be trying to make it right." He raked a hand through his golden locks. "It's basically all I've done for the last two years, and yet, you still treat me like a reckless teenager."

"The election." My breath turned to a whisper as the lump in my throat blocked the air. I clenched my molars, managing my emotions. I wouldn't let him see me as weak.

Frowning, he furrowed his brows. Then his eyes got big with realization. "Are you talking about the student government election in . . . *high school*?" He emphasized high school like he wasn't sure if he was correct.

"Unless you managed to stab me in the back during some other election."

"Carleigh, I was an idiot kid with a major crush on the captain of the cheerleading squad. When she asked me to help her, I didn't consider not agreeing. Honestly, I didn't think it'd matter."

My muscles tensed at his words, and I gripped the edge of the wooden seat. "Is that supposed to excuse your behavior?"

"No, of course not. I was just trying to explain that I wasn't trying to hurt you, only help myself. But I guess the result was the same. I'm sorry that I didn't realize it. I would never do something like that now."

"How am I supposed to know that? After I lost the election, you didn't even notice that our relationship was different. You were—are—always more concerned with other people's feelings than mine. This whole conversation is because you don't want me to mess things up for you."

"I didn't see it that way. I'm sorry." His shoulders rounded. "I always see you as so strong. You act like nothing bothers you."

"Losing bothers me, especially when it's because someone cheated." Flares of injustice shot up my spine.

"I get that, and again I apologize. I should've done it years ago, but I can't go back in time. If I could, trust me, I'd smack fourteen-year-old Brad on the back of the head and tell him to act more like his sister." He tapped his head. "It would've served me well to have taken that advice."

"I'm pretty sure Mom and Dad mentioned it."

"Yeah, well, that only made me want to do the opposite. Not that I'm blaming them for hurting you, but it was hard growing up in your shadow."

My anger tempered with his admission. Clearly, we both had unresolved issues with our parents. "Everyone always loved you. Even when you were getting in trouble, people couldn't get mad at you."

"You're forgetting how angry Mom and Dad would get."

"But it seems you're back in their good graces."

"I don't want to be at odds with you." He folded his hands on the table. "Will you forgive me and give me a chance?"

"I can forgive you, and I'll try not to let the past influence our current relationship, but it isn't going to be easy." I released my hold on the chair, trying to let go of the resentment.

"Thanks for giving me a chance. How about I start by telling you my ideas for the bachelor party?" He gave me that lopsided grin that I'm sure disarmed most women.

If I helped plan a bachelor party, did it mean I was giving up? Not really. Why couldn't we all go out and have fun? Besides, it might give me another opportunity to persuade Lawson if he was still engaged by the night of the party. My only concern was Wyatt, and not because I cared about his suspicions. He'd nearly taken Lawson down in college, and while my parents had gotten control of Brad before he joined Wyatt, I had no desire to hang out with the guy. "Can I ask you something first?"

"Sure."

"Do you think Wyatt's for real? He seemed pretty unhinged when I saw him last night."

"He seems to be doing well and making an effort to turn his life around. I was hesitant at first, but with my history, I couldn't deny him a second chance."

"Got it. I'm just not looking forward to him crashing our party."

"Well, I wasn't thinking about a traditional party."

"What were you thinking?" I asked.

He reclined in the chair, folding his hands over his middle. "Savannah Bananas."

"I'm sorry, what?"

"Savannah Bananas." He leaned forward. "Surely you've seen them on InstaTok. They have millions of views."

"I don't have InstaTok. Are they a dance group?"

"It's a baseball team."

"What happened to the Sand Gnats?" I filled my fork.

"You have been away for a long time. The Savannah Bananas started out as a summer team after the minor league team left, but it's more like a variety show than a baseball game. They're sold out most of the time, but the network could score some tickets for us."

"Nice. I suppose this is one perk of being a big TV star."

"Somehow I doubt our little show will make me a big star, but the network does like to pamper us, and I'm going to enjoy the benefits until they realize that while I know construction, I know zilch about making a successful show."

I lifted my mug in a toast. "I'm here for it."

"Great." He tapped his travel cup to mine as he rose from the table. "I need to get to the job site."

"Send me the details for the game, and I'll take over the planning, so you don't have to split your time. Thanks for getting the ball rolling."

Brad glanced back from the opened door. "Carleigh, I'm glad you're here. I hope we can be friends."

"Okay." I nodded, and he left and not a moment too soon. I couldn't handle much more emotion. After I finished my breakfast, I checked my phone for messages. Before I'd gone to bed, I'd texted Spencer, thanking him for the picture, but with Lawson's allegations nettling me, I'd deleted the perfectly innocent heart emoji.

Spencer: Good morning. I hope you found coffee.

Me: Not only did I find coffee, but I also found my brother and his fiancée.

Spencer: Yikes!?!

Me: Zoe made Nana's cinnamon cake—so good—and I just had a long talk with Brad.

Spencer: Good too?

Me: Maybe. He apologized.

Spencer: That's a start.

Me: Yep.

Spencer: Jordan and Cooper's new place in Courthouse is great.

Me: How do you know?

Spencer: Cooper invited me to cards night with the guys.

Me: Nice.

Spencer: In other news, Dan stopped me the other day and asked about our lease renewal. He said neither of us returned it.

Me: I totally forgot before I left.

But why hadn't Spencer signed it? And why had he mentioned Cooper and Jordan's condo?

Spencer: They need it by the end of the month but would like it earlier.

Me: OK. Will you scan mine to me?

What followed had my skin crawling. The dots appeared indicating he was typing, but then they disappeared, and then they returned. Why couldn't he just send the thumbs-up emoji? Finally his text came through.

Spencer: I'll send yours, but I'm considering my options.

I started to ask what he meant, but I didn't want to hash out our living arrangements over text messages. Before I could tap the icon to call him, another text appeared.

Spencer: Talk later. Got a meeting.

"Noooo." I fell back against the pillows. If he was going to consider his options, he shouldn't have waited until the last minute. *Ahhhh!* I needed to get back to DC and Spencer. After grabbing my laptop, I hopped on the Wi-Fi. It was time to find Lawson a new job.

Chapter 12

Game night. Two words that usually brought me joy, but when Willa included me in the group text, I wanted to crawl under the bed. How was I supposed to convince Lawson that he was wasting his potential at Magnolia Bluff—yes, I'd decided to use my parents' line—if I couldn't get him alone?

For two days, Willa had arranged dinner for us with Lawson. Not to be deterred, I'd used the occasions to exploit Willa's past. When she confessed to not only being a cheerleader but also homecoming queen, I'd tried to give Lawson a knowing look. But he was too busy gazing at Willa while he pointed out how generous and friendly she'd always been, so it only followed that she'd been elected to wear the crown.

While Willa may have cultivated her hospitable persona, her people-pleasing tendencies left her vulnerable, or so I thought. When I'd mentioned that the college football schedule conflicted with the wedding and guests might be disappointed to miss the games, Willa agreed, thanked me, and jumped into action, texting the wedding coordinator and requesting a television be set up in the library.

But when I realized Willa was determined for us to be friends, I changed my strategy. I borrowed all her hair conditioner, most of which

I'd poured down the drain. Her response was to smile and dismiss it as not a problem. And to my amazement, it wasn't. Her hair was just as perfect as ever, defying the laws of nature. Maybe she was the Polished Princess Barbie. Of course, we couldn't all be so blessed. When I walked outside into the humidity, my wavy hair morphed into a frizzy mess.

After dinner last night, I'd suggested Lawson join us for a movie, and I'd chosen an action adventure with a lot more gore than I usually liked, hoping Willa would refuse to watch it. Instead she curled up next to Lawson and every time something gross or scary happened, she buried her face in his chest—total fail.

I thought for sure when she discovered her stash of chocolate was missing, she'd lose it. But Willa simply shrugged and said it was better for her wedding diet. I was beginning to wonder if the woman could be ruffled, but I wasn't a quitter. I just needed a new plan.

It would've been nice to vent to Spencer or even talk to him, but he'd been slow to respond, leaving my insides in knots. My anxiety wasn't fair, and at the same time, completely illogical. Obviously, Spencer's life didn't cease just because I had an abundance of free time.

Still, my imagination whirred, conjuring up all kinds of worrisome scenarios to explain his silence. I knew he was busy, but being in the literal woods left me with a new understanding of the phrase *hearing nothing but crickets* as I was actually hearing the persistent chirping creatures.

While a game night with all the happy couples didn't top my list of interesting activities, I could use it to my advantage. I just needed the perfect game. However, an internet search for games to get rid of your best friend's fiancée only resulted in activities to play with girlfriends or ways to cope with your best friend's significant other's mistreatment. But while I scrolled through the results, an article listed games to play with friends. When I saw charades on the list, my next search was for clues that would stump Willa, and if my plan worked, the game would prove how wrong she was for Lawson.

With renewed focus, I spent the rest of the day preparing. Zoe and Brad arrived first with a platter of desserts. My brother's fiancée was definitely growing on me. After putting the platter on the table, Zoe peeled off the plastic wrap. "I'm so glad we're getting together, but Wren texted, and Nathaniel isn't going to make it."

Brad snagged a brownie. "Did you really think he would?"

"Actually, I did." Zoe passed him a napkin. "Wren said he turned in his latest book to his editor yesterday, so I thought he'd want to celebrate."

"I'm sure he does, but not with us," Brad said.

"Why not?" I asked.

"He's not a fan of crowds and likes his quiet." Zoe nodded, giving Brad a look that said to be nice.

"This is a crowd?"

"Zoe's being kind. The famous author only enjoys us in small doses." Brad ate half his treat in one bite and reached for a cookie.

Zoe smacked his hand. "Don't eat everything before everyone gets here."

I laughed. "Willa won't eat anything, so you can have her portion."

"I should probably join her on the bride-to-be diet." Zoe patted her belly.

"Please tell me you aren't serious," Brad said between bites.

"Don't worry, you'll still get your daily dose of sugar." She turned to me. "I stress bake, and I can't imagine anything more stressful than planning a wedding while launching a television show." She moved to the sink. "I'm going to make some coffee."

Brad snuck a cookie and crossed to the couch. "Where is everyone?"

"I'm not sure." I passed Zoe a filter from the drawer.

"Willa texted. She and Lawson were finishing up a pre-marital counseling session. They should be here soon." Zoe opened the coffee canister.

"Really?" My chest clenched. It all sounded so official and final.

"Last meeting, I think." Zoe scooped grounds into the basket. "I can't believe how quickly everything is going. In a couple months, it'll be our turn." She finished prepping the coffee and pressed the brew button. "Which reminds me. Carleigh, we need to get your measurements. I can do them or Willa is an expert, or if you have time, we could pop over to the bridal shop in Savannah."

Before I could answer, the door opened, and Lawson held it, while Willa and a woman with shoulder-length brown hair strolled inside.

"Carleigh, this is Wren Sullivan, my design partner and best friend." Zoe hooked arms with Wren, guiding her into the kitchen area.

"Nice to meet you." I extended my hand.

Wren shook my hand. "So hugging people the first time you meet them isn't a family trait?"

"You have to forgive Brad. We've tried to tame him," I said.

"Hey, it wasn't the first time we'd met." Brad joined us. "I'd been talking to y'all for months."

Zoe leaned against his side. "I, for one, didn't mind my Brad-greeting, especially since I was in the throes of a panic attack."

"And it all worked out for the best." Brad gathered Zoe in his arms and kissed her.

Wren and I exchanged a look and laughed. She was definitely the steady one in their design partnership.

"Oh, Zoe, thank you for bringing dessert. You're the best." Willa smiled sweetly, and I wanted to groan. No one was this benevolent.

But two could play at this game, and I would enjoy the fruits of Zoe's labor. With a napkin in one hand, I began selecting items from the platter. "I don't know how I'll choose."

"Get one of each, sis. That's what I do."

"I just might." I pinched off the corner of a blondie and popped it in my mouth. "You have to try this." I held up the square to Lawson.

"Good to see your sweet tooth is still around." He grinned.

"Always." I placed the morsel in his mouth.

Willa's gaze flitted between us. "What game should we play?" She clasped Lawson's hand and pulled him away. *Interesting*.

"Charades." I smiled widely. "Lawson, remember how we used to play in college?"

"Carleigh was brutal. She was known for choosing the most obscure titles."

"It made it more fun."

"Only because your team always won."

"Are you afraid of losing?" I arched a brow, staring him down. It was a totally normal exchange for us, but out of the corner of my eye, I could see a flash of concern cross Willa's face.

"Not at all." Lawson wrapped an arm around Willa.

"Well, I am." Brad smirked. "So I want to be on your team, sis."

"Zoe and Wren, do you want to be a team or split up?" I asked.

"I don't think we'll have a chance on our own." Wren nibbled the edge of a cookie.

Zoe nudged Lawson. "I'll go with the scary siblings."

"Great. I've already got the paper cut into strips." I passed Willa a bowl with a pen and paper inside it. "Everyone has five minutes to come up with their challenges."

"How about ten? Since I'm assuming you've been brainstorming yours all afternoon." Lawson tapped the pen against his temple.

"Fine, and for your information, I do have to keep up with my job, while I'm here. The world doesn't stop just because I left civilization."

"Got it." Lawson popped the end of the pen, like he was opening a switch blade. "May the best team win."

One thing my brother and I do have in common is our competitive nature. The joke at our house was always that second was the first loser. Poor Zoe hurried behind us as we hustled into my room and closed the door.

"Lawson was right. I do have several ideas." I started filling out the slips. "The trick is choosing songs and movies from when Willa was under ten and wasn't paying attention. What about Wren?"

"Wren only knows Southern books and movies. Otherwise, she's been sheltered." Zoe bounced.

"Perfect."

"*Forrest Gump*?" Brad suggested.

"*Decent* and *The Shawshank Redemption*," I added.

"Is that a movie?" Zoe cringed.

Brad paced. "You probably wouldn't like it."

"I'll take your word for it." Zoe perched on the end of the bed, while Brad and I rounded out our list with movies, music, television, and book titles that were either impossible to perform or out of Willa's frame of reference. We were a hundred percent going to best them.

When we emerged from the room, Lawson's hair was disheveled as though he'd been tugging on it. For a moment, I felt sorry for him, but it passed.

"Ready?" I grinned.

"Who goes first?" Zoe asked.

"Carleigh is our guest, so she should decide." Willa nodded, and all the bubbles bouncing around happily inside me burst.

"I guess it doesn't matter. We can each take a turn acting out a challenge for our team, and if there's a tie at the end, we'll go into a sudden death round," I said.

"Sounds fair." Lawson held out the bowl. "Since you're so confident, you go first."

"Great." I lifted a slip of paper from their bowl. In unbelievably beautiful penmanship—seriously, it looked like the example in the books we used to learn cursive—I read the words: *Dancing Queen*. Giddiness fizzed inside me, but not wanting to take anything for granted, I maintained my composure.

"Your time starts now." Lawson tapped the button on his phone.

First, I performed the sign for song by drawing my hand from my mouth and opening it like I was singing. Then I held up two fingers for two words.

"It's a song, two words in the title," Brad said.

I dropped a finger and broke into a seventies style finger point dance.

"First word is . . ." Brad scrunched his brow.

"John Travolta?" Zoe wondered.

Shaking my head, I held up two fingers then placed an imaginary crown on my head.

Zoe jumped off the sofa. "Dancing Queen!"

"Yes!" I smacked her lifted palms and then Brad's. "And that's how it's done." I did a little cha-cha as I made my way to a seat. "Your turn."

"I'll go first." Lawson reached into our bowl.

He passed it to me, and I read it silently. It was our ringer, *The Shawshank Redemption*. "Ready. Go." I started the timer.

Willa and Wren interpreted Lawson's initial moves, learning that it was a movie with three words in the title. They figured out the first word was 'the' when Lawson made the sign for a small word, but their correct guesses didn't concern me. The hard part was coming.

Lawson raised two fingers for the second word, then indicated it was two syllables. Where was he going with this?

"First syllable." Willa bounced on the edge of the couch like she'd guessed the secret ingredient for Chick-fil-a sauce.

Nodding, Lawson held his arms out wide and then wrapped them into his chest, acting like he was draping a shawl around his shoulders. *What?*

"The Shawshank Redemption!" Willa jumped to her feet.

What the what?

"Wow. Amazing guess." Zoe clapped.

"Your faces." Laughing, Lawson pointed at me and Brad.

"How?" Brad asked.

"It's a long story, but you know how you have these inside jokes when you're with someone." Lawson clasped Willa's hand and kissed her cheek. "Sometimes we just know what the other is thinking."

"But shawl"—I emphasized the *all* sound at the end of the word—"isn't the same as shaw in Shawshank."

"Yeah, we were watching a comedian the other day, and he was describing how Southerners don't always pronounce all the sounds in words." Willa smiled.

Lawson continued. "Then he did this whole monologue, leaving out all the sounds."

"Shawl was one of them." Willa giggled.

Lawson chuckled, glancing at the rest of us who'd failed to grasp the hilarity. "Like I said it was one of those things." He held out their bowl. "Anyway, it's your turn."

Zoe hopped to her feet. "I'll go."

"I sure hope you can read her mind like that." I jabbed Brad in the ribs.

He moved to the edge of his seat. "We got this."

After Zoe got in position, Lawson started the timer. We sailed through the first signs, learning it was a two-word movie title. Then Zoe slapped her cheeks with her mouth and eyes wide open—à la Kevin McCallister.

"Home Alone!" Brad and I shouted together.

"Yes." Zoe gathered us in a group hug.

"I guess I'm up." Willa plucked a strip and read the clue.

After I started the timer, she gave the signals for a two-word movie title and then held up two fingers for the second word. She pushed her arms forward in what I guessed was a park swing, but it was evident to Lawson.

"Jurassic Park." He reclined on the couch like he was relaxing.

"I knew you'd get it." Willa jumped in his lap and planted a kiss on her fiancé's lips.

Chuckling, Lawson shifted Willa to one leg but kept her snuggled close. "Do you want the explanation?" He shot me a challenging gaze.

"Nope." I patted my brother on the back. "Brad, it's your turn."

"Don't worry, sis. I won't let you down." And he didn't, easily acting out *Boys in the Boat*. But as the game ended with Wren failing to act out *The Fresh Prince of Bel Air*, I didn't get the buzz of adrenaline I relished with a victory. Winning had never felt so inconsequential.

When everyone had finally left for the night, I settled on my bed with a plate of Zoe's desserts. I needed to comfort the monster gnawing a hole within me. I'd tried to focus on the Braves game with the guys but couldn't help listening to the girls discuss wedding plans and married life. It seemed there was a real probability, upwards of sixty percent, that I was losing at the game of life.

What I really needed was to talk to someone who wasn't living in this bubble and could reassure me I could still rally for a win, even make a run for the championship. Chewing on a lemon bar, I rolled my phone over my knee as the tart lemon blended with the powdered sugar and buttery crust. My taste buds skipped to a happy melody that was in direct conflict with my frowning body. Only one person would give me the perspective I craved. It was either call Spencer or satisfy myself with calories I'd regret later.

Shuddering, I swiped my phone screen and tapped on Spencer's contact.

"Hi," he answered.

"Hey," I said, and then there was nothing. What did I say next? Blurting out that I needed him to validate my life choices seemed like the wrong place to start, and I didn't want to get into a debate about our future living situations. I definitely didn't want to discuss Lawson and Willa's pending wedding and the failure I was at bringing them clarity. Asking him how he was doing would be polite, too polite, and he'd think something was up.

"Carleigh?"

"Yep."

"Did you need something?"

Did I need something? Yes, I needed him to come down here, but he'd seemed pretty determined not to join me. I glanced at the unfilled closet. *Clothes!* I needed clothes.

"Actually, I do, but I hate to ask you to do anything else for me."

"I don't mind helping you. What bothers me is that you think I don't want to be there for you. In truth, I hate it. Before all this stuff, you never hesitated to ask me for almost anything, and I knew you'd be there for me in the same way."

"I'm sorry. You're right." With my stomach twisting, I moved the plate of leftover treats to the dresser. "What's wrong with me? You're the best. I don't doubt you at all. You're always generous and patient and kind and—"

"You don't have to flatter me. I already said I'll help. So what is it?"

Ignoring his gruff tone and hoping if I talked normally, he'd respond the same way, I continued. "Well, it seems I'm going to need my pink and white gingham dress for the shower."

Spencer chuckled. "As much as I want you to abandon this whole scheme and come home, I kind of love that you have to go to the pink party. And I'll pack whatever clothes you need, but you have to promise to send me pictures, especially if at any point, there are hats involved."

"This isn't England. It's Georgia."

"Fully aware, but from what you've said, I think hats will happen, and I don't want to miss my chance to obtain ammunition for some friendly teasing in the future." At least he was talking about the future and joking with me.

"If this is you trying to make me comfortable asking you for stuff, it seems counterproductive."

"Not at all, but you do sound a little on edge, so is there something else you want to discuss? Because while I believe that you've humbled yourself a lot to ask for a dress, I know when it's a cover. I may have been less than supportive lately, but Carleigh, I'm your friend."

"Do not say I can lean on you, or I will hang up."

"Never," he said.

Sighing, I fell back on the bed and covered my face with a throw pillow. "I feel like I'm down four games in the set, and I'm losing the current game 40–love."

"You aren't losing any games, metaphorically or otherwise."

"I lost at darts to Lawson the other night."

While I waited for him to respond, I could almost hear him banging his head against the back of his couch as he no doubt gathered his patience. "Fine. You lost at darts but only because you're out of practice."

"So what you're saying is I need more training?"

"Carleigh, can we please stop talking in metaphors? I'm getting lost, and I'm pretty sure you're trying to hide whatever is bothering you, so say it in plain English."

"Logically, I understand that I've accomplished a lot in my life, but I'm worried that I still need to do more and that I might be falling behind and never be able to catch up and succeed at it all." I pressed my palm to my belly, trying to ease the churning. "Also, I've had an excessive number of desserts and feel nauseous."

"I wish I was there to make you some peppermint tea."

"I wish you were here too." But I stopped short of begging him to come.

"As to your other concerns, I don't know if I have the right wisdom for you. I will say this: you are an amazing woman with so much to offer the world, and you will figure this out, and you won't be too late. Someone told me the other day to give myself some grace. You should do the same."

Why did Spencer need to give himself grace? Who had he been talking to? I could ask him, but if he wanted me to know he'd tell me, right?

"Carleigh?"

"Sorry, I was just thinking about what you said, and I'll try."

"Okay, I was worried you'd fainted."

"Ha ha." I rolled to the edge of the bed. "If I send you a list, can you ship the clothes overnight?"

"Sure. Do you feel any better?"

"I think so, but if you come down here sooner rather than later, I won't complain."

"It just wouldn't be a good idea right now. I've got some stuff I need to deal with here. But I'll see you soon."

"Okay. I'm going to look for some tea or an antacid. Bye." I ended the call. Instead of feeling relieved, all the things Spencer hadn't said swirled through my mind.

Chapter 13

With my sentence determined and no chance for an appeal, I ordered the high-end blender from Willa's bridal registry and told my mom that I'd be at the shower. The last thing anyone needed was Laura Chastain making a big deal about my secret visit, so I suggested we have lunch. But to my surprise, Mom informed me that while she'd love to meet before the party, she was busy assisting the television production company with logistics for Zoe and Brad's show. In an interesting turn of events, she'd been hired as the location liaison. Who knew all those years serving as the class mom would prepare her for a career in television?

Mom expressed her disappointment that I wasn't staying with them but understood that the Retreat was probably more relaxing. While I agreed with her in theory, I'd yet to experience the serenity.

It was entirely too hot to enjoy the outdoors, and with the infernal silence, the voices in my head didn't need to shout to be heard. All the things I never thought about were like hot spots in my brain, ready to rage into a roaring blaze with the slightest spark. While I kept dousing them with logic to control the spread, I was barely keeping the fires contained.

My instincts could be trusted to solve problems. They'd never failed me, but overcoming the anxiety was taxing my patience. If only I could've given myself the grace that Spencer had suggested. When I tried, I started worrying about why he needed to talk to someone and why that person thought he needed to give himself grace. I should've just asked him, but the hairs on the back of my neck warned me against it.

Instead, I buried myself in completing employee evaluations and scouring the news in an attempt to predict the next big political issue. The tasks filled my days, and at night, I'd discovered an app that created the sounds of the city to help me sleep. Keeping busy might not solve my problems, but it didn't hurt.

On the morning of the shower, I took a picture of myself in my pink ensemble and sent it to Spencer.

Me: Thanks for sending the clothes. About to leave for the pink party. Pray for me.

Spencer: You could try to have fun.

Me: I will, but only because later I can be catty with you.

Spencer: Glad I'm useful for something.

Me: You're also a wonderful packer, cat sitter, dance partner, coffee maker . . .

Me: Should I go on?

Spencer: I'm not going to stop you . . .

Me: You do too much for me. I'll never catch up.

Spencer: No one is keeping score.

Spencer: Not everything's a competition.

Me: It's not?!?

Spencer: Go to your party!

As I read his last message, Mom knocked and strode through the door. "Good morning, honey." She hugged me. "You look so pretty. I love to see you smiling. Did you get some good news?"

"It was just a text from Spencer." I stored my phone in the small hot pink satin handbag that Spencer had ordered and express shipped to me with a note that he hoped it wasn't too *fabulous* for the elegant affair.

"He's coming for the wedding, right?"

"Yes, and before you ask, we're still just friends."

"I was only going to say that it would be good to see him." She squeezed my hand. "We miss you. It's been a while."

"I didn't think I'd be able to come early, but I made it happen so I could be here for Lawson." With a slight shrug, I strode to my bedroom. Mom wasn't as perceptive as me, but she was still a mom with that special power to perceive if I was up to something. Hopefully, she was out of practice.

"I was surprised you could take so many days off."

After retrieving my wrapped gift from the dresser, I returned to the living room. "It was a good time because Congress is in recess."

"I suppose." Mom tapped a finger to her chin. "I hope you realize how blessed Lawson is to have found a woman like Willa."

"What are you getting at Mom?"

"I just want to be sure you aren't having any regrets about your friendship not becoming more."

"Just like Spencer, Lawson and I have never been more than friends. I only want what's best for him." But the best for him wasn't Willa or Magnolia Bluff. I lifted my bag from the table. "Ready?"

"Yes. Have you met Linda?" Mom followed me outside, thankfully dropping her suspicions.

"Not yet, but I'm looking forward to it. She sounds like quite a character."

"She's Chastain Construction's biggest and most influential client."

"Her company might benefit from my services also, especially if they plan to do any further development in the southeast."

"Carleigh, please keep the conversations pertaining to your job or politics or anything involving regulations or legislation to a minimum."

"Mom, I can network gently." We stopped at the front door.

"I have no idea what that means. You don't do anything gently, so please just pretend you're on an actual vacation." Mom rang the bell.

"I will, but I've made some profitable connections on *actual* vacations."

"When was your last vacation?"

"I was on Sea Island last year, remember?"

"Yes, you squeezed us in for lunch between your *work* meetings."

"Well, I also spent a half day at the spa."

The door swung open, and Wren ushered us inside. "Sorry for the delay. We had a glitter incident."

"Sounds like Zoe was involved." Mom laughed.

Wren held out her hands for the gift box. "Let me take that."

"When we were antiquing a few weeks ago, Zoe and I found a gorgeous set of silver candle stick holders for Willa." Mom leaned close, lowering her voice. "I had them engraved with *G* for Grant."

"Wow, that was a rather permanent alteration."

"Marriage is a rather permanent situation." Mom narrowed her eyes at me. "Don't you agree?"

"Of course. I was just making an observation."

"Good." Mom passed me a flute of sparkling rosé from the table in the foyer. "And hopefully, one day we'll be toasting your permanent connection, but no pressure."

"Of course not." I clinked the edge of my glass to hers. "And for your information, I have been focusing more on acquiring a husband. Although with Willa spoiling my marriage pact with Lawson, it has gotten more challenging. But I don't mind a little competition." I smirked.

Mom coughed, choking on her bubbly.

"Just kidding." I patted her back. "Relax. I don't plan to marry Lawson." As the words left my mouth, the finality of them dropped in my belly.

"Just be careful with your sass. Everyone won't find you hilarious." With a curt nod, she pivoted.

"Yes ma'am," I said to her back, following her like a scolded child.

As we entered the great room, a woman wearing a fuchsia tulle fascinator beamed at us. "Hi, Laura, so good to see you." She embraced Mom.

"Linda, everything looks fabulous. Y'all outdid yourselves with this theme."

It was even more blush and bashful than I'd imagined. Willa hadn't been exaggerating. If anything, she'd understated the decorations. Ballet pink tulle wound around the curtain rods, while rose-colored sheers hung down the sides. The tablecloths were various shades of pink, giving the impression of a sample paint card. Besides the rosé, there was a raspberry punch. Each table had quotes from *Steel Magnolias* displayed on signs. The chairs had even been covered in blush fabric.

"It's all so tacky, but I decided that if we were going to do it, we might as well go all the way. Wait until you see the food," our hostess said.

"I'm sure it'll be delicious with my future daughter-in-law's desserts."

"Zoe went over the top with these." Linda turned to me. "And you must be the elusive Carleigh. Willa has been telling me about you. I hope you're enjoying your stay at the Retreat."

"Absolutely. It's picturesque and so peaceful. Thank you for allowing me to stay in your guest house. It's lovely."

"Pish posh." Linda waved her hand dismissively and then chuckled. "I don't think I've ever used that phrase, but with this contraption on my head, it felt right."

"It's so fun."

"I'm glad you like them because they're an option for the party favor. We also have sunhats." Linda gestured to a table at the far side of the room. "Come with me, and we'll find you the perfect one."

At the hat table, Linda introduced us to a couple of Willa's friends who were giggling as they took selfies with different headpieces. They seemed so young and naïve. How could Lawson be almost married to a girl their age?

After the introductions, I lifted a straw hat and placed it on my head, focusing my attention on Linda. "What do you think? The color reminds me of the cherry blossoms that line the Tidal Basin in the spring."

"That's right. Lawson mentioned you work in DC," Linda rearranged the headpieces.

"I help developers all along the coast with various Federal issues. I'm a lobbyist."

"How interesting. I'd like to hear more about your clients."

"Carleigh." Mom touched my arm. "I want you to meet Kara Monroe. She's Willa's former boss and the wedding coordinator."

"Okay." Taking the hint from Mom, but unwilling to not take the next step, I smiled at Linda. "I look forward to setting up a time for us to chat."

On our way to meet Kara, Zoe and Willa intercepted us and insisted we take several photos with our hats. Then Zoe asked for Mom's help to set up the shower games.

Meanwhile Kara approached us with an extended hand. "You must be the best woman that I've heard so much about. I'm Kara Monroe."

"Carleigh Chastain." Nodding, I shook her hand. "Hopefully, they're only giving me compliments."

"Of course," Willa said a little too quickly. However, her expression showed no hints of concern. She simply sipped her punch.

Not to be out played, I drew on my best etiquette and replied. "It probably wasn't ideal having a house guest right before the big day, but Willa insisted, and it's been so fun getting to spend time with everyone."

"No complaints from me." Willa pointed to something over my shoulder. "My aunt and grandmother just walked in. I'll talk with y'all later."

"It must have been hard losing Willa to the club," I said to Kara.

"Actually, I sold the business and only work part-time with the new owners, but Willa and I have remained close friends."

"That's nice and so special that you can coordinate the big day."

"Look, I'm going to be straight with you. I've dealt with this whole best woman business before, and it's rarely as simple and mature as everyone makes it out to be. Maybe y'all are different, but be aware, I don't let anything or anyone upset my events, especially the weddings."

"Sounds like they have the best person for the job." I smiled sweetly. "I'm going to check on my mom." Bless her heart, Kara thought she was a match for me. I crossed the room, ready to charm everyone. If it meant taking selfies, giggling, or even losing the shower games, no one would believe I was more than a great friend by the time this shindig was over. As a matter of fact, I needed to make plans with Zoe for that girls' night. It was going to be one for the books.

As soon as I returned to the cottage from the shower and was in the safety of my room, I sent Spencer a picture of me in my new hat.

I watched the screen for his response, expecting a witty comeback, but when the phone went to sleep from no activity, I gave up and changed into a tennis dress. It'd been over a week since I'd hit a ball, and I needed to release some of the energy I'd pent up from playing the part of Willa's new incredibly sweet girlfriend. Lawson had told me I could use all the club's amenities, so I put on a moisture wicking hat and jogged up to the courts.

After borrowing a racquet and getting directions for the ball machine, I set everything up for my workout. It would've been nice to play against someone, but Lawson was helping Willa move all the gifts to his spare room.

After pressing the start button on the remote, the ball machine whirred and shot a ball across the net. I slammed it back, imagining my opposition. As I focused on hitting each ball, all my worries faded, and though my pulse increased, my body relaxed for the first time since I'd left Spencer at the airport. When the machine emptied, I grabbed a basket and began collecting the balls. If I went one more round, maybe Spencer would've texted or maybe Lawson would be available for a quick game.

"Hi." A male voice interrupted my thoughts.

I spun around to find Wyatt leaning against the building, spinning a racquet in his hands. "You played in high school, right?"

"Yes. I was on the team." I returned my focus to the scattered balls. What was he up to? I certainly didn't plan on reminiscing with him. Besides Lawson, we'd had absolutely nothing in common in high school.

"It looks like you still play."

"Yep."

"After I moved out here and made sure it was okay for staff to use the courts, I took it back up."

Did Wyatt think I cared about his hobbies? Ignoring him, I caged the last of the balls. Hopefully, he'd go away, but as I walked to the machine, I glimpsed him out of the corner of my eye.

"It's become one of my favorite activities."

Without acknowledging his statement, I loaded the balls into the machine. He wasn't asking me questions, and I wasn't looking for a conversation.

"Are you really not going to respond?"

"I don't have anything to add."

"I seriously doubt that. From what I witnessed the other night, you have an arsenal full of opinions about me."

"Frankly, I don't think about you at all, and I'd like to keep it that way."

"Well, that's not going to be easy, at least not in the immediate future, so how about we call a truce? I'll overlook your snobbery if you can forget my past. And for the record, you're getting the easy part of the deal because I've changed and I'm trying to make a better life for myself."

"I'm not a snob, but I do protect myself and the people I love. The same cannot be said for you. I'm sorry if that's hard for you to accept.

I've spent my life reading people and their motives. My instincts tell me to beware of you, and I trust them."

Wyatt pushed off the wall. "Carleigh, why are you so bitter?"

"Pardon, me?"

"Why are you so bitter?" He strode toward me.

I pointed my racquet at him like a sword. "Are you planning to stay here and sling unfounded accusations at me?"

He raised his free hand in surrender. "You could consider the possibility that I've changed. Your instincts aren't always so accurate when it comes to matters of forgiveness and grace." Dropping his hand, he backed away. "I'll leave you to it. If you ever want to play against a person instead of a machine, let me know." He sauntered off.

How dare he question my instincts? I'd witnessed the way he'd burdened several lives. There was zero chance his memory was anything more than hazy, and I wouldn't leave myself vulnerable to him.

Chapter 14

Unfortunately, the next morning, Wyatt's accusations still needled me, so I texted the one person who knew me best.

> Me: Am I bitter?

> Spencer: Not a word that I'd use to describe you unless someone has more than ten items in the express lane at the grocery store. You simmered for days the last time that happened.

> Me: Ha ha.

> Spencer: Why?

> Me: Wyatt, Willa's brother, told me I was because I don't trust him.

> Spencer: I don't have enough information. Do you want to talk?

Did I want to hash this out with him? My insides twisted around the memory of our last chat about grace and where a conversation like this might go, especially with this ultra-introspective version of Spencer. He'd always been thoughtful with his advice, but lately he kept diving deeper. Did I want to answer probing questions over a baseless comment from a person I held no respect for? Nope. I pressed my palm to my stomach, quelling the quivers. The sensation was just my internal compass directing me away from this discussion.

Me: Unnecessary. I don't know why I'm letting this bother me.

Me: Yesterday, I played tennis with a ball machine.

Spencer: Did you win?

Me: In a way.

Me: How are you?

Spencer: Fine, but I've got to go.

Didn't he just ask if I wanted to talk? I stared at the phone like I'd be able to see what he was doing and test the veracity of his statement. Although, if I really wanted to know the truth, I only needed to ask the right question.

Me: Please send me the lease renewal.

Me: If you're too busy, I can call Dan.

Spencer: <thumbs up emoji>

And with that, the conversation was finished, and I had my answer . . . sort of.

With the promise of coffee and breakfast, I crept out of the cottage as the first rays of the sun glistened on the still dark waters of the river meandering through the whispering grasses along the shore. I paused and inhaled deeply, on the verge of becoming a fan of early mornings and nature. Exhaling my worries over Spencer, I hurried to the carport. The night before, Lawson had requested a second dance lesson at his place before his first meeting at the clubhouse.

Finally, I'd have a chance to present him with the possibilities I'd found for his career. With the results of my research, there was a better than even chance he'd be handing in his resignation by the end of the day.

Not wanting a repeat incident with the golf cart, I borrowed one of the club bikes and pedaled through the pine forest to his house. The brisk morning air energized me as it blew against my skin, and for the briefest of moments, I considered whether I should take up cycling instead of coffee. But as I parked the bike, the hint of roasted beans met my nose, and I grabbed my proposal from the bike's basket.

Knowing my need for caffeine, Lawson met me on the porch with a large mug of coffee. "Good morning."

"Good morning." I traded him the project folder for the coffee. "Thank you." I took a sip, and as the hot liquid made its way through me, my brain alerted.

Lawson thumbed the corner of the cover. "What's this?"

"Just some thoughts I wanted to share with you." I lowered into a rocker and continued enjoying my beverage.

"Okay." Lawson leaned against the porch railing and flipped open the booklet. "This is a list of open positions." He turned the page. "And club descriptions for each one." He turned another page. "Wow, you made a list of pros and cons. Did you do this for all of them?" He studied the page.

"I wanted to help you see that you have lots of options. The Retreat is nice, but this isn't what you dreamed of for your career. There's a top golf resort in Maine where some pretty influential people vacation. It would be perfect for you." I drank my coffee quietly, giving him a chance to review the information, and hopefully, see the wisdom in it without me having to say anything else. These were not the kinds of positions that he'd be able to resist, regardless of his infatuation with Willa.

But without reading all the documents, he closed the book. "I appreciate the time and effort you put into this, but Willa and I are happy here. We both have fulfilling jobs, and we see ourselves being a part of this community for the long term. While it's not as prestigious a place, we like the idea of starting something from the ground up. Maybe we'll decide to leave one day, but that'll be a decision we make together."

As Lawson spoke, my chest tightened. Why was everything about Willa? I shouldn't be surprised though. If Lawson was anything, he was loyal. That's one of the things I loved most about him.

I gripped my coffee cup. "The decision to take a job at Magnolia Bluff was easy for Willa. This position was a huge promotion for her, but you made a lateral move to get away from a bad situation. It made sense at the time, but—"

"But nothing. Willa was well on her way to opening her own business when Linda offered her the job. She might not be as ambitious as you, but she does have goals. We both do."

"So you won't consider a move?"

"Right now, I can't imagine it. I have a quality of life here that I won't be able to find anywhere else. My priorities aren't what they were ten years ago. I hope you understand."

"Of course. I just want you to be happy." Smiling, I raised my mug to emphasize my agreement, but I was feeling anything but cheerful.

"I am." Lawson opened the door. "Come on, breakfast is almost ready."

"Great. I'm starving." I followed him.

"You're in for a treat. I've got quiche Lorraine."

"You make quiche?" I stopped, staring at him. Who was this man? Maybe Lawson had been brainwashed, and that's when he started whisking eggs with cheese instead of popping frozen waffles in the toaster.

The Retreat could be a cult where the members live in isolation and follow a supreme leader. Magnolia Bluff was out in the middle of the woods, and Linda seemed like she could command a following. Although I'd never heard of a faction where everyone had the freedom to choose from a menu of recreational activities or could simply sway on a swing and watch the sunset. Still, there were an inordinate number of people pairing up out here and everyone did seem unreasonably blissful.

As Lawson put on oven mitts, he glanced at me. "Relax. I didn't make it. Chef keeps a selection in the freezer for the residents to buy and heat up at their cottages.

"Oh, that makes more sense." So my cult idea wasn't exactly on point, but Lawson had changed. Goosebumps prickled my arms, unsettling me. My instincts were telling me something was wrong, and I intended to figure out what it was. After our dance lesson, I took a long bike ride and stopped at the dock. Everything glimmered in the morning sun, and I took a picture of an egret standing regally on the opposite bank among the bright green marsh grass. In a somewhat desperate attempt to convince Spencer to come early, I sent him the picture of the beautiful setting.

Spencer: New friend?

Me: Would you like to meet him?

Spencer: We'll see.

Me: Lawson refused to look at the jobs I found him.

Spencer: Okay

Me: He likes the pace here.

Spencer: Good for him.

Me: Seriously?

Spencer: Yep

Whatever. I mashed the button on the side of my phone, putting it to sleep. But I couldn't ignore the way my heart had grown heavy and was sinking inside me. I didn't want to fight with Spencer, but his indifference was killing me.

Chapter 15

W hen conducting covert operations, it's imperative to follow three rules: one, destroy all the evidence; two, always maintain your cover; and three, never underestimate your target. At least that's what I'd learned from reading spy novels. Unfortunately, when I witnessed Willa leap from her golf cart as it rolled to a stop in front of the clubhouse, I saw a familiar booklet in her hands and knew I'd failed to follow two of the rules of espionage.

Lawson, Wyatt, and I'd just returned from the bachelor party at the Savannah Bananas baseball game. As expected, it'd been the highlight of my time in Georgia, and if I'd been in favor of Lawson marrying Willa, it would've been the exact activity I'd have planned to celebrate the groom. During the game, I found myself completely forgetting to worry, and instead laughing at the antics of the players and other performers. The whole crowd was a part of the show.

So when the kiss cam landed on Lawson and me and the fans cheered for us to smooch, smooch, smooch, I jumped in Lawson's lap and pretended to kiss him passionately. My hand was over his mouth the entire time, but the crowd roared with applause. Even Wyatt's presence couldn't dampen my spirits. Although in a strange role reversal, he was rather reserved, while the rest of us devolved into what can only be described as silly.

Exhaustion from laughing might be my new favorite thing, and I relished in the afterglow as we drove back to Magnolia Bluff. Lawson, Wyatt, and I'd met at the clubhouse to drive together to Savannah. When we returned at almost midnight, I was still in such a good mood that I didn't even mock Wyatt when he roared out of the parking lot on his motorcycle, the epitome of the bad boy cliché. Lawson offered to drive me to the cottage after he checked on the clubhouse, but it was a relatively cool night, and I was content to stroll down the path as I texted Spencer.

Me: Savannah Bananas game was awesome. If they come to DC, we have to get tickets. You should check them out online. Good night.

As I'd slid my phone in my pocket, I heard the buzz of Willa's golf cart, and I'd ducked behind the azalea shrub. She dashed into the clubhouse, and I waited for the door to click shut before I crept inside the building.

Waving her phone in the air, Willa paced the length of Lawson's office. "I know you said y'all are just friends, but this video doesn't look that way."

Did she really think I'd stoop so low as to kiss her fiancé? I might not want them to get married, but I didn't break the rules. Still if she doubted him, things weren't so perfect.

"What video?" Lawson held out his hand. "Can I at least see it?"

Willa gave him the phone. "I was checking social media to see if y'all made any of the posts because everyone says the videos from the games are hilarious. To think, I'd been staying up to surprise you. I must be the biggest fool."

"You aren't a fool. This looks a lot worse than it was."

"Did you kiss her?"

"No. We were all having fun, and Carleigh may have gone a little overboard, but I promise you that no one's lips touched. Wyatt would've punched my lights out if I'd kissed another woman."

"I thought he was getting a hot dog or something, and I didn't want him to kill you, so I didn't call him and ask."

"Thanks for that. I promise you don't need to worry about Carleigh. We're just friends."

"Yeah, you might be just her friend, but I'm not convinced that she views you in the same light, especially after finding this at your house when I was dropping off presents this afternoon." She slapped the presentation folder on the table.

"Let me explain. Those were just some suggestions that I'm not interested in pursuing. Without me asking, Carleigh—"

"Don't get me started with that woman. I knew this presentation must have been her creation, especially after that performance tonight, and everything else."

"What do you mean? What else?"

"Seriously? Out of the blue, the busiest woman in the world suddenly has three weeks to spend down here just hanging out with her best *friend*. Give me a break. The movie might be from the late nineties, but I've seen it. Just because I'm nice and young doesn't make me naïve. I'm an event planner. I've dealt with my share of jealous ex-girlfriends and other wedding disrupters. Why do you think I insisted she stay with me? I wanted to keep an eye on her. Oh, and I'm perfectly aware that she's been sneaking out and going over to your place in the dark of night."

"I-I don't know what to say." Lawson hedged.

I kind of wanted to give Willa a high five. She had a lot more gumption than I'd given her credit for, but it meant I was going to have to up my game.

"Tell me nothing is going on," Willa said.

"I promise nothing is going on. Carleigh took dance lessons with Spencer and has been teaching me the Carolina shag, so I could surprise you. I didn't question why she came early. I was just glad to have my best friend here to celebrate with us, and though she adamantly denies it, I think she has feelings for Spencer."

Not that again. I rolled my eyes, shaking my head. Although . . .

A rush of adrenaline swept through me, and I almost gasped with the brilliance of the idea. Covering my mouth, I hurried from the clubhouse before I got caught and couldn't carry out my newly inspired plan. If I played the role right, I could still save my cover and complete the mission. For the first time, I was grateful that Spencer had refused to come with me.

While I rarely delegated jobs to people who hadn't proven their worth—actually I never took a chance on an unknown person—I needed insider help. Still, I surprised myself the next morning when I picked up my phone to text my future sister-in-law.

Me: Hi. Circling back to you on the girls' night. We're running out of time.

Me: It should be a surprise. A sleepover?

Zoe: Yes, yes, and yes!

Me: Can you take care of the food? I'll get everything else.

Zoe: Perfect.

Me: Tuesday night?

Zoe: That works. I'll let Wren know.

Me: Thanks.

My experience with bachelorette parties was as limited as my participation in slumber parties. Not counting my freshman year with a roommate in the all girls' dorm at the University of Georgia, my last sleepover was in middle school. But what I lacked in experience, I could make up for with research, and the internet didn't fail me.

By lunch, I'd ordered everything we'd need for an upscale party that wouldn't include Zoe sprinkling glitter on me. Instead, there'd be matching peach pajamas for Zoe, Wren, and me, while Willa would get the white version. With express shipping, the outfits would be delivered before the party. It cost a little more, but it'd be worth it.

Since Wren was an artist, I planned for her to lead us in a painting class, and we'd each have our own canvas and tabletop easel. To add elegance to the affair, or at least that's what the website claimed, we'd have strawberry champagne punch. But the pièce de résistance was the adorable game of Pin the Veil on the Bride. No one would ever be able to say Carleigh Chastain didn't throw the best bachelorette party ever. This event would be deserving of a Pinterest award if there were such a thing.

Four days later on the evening of the party, I arranged everything, then surveyed the scene and patted myself on the back. It was all coming together better than I'd imagined. Maybe I'd take up event planning. It wasn't so hard.

Then my phone vibrated with a text from Spencer, making my stomach quiver with nerves. I hadn't heard anything from him since my text about the game, and he felt so distant—not just because three states separated us, but there was something else. He wasn't filling me in on his life like normal. Up to this point in our relationship, he'd never hidden anything from me, but something was up. I didn't know if I wanted to deal with it, but when the phone buzzed again, I held my breath and swiped the screen.

Spencer: I found some videos of the Savannah Bananas.

Spencer: Carleigh??

Me: Sorry, I was working on something. Funny right?

Me: The game. Not that I was working.

Spencer: I watched a video from the night you went.

Me: Ha ha. Can you believe we made the feed?

Spencer: Yeah.

Me: I went a little over the top.

Spencer: You think?

Me: Actually, it's part of my new plan.

Spencer: Really?

Me: Yes, and this new angle will be successful.

Spencer: Can you talk?

Cringing, I shook my head like he could see me. Talking to Spencer wouldn't go well. I couldn't lie to him, and I hated hearing the disapproval in his voice. But with fantastic timing, a noise at the door gave me an honest excuse.

> Me: Not right now. I've got a big night ahead and someone just knocked.

After I made sure my phone was silenced, I dropped it onto the couch and rushed to the door. If everything went right, Spencer might even get a good laugh over the scenario.

When I opened the door, I found Zoe's arms overloaded with trays of food and a basket looped over her arm. "Let me help you." I lifted a ceramic platter of chocolate-covered strawberries.

"Thanks." Zoe continued inside. "I may have overdone it, but when else are you supposed to indulge?"

"Hopefully, Willa will put her diet on hold for one night. What's in the casserole dish?"

"Shrimp and green noodles. Your mom gave me the recipe. I guess it's from a restaurant on the coast that closed decades ago, so it's kind of like a secret."

"It doesn't sound that unhealthy."

"That's because you didn't see the amount of cream that went into it. Trust me, it's going to be decadent."

"But also upscale, so it fits right into my theme." I uncorked the champagne with a satisfying pop and began making the punch.

"You thought of everything." Zoe arranged slices of strawberries on top of chocolate frosted cupcakes. "Willa is going to be amazed."

Wren arrived a while later with painting supplies. A little later when the bride-to-hopefully-not-be walked in the door, she was stunned.

With eyes shimmering, Willa splayed a hand over her chest. "Y'all, this is too much."

"Carleigh organized it all." Zoe wrapped an arm around Willa's shoulders and guided her into the kitchen.

"Thank you." Willa sniffled as she stepped forward and hugged me.

"You're welcome, but Zoe was the one who gave me the idea." As I patted her back, something like guilt pinched at my resolve. Willa was a sweet girl, and I didn't want to hurt her, but marrying Lawson wasn't in her best interest either. She was so young and had so much life ahead of her. I was doing her a favor. I shifted out of her embrace, picked up two flutes of punch, and passed one to Willa. "Let's start with a toast."

Zoe lifted her glass. "To my new friend. May everything on your big day be filled with love, joy, hope, and happiness. Best wishes for a wonderful wedding!"

"Best wishes!" We clinked flutes and took a sip.

The champagne's bubbles danced with the fruit juices on my tongue. It was such a refreshing drink, perfect for a summer picnic. I could make it the next time Spencer and I went to a concert in the park. It was one of our favorite things to do together. They always held them during the golden hour, creating this magical ambiance. I could see Spencer lounging on my blue and white quilt, his eyes deepening a shade as he granted me a lazy smile, and a pleasant flutter tickled my heart.

"Carleigh. Carleigh?" Zoe's voice interrupted my daydream. What had she asked?

"Um, sorry. This drink is just so yummy." Holding up my glass, I looked through the sparkling rosy liquid with the slices of strawberry floating about. "And pretty."

They all exchanged looks.

"What? Don't y'all like it?" I asked.

"The drink is delightful." Willa took another sip, arching her brows at Zoe.

"Absolutely, but you seemed to be delighting in something else." Zoe grinned. "Or someone else . . ."

"Was it Spencer?" Willa asked in a teasing voice but her narrowed eyes told a different story. Before anyone caught her skepticism, she playfully clinked her glass to mine and then emptied it.

My cheeks heated like I had something to hide, but why wouldn't I be smiling dreamily about a sunset picnic at a summer concert? Still my apparent physical response to their teasing would make what I needed to say seem a lot more plausible. But I couldn't just divulge my secret-not-secret all at once. It'd be more believable if they chipped away at my defenses.

"Maybe." I lifted the pitcher of punch. "Refill?"

Willa held out her glass. "Sure."

"If it wasn't Spencer, who was it?" Zoe nudged Willa.

"Leave Carleigh alone." Wren pointed at Zoe and Willa. "She's entitled to her secrets."

"Of course, but if there's someone else besides Spencer, we may need to adjust the seating chart for my wedding reception." Zoe tapped Willa's flute like this should be reason enough for me to spill the tea.

Normally, I'd have pointed out the holes in her argument, but it didn't seem worth it to continue pretending when I wanted them to think Spencer was more than a friend to me.

"Y'all can't tell anyone." I ducked my chin shyly.

"Really?" Wren's eyes got wide. "They were right?"

"I mean Spencer is my best friend, but lately things have changed. No one knows, not even Lawson." Sadly, my description of the current state of Spencer's and my relationship leaned more toward the truth than a lie. Our friendship was barely recognizable since the start of summer. Whether that was for the good or bad made my stomach knot, but for now, I'd let the girls draw their own conclusions.

"I knew it!" Zoe high-fived Willa.

"Okay, okay, but seriously, please don't tell anyone. Spencer is a very private person, and we're still figuring things out." Also, not a lie.

"This makes me feel so much better." Willa smiled.

"Why's that?" Wren asked.

Willa wrinkled her nose. "Even though I said I wouldn't, and I totally trust Lawson, I have to confess that after your fake kiss with him, I worried your feelings had changed. This is such a relief. Now we can all be friends."

Zoe lifted her glass. "To girlfriends!"

"To girlfriends!" We all followed her lead.

In all my life, I never thought I'd utter those words, but here I was, and now, I'd seal the deal with party games. I lifted one of the bunches of white tulle I'd glued to a magnet earlier in the day. "Who's ready for Pin the Veil on the Bride?"

As suggested from one of my searches, I'd sketched the outline of a bride on a large piece of paper and taped it to the refrigerator. I affixed the pretend veil to the bride's head, demonstrating the game.

"How adorable." Zoe clapped. "We have to save it for my party too."

"For sure." I passed everyone their own tulle-covered magnets.

"Wren, you go first, since you're the only one who's been a bride." Willa sipped her punch.

"Great idea." I gave my satin sleep mask to Wren, and she slid it over her head.

"Right this way." I guided her to a spot a short distance from the refrigerator. "Are you ready?"

"Wait, that's too easy. You need to spin her around three times. That's how you play Pin the Tail on the Donkey. Right?" Willa asked.

"You're right. I totally forgot." Because I hadn't pinned any tails on anything in too long to remember. Of course, the child bride probably played the game at her last birthday party. Why didn't Lawson see how mismatched they were? I clasped Wren's shoulders and rotated her in a circle, counting aloud, "One, two, three." I pointed her toward the kitchen and lowered my hands. "Go for it."

Wren staggered a bit but made it to the fridge and stuck the magnet on the bride's shoulder. She removed the mask and held it out. "Who's next?"

"You go, Zoe," Willa smiled.

Zoe took the mask and put it on. After the requisite spinning, she crossed the room and placed her magnet on the side of the bride's head. After tugging off the mask, she laughed. "I guess that would make an interesting statement."

"I'll go last," Willa said, pointing her glass at me. "You go."

After I positioned the mask over my eyes, Zoe spun me. I lifted my hands in front of me and walked until I found the target and mounted my magnet veil. When I looked, I'd put the magnet on the bride's neck. "Looks like you can still win." I gave Willa the mask, and she handed me her empty flute.

"Ready." I placed my hands on her shoulders.

"Absolutely." She pressed her hands to her cheeks. After I turned her in three circles, she teetered slightly. "Wow, I'm a little dizzy." But she began shuffling toward the paper bride, then she stopped. "Oh, no."

"Are you okay?" I stepped in front of her and touched her hand.

As she ripped off the mask, the color drained from her face and she grabbed her stomach. "I think—" She heaved, and red liquid spewed from her mouth all over me before she dashed to the sink, where she continued vomiting.

Zoe ran to her side and began rubbing her back, while I watched in shock as the regurgitated punch dripped down my body. Apparently, she hadn't grown out of everything. How had I ended up as the recipient again?

"I'm so sorry, Carleigh." Willa hunched over the sink.

"Here." Wren tossed me a towel before she filled a glass with water. "Rinse out your mouth. You poor thing."

"I should've known better than to put on a blindfold and turn in circles with my motion sickness, but I thought I'd be fine."

"Maybe you shouldn't have had two glasses of champagne punch, but it's mostly juice." I wiped off my arms. "There's hardly any alcohol."

"I didn't taste the champagne and thought it was plain strawberry punch." She crumpled onto a kitchen chair. "It looked like the non-alcoholic drink from the shower. I thought y'all used a similar recipe. Oh, and I've hardly eaten all day."

"You were doomed." Zoe opened a box of water crackers and gave it to Willa. "Eat some of these."

"Thank you. I'll be better as soon as my stomach settles."

"There's some sparkling water in the fridge. That'll help." I moved to my bedroom door. "And we can all change into our party pjs."

"Carleigh, I'm so sorry." Willa tucked her bottom lip between her teeth, and my chest tightened with regret. She looked so pitiful. I didn't want to hurt her. She was a sweet girl with so much ahead of her, and nothing was making sense. How would this all turn out for the best?

"No worries. It happens." Evidently, more often to me than others but maybe I deserved it. I trudged into the room and closed the door, my own stomach churning. What if they went through with the wedding? Everything felt so off-balance, and I didn't know how to deal with my concerns. I couldn't just ignore my instincts, but for now, I'd focus on getting through this night.

Chapter 16

While I did make it through the night, I didn't escape a makeover by Zoe complete with glitter makeup, nail polish, and hair spray. Then, she'd insisted we take pictures in our coordinating pajamas, and Willa even agreed to indulge in the high-calorie food. Since the girls believed Spencer and I were an item, I could freely check my phone for a message from him.

But there was nothing, and even as a trail of goosebumps lined up on my arm, I ignored the warning. I should have learned my lesson after the airport surprise, but the glitter and exhaustion had weakened my defenses.

Since I didn't have anywhere to go in the morning, I told the girls I was sleeping in, which was what I was doing, complete with eye mask and city sound app playing, when a tapping at the door jarred me awake.

"Yes?" I pushed the sleep mask onto my forehead.

The door opened a crack, and Willa stuck her head inside. "Carleigh, I'm sorry to wake you, but you have a visitor."

"What?" I reached for my phone, but it'd died during the night. "What time is it?" I found my glasses and pushed them on.

"Ten o'clock." She gave me a polite smile, but it didn't fool me. I used the same one when I needed to keep people calm. Something was wrong.

"Is it my mom? Because I can't with her right now." I massaged my temple. Undoubtedly, I was too old for slumber parties. My head hadn't hit the pillow until some early morning hour.

"No." She glanced over her shoulder. "I think you'll be happy about this person."

"How certain are you?" I pushed onto my elbows, waiting for her to tell me who this mysterious visitor who'd interrupted my peaceful sleep was, but she just stared back with that serene, but difficult to read, expression.

"What do you mean?" she asked.

"What's the numerical likelihood that I'll be happy?"

"Nine-nine point nine percent." She smiled, nodding. "So, I'll let everyone know that you're coming."

"Wait. Everyone?" I bolted upright. Were we hosting brunch or something? I certainly hadn't included any morning plans for the party. In fact, I'd hoped that by the time I got up, they'd all be gone.

"It's just Zoe, Wren, and the visitor. See you in a sec." Willa closed the door, and I searched my brain for anyone that would require all this secrecy.

When no one came to mind, I grabbed my glass of water from the bedside table. After I swished the water around my mouth, I popped in a mint and stood, avoiding the mirror. Whoever it was would get the full sparkly Carleigh experience, since the only way to the bathroom was through the living room. I should've taken a shower before bed, but I'd been too exhausted by the end of the second Julia Roberts rom-com.

As I gripped the doorknob, I sighed. I should've stayed at the bed-and-breakfast and avoided these unwelcome morning surprises. I turned the knob and opened the door.

"Surprise!" the girls shouted.

"Good morning." An exhausted-looking Spencer gave me a little wave.

Wait. *Spencer?* It couldn't be. I must be seeing things.

Trying not to choke on the mint, I blinked twice, took off my glasses, and then put them back on.

Yes, it was Spencer, but his normally tamed and styled hair flopped over his forehead and dark circles puffed under his broody gray eyes. My chest tightened as I tried to put together the puzzle that stood before me. *What? How?* Then a lightness floated through me, releasing the worry. It was so good to see him.

Until one of my party guests cleared her throat, and I remembered that we weren't alone. I shifted my focus from him, surveying the expectant faces. The faces I'd told only a few hours earlier that Spencer and I were in a romantic relationship.

Waves of heat overwhelmed my body as I swallowed what was left of the mint. I had to do something. With no other choice, well, no other choice that I could ascertain in my sleep-deprived, very confused, slightly grateful state, I ran across the room and launched myself at Spencer.

As I wrapped my arms around his neck, I closed my eyes and pressed my lips to his. To my surprise and relief, he kissed me back with a tenderness I'd never experienced. With strong arms, he gathered me in an embrace that seemed certain, almost encouraging. For a moment, nothing else mattered and tranquility eased my nerves. But only for a moment because this was my best *friend*.

Realization zipped through me, and I snatched my lips from Spencer's, rolling them together, while I moved my quivering hands to his chest to stop my body if it decided to indulge in another round of pleasure. My lips buzzed for more, but my brain reasoned that it was just a physical sensation, and one that hadn't been satisfied in quite a long time. It couldn't be anything else because this was Spencer, and we were just friends.

However, he was breathing like he'd just finished a sprint as his gaze shifted to our audience then down to me. His lips twitched into a smug smirk as he arched a questioning brow.

Before he could say anything that would blow my cover, I said, "It's okay. They know our secret and promised not to tell anyone."

"Our secret." He nodded, with a very satisfied grin like he knew something I didn't and was going to make me pay for my hasty actions. "Well, that's a relief."

Dropping my hands, I turned to see if anyone was being fooled by our performance. Surely, they'd recognize the signs of a first kiss even if it hadn't felt like one. "So I guess y'all met Spencer."

"Y'all are adorable." Willa snuggled with Queenie who'd also made the trip and fallen under Willa's charms. "Your kitty is so sweet."

"I need coffee." My shoulders fell as I shuffled to the machine. "You look like you could use a cup too."

"Thanks." Spencer joined me at the counter. He lifted my hair over my shoulder and leaned close to my face, sending tiny thrills tripping down my spine.

What was wrong with me? I gripped the handle of the pot.

"Is this glitter?" He brushed my cheek.

Sighing, I shifted away from his touch and poured two mugs of coffee without spilling a drop—which under the circumstances, I saw as a huge accomplishment. "Zoe gave me a makeover." I passed him a mug, hoping that the normality of the gesture would center me.

"Spencer, you have to join us for breakfast." Zoe opened the oven and began moving pans to the stove. "I made egg sausage casserole and blueberry muffins with streusel topping."

"Breakfast sounds great. I haven't eaten anything but trail mix from a gas station sometime last night."

Zoe sliced the casserole. "You must be starving."

"You're in for a treat." Willa crossed the room and passed everyone a plate from the stack in the center of the table. "Zoe makes the best food."

Spencer held out his plate for Zoe to fill. "It seems my timing was perfect."

"Speaking of timing. When did you leave?" I asked.

"After your last text, I needed to see you in person, and Queenie agreed, so I packed our bags—by the way, she doesn't travel light—and we hit the road."

I placed my mug on the table. "You drove straight here?"

"We stopped at a hotel, and I slept for a few hours." He pulled out a chair and sat. "Traffic was light, so it was easy."

"It's a miracle your car made it." After I placed a muffin on my plate, I joined him. "Spencer's been driving the same Honda Accord since we met."

"And she hasn't failed me yet."

"I'm not sure testing her longevity by driving to Georgia was the best idea."

"My options were limited if I wanted to get here fast."

"A plane?" I suggested.

Zoe gave me a nudge as she took a seat. "I think it's sweet."

"Thanks, Zoe. You'd think my *girlfriend* would be happy instead of second-guessing my choices."

Girlfriend. Nicely played, Spencer, turning Zoe into an ally.

I pinched off a piece of muffin. "It just worries me to think about you driving that old car all the way here. Anything could've happened, and you were supposed to come in less than two days, anyway."

"I couldn't stand to be apart any longer." He squeezed my hand, giving me puppy dog eyes.

While I desperately wanted to give him a strong side eye, his words and gestures elicited a round of *awws* and *how sweets* from Zoe, Wren, and Willa.

With great determination, I refrained from gagging and settled for batting my lashes at my *boyfriend*. "You're the best of the best."

When I saw the corner of his lips twitching, I knew he'd comprehended my entire message, but he didn't let on.

"Do you have somewhere to stay?" Willa folded her napkin. "Lawson has a spare room."

"Thanks, but I was able to get my room early at the Kensley Inn, so I'm all set as long as Queenie can stay here."

Willa scooped up my enamored cat. "Of course she can."

Wren stood. "I'm sorry I can't visit longer, but Nathaniel has already texted three times."

"Aww, he misses you." Zoe held up a container. "Give me a sec, and I'll make you a to-go breakfast for him."

Wren gathered her stuff. "Thanks. He loves your muffins."

"What do you have planned for today?" Spencer released my hand, and I unexpectedly felt chilled.

"Sleeping and then cleaning up around here." I leaned close to him and whispered, "So you don't have to worry about me getting into any trouble."

"Hmm. Worrying about you has become an unfortunate new pastime for me," he said quietly. "Can we talk alone?"

Nodding, I swallowed the lump that'd formed in my throat. I didn't want him to worry about me. But the fact that he cared about me so much that he drove all the way to Magnolia Bluff with my cat twisted my heart in unfamiliar ways. I shifted back in my chair. "I'm sure you want to get cleaned up and take a nap."

"No doubt, but I have some rather time-sensitive issues that I need to discuss with you."

"You go take care of yourself and come back when you're ready. I'll be here." I pushed away from the table. "Do you need directions?"

"I'm good." He stood and held out his hand to me. "Walk me out?"

"Sure." I took his hand and let him lead me from the cottage.

Once we'd rounded the corner of the house and were out of sight, Spencer dropped my hand and dragged his fingers through his hair. "Carleigh, I know I played it off, but I'm more concerned now than when I arrived."

"Don't be. I have everything under control. Besides, I'm not the one who jumped in the car and drove ten hours on a whim."

"It wasn't a whim. I tried to ignore your texts and the video and well, everything, but I couldn't, and then there's this whole situation. I definitely didn't expect to find you wearing matching pajamas and hosting a sleepover. We won't even discuss the way your entire head is reflecting the sun like the chandeliers that artist you like so much makes."

"Chihuly."

"What?"

"Chihuly is the name of the artist with the colorful blown glass chandeliers. Oh—" I lifted a finger. "That's a great idea. They make Chihuly-inspired glassware. Zoe would love it. Remind me to order a set for their wedding gift."

"Are you really trying to change the subject?" He glared at me, massaging his neck.

"I didn't know we'd chosen one, but I'm tired and quite frankly, not fully recovered from the shock of you appearing out of nowhere with no warning. It's not like you at all."

"I know." He sighed, dropping his hand. "But I'm not the only one acting out of character."

"Fair point." I shrugged. "It's all this peace and quiet. It's making me so anxious."

"Do you know how backwards that sounds?"

"Yes, but here we are."

"Yes, we are, and while we're here, not that I'm complaining about your greeting, but seriously, is kissing your *friends* a new thing for you?"

I rolled my eyes. "Are you serious?"

"The kiss cam."

"I knew what you meant." Chuckling, I waved my hand dismissively. "That was all fake. I can't believe you couldn't tell, but neither could Willa. Maybe I should try acting. Anyway, that's why I told her we were together."

"Fine, but what just happened in there"—he flung an arm toward the cottage as he stopped beside his car—"wasn't fake."

"I know, and I'm sorry."

"We need to talk about—" Squeezing his eyes shut, Spencer clasped the back of his neck—"about all of this. We can't put it off any longer."

"Um, do you really think this is the best time? I just don't want one of us to say something we'll regret. You're exhausted. I'm seriously sleep deprived and covered in glitter." I swept my fingers through my hair, creating a shimmering shower.

"Fine." He dropped in the driver's seat, clearly not amused. "Just promise me you'll lie low until I get back. Your judgment seems to be less-than sound, especially when it comes to where you plant your lips."

"I promise I won't kiss anyone else until I see you." I winked, trying to lighten the mood. "But then all bets are off."

"Should I be glad you're joking or worried that the glitter is affecting your sanity?"

"I'm fine. See you in a bit." I backed away. "Oh, and Spencer, I am beyond happy you're here. Best surprise ever! I'm glad we're not keeping score because I'd never catch up."

<h1 style="text-align:center">Chapter 17</h1>

When the sun was starting to dip behind the pine trees and Spencer hadn't reappeared, I began to worry he'd given up on our conversation. Not that I wanted to hear what had been so important and was so time sensitive that he'd needed to drive to Georgia instead of waiting to fly down for the wedding. I didn't need to be scolded. I felt confused and guilty enough.

Queenie sauntered across the cottage and leaped onto the sofa next to me. She certainly didn't mind that the change of plans meant she wasn't at the kitty hotel. I scratched her head. "What's going on with Spencer?"

She shot me a side-eye like it was so obvious.

"What?" I stuck my tongue out at her as Willa walked in the front door.

"Hi." I put Queenie in my lap, holding her close. Not one for being constricted, Queenie whined and wiggled until she had both of her front paws on top of my arm, but she didn't leave me. Likely because I scratched her in the exact place to gain her submission.

Willa dropped her bag on a chair. "I thought you'd be with Spencer."

"Me too. I'm sure he'll be here soon."

"So, you didn't give a lot of details last night." She grabbed a sparkling water from the fridge and joined me on the couch.

What kind of specifics was she hoping to elicit? I wasn't even sure how I'd ended up here. Kissing Spencer hadn't been part of the original plan, even if it had been nice. *Ahhh! Stop it, Carleigh!* But the damage was done. Tiny fireworks exploded inside me.

"Not much to say. We've been friends for a long time. It just kind of happened." I shrugged like it was no big deal that I'd kissed my best friend. Where was he anyway? I checked my phone to see if I'd missed a text from Spencer, hoping Willa was buying my explanation and desperate to end this conversation. Seeing nothing from Spencer, I typed out a message as I spoke. "I'm sure it was the same with you and Lawson."

> Me: Please tell me you are OTW. Hurry.

I lowered my phone.

"I mean, we were friends, but it all happened so quickly." She opened her drink.

"No kidding. That doesn't worry you?" While I seriously doubted she'd call off the wedding now, her answer might give me a measure of peace about the arrangement. Better still, if she was talking about herself, she wouldn't be grilling me.

"Not really. Like I told you, I've had a thing for Lawson since I was a kid, which I thought was just a crush, but it wouldn't go away. Trust me, I didn't want to fall for him. My career was about to take off, but God had other plans, and I adore my job here."

"And you aren't concerned about working together every day and living together? It seems like a lot of stress to put on a new relationship."

"We won't just be living together. We'll be married, and there's a big difference. Besides, we work well together, like Brad and Zoe."

My phone vibrated with an incoming message.

Spencer: I just woke up. Sorry. I'm throwing on clothes and will be on the way.

I held up my phone. "He's on the way."

"That's great." She sipped her drink, tilting her head to the side like she was deciding what to say next.

Before she could speak, I lifted my hand and rotated my finger. "So, circling back to something you said about your career. Aren't you worried that this job won't always be satisfying? I get that now it's all new and you're getting to be creative with the planning of the events, but what about later?"

"I guess that's a risk you take with any job. I plan to keep things fresh here, so we won't be doing the same thing year after year. Although I do hope we can develop some events that become traditions, especially for the holidays. And we plan to be a venue for weddings and corporate events. It's going to be a busy place. In fact, I'm more worried that I'll get overwhelmed, but Lawson will have my back."

"He's one of the most loyal and dependable people I've ever met." I shifted a snoozing Queenie onto the couch but remained silent. If Willa was like most people, she'd start talking again to avoid any awkwardness.

"It's one of the things that first attracted me to him when he was taking care of Wyatt. It seems so crazy, and only God could have orchestrated our meeting all these years later at the right time and place, so I guess that's why I don't doubt our future. I have faith that if God brought us together in this strange way, He'll be there to guide us when things seem uncertain."

I nodded, surprised by her response, so I gave her my standard answer when I didn't agree with people but didn't want to offend their logic. "You definitely have given this a lot of thought."

"I'm glad we got to talk. Slowing down and having the chance to form meaningful friendships is one of the things about Magnolia Bluff that I've come to love, but we've been so busy with the wedding planning and preparing for Lawson and me to be gone for a week that I've barely gotten to know you."

"No worries. I'm sure we'll have other chances to hang out."

"Like Zoe and Brad's wedding."

"True." With a renewed tension gripping my lungs, I stood, desperate to be alone in the open air where I could get a deep breath. "I'm going to wait outside for Spencer. We might catch the last of the sunset."

"The moon and fireflies are pretty great too."

"Good to know." Trying to act untroubled, I strolled out of the cottage. As I walked to the driveway, I inhaled and exhaled deeply. With a warm breeze rustling through the palmettos, my body relaxed, but my mind still swirled with doubts.

Willa seemed so sure of her future with Lawson at Magnolia Bluff, but hadn't I been that way when I was twenty-six? Everything had seemed not just possible, but inevitable. If I worked hard, I'd be successful and would eventually have it all, and my life to this point had been pretty great. I wouldn't change the way it'd gone so far. Hopefully, Willa's faith wasn't misplaced naïveté. I really did wish the best for her.

My vibrating phone brought me back from my thoughts.

Lawson: Any chance we can squeeze in one more dance lesson?

Me: When?

Lawson: Tonight, but a little bird told me that you had a visitor appear out of the blue.

Me: So much for secrets among girlfriends. I should've known better.

Lawson: It wasn't Willa, by the way. This is a small town. I heard the news from no less than three people before I finished my lunch. News travels fast, especially of the romantic variety. We're considering a new slogan: Magnolia Bluff, where love is always in bloom.

Me: Ignoring all of that.

Lawson: Not surprised, but I'm here for any confessions.

Me: I still can't believe you're getting married in a couple of days.

Lawson: I hope you can see that this is the life I want. I'm happy.

Me: That's all I want for you. Could we meet tomorrow morning around eleven?

I sniffled, stupid, stupid tears filling my eyes.

Lawson: Sure.

Trying to displace the droplets on my lashes, I blinked, but it was useless as the waterworks continued, causing the words on the screen to blur.

Pull it together, Carleigh. You don't want Spencer to see you like this . . . again.

But if anything, recent events in my life had proved I'd become a very unlucky person with terrible timing. As Spencer steered into the driveway and parked, I wiped under my eyes, removing the residue, but I couldn't stop the dripping. My tear ducts were in serious need of a plumber. Still, maybe he wouldn't notice in the dim lighting.

As he got out of the car, I tried some extra big blinks, but it didn't help.

"Hi." I waved in a fake-it-till-you-make-it ridiculous kind of way.

"What, no kiss this time?" Chuckling, Spencer eliminated the space between us with his long strides.

"Nope." My chin dropped to my now quivering chest. *Fantastic*. I was having a full-on meltdown.

"Carleigh?" His feet came to a stop in front of me. "Are you okay?" He pressed gently on my chin as if to lift it, but I resisted, so he did what best friends do. Saying nothing, he drew me into a hug, rubbing my back, while I pressed my cheek against his chest, soaking his shirt.

When I finally got a hold of myself, I twisted the button of his golf shirt. "Is it enough?"

"What?" His voice was thick, like he might have been fighting his own emotional boundaries.

"I've done all this work and been successful at my job, youngest person to make partner at the firm, top of our law school class, chair of the foundation for the animal shelter, named as thirty under thirty by the University of Georgia. I've made a lot of difference for a lot of people. But is it enough?" I splayed my palm over the fish logo embroidered on his shirt. "I'm missing something, but it's not just about getting married and having a family. Until this visit, I've always felt fulfilled and pretty happy."

Spencer's chest rose and fell as he took a slow deep breath. "I want to tackle this with you, but is that what you want right now?" His fingers wound around the ends of a lock of my hair. "Because I don't want this to turn into a fight." He knew me so well, and if I was this emotional and letting him see me this vulnerable, I'd get defensive.

"Me either. Actually, tonight, I don't want to talk about the future or weddings or houses with white picket fences or even the suburbs."

"That's oddly specific." He patted my shoulder. "But I get it, and if that's what you need, I'm fine with sticking to other topics for tonight."

"Thanks, and I promise, tomorrow, I'll give you all the time you need, sans tears, to tell me whatever it is you want to tell me."

"I don't mind your tears, but I know you hate them." He brushed the dampness from my cheek with his thumb, sending an entirely different sensation fluttering around my heart.

"It makes me feel exposed, especially when I don't understand the cause." I shifted out of his embrace, a sudden coldness sweeping over me, but I couldn't stay all wrapped up in his arms. "And I don't want to delve into that now."

"Got it. The inn keeper recommended having supper"—he smiled—"at the General's Diner. It's on the town square. Haslemere feels like it could be the set of a television show."

"I haven't been there yet, but I've heard they have the best peach milkshakes."

"Even better." He quirked a brow, giving me a once over.

I touched the side of my face. "Oh, do I look all splotchy?"

He chuckled. "No, I was just noticing that you're not shimmering anymore. I kind of miss it. Are you sure you don't want to apply some glitter before we head out?"

"Maybe that's what I'm missing." I laughed, relaxing as I relinquished my guard.

With only one restaurant, Haslemere didn't scream burgeoning metropolis, but as we turned at the stoplight, the charm of the small town had me blinking away tears. Evidently, I'd become a full-blown sentimentalist. Next, I'd be crying at television ads.

But my weepy mood was soon replaced by laughter and easy conversation with my best friend. As I gave him an account of the sleepover, Spencer chimed in with just the right commentary. The food didn't hurt either—juicy bacon cheeseburgers with shoestring fries for the win. After dinner, we strolled around the square, reminiscing and sipping peach milkshakes. A person can't be sad with vanilla ice cream and sweet Georgia peaches enveloping each taste bud with perfection. And if all that wasn't enough, as Spencer walked me to the cottage door, fireflies delighted the darkness with sparks of gold. *Enchanted* described the entire night. Even the crying because it forced me to experience everything with an intensity that I normally avoided.

Chapter 18

As Spencer joined me on the backyard swing the next morning, his eyes were that broody shade of gray, promising a difficult discussion and proving all good things come to an end.

Eager to hold on to our bliss, I pointed to the dock. "We could go kayaking."

"Nice try." Spencer arched a brow. "I've put this off as long as I can, but I'm glad we had last night."

"Um, that sounded foreboding. Are you sick?"

"Not in the ways you think, but if I don't get this out, I am going to develop an ulcer."

"I'm sorry to be causing you anxiety. Thanks for being patient with me." Setting the swing in motion, I nudged his side. "I know I've said it before, but I don't know why you put up with me."

"And there it is." He glanced over at me. "Carleigh, I've done something that I'm not sure you're going to like, and I thought I could manage it or find a solution for it, and then when I saw what appeared to be you making a play for Lawson, I knew—" The soles of his Sperrys skidded across the ground as he bent forward, resting his elbows on his thighs and catching his head in his hands as we came to a stop. "I knew I couldn't let that happen because I don't want him to be with you."

Sighing, I dropped a hand on his shoulder. "I told you it was all a show for Willa, so you don't need to worry."

"You don't understand." His shoulder collapsed under my hand. "I don't want you to be with anyone other than me."

"Pardon?"

He turned his head, taking me in. "I'm sorry, but over the weeks since your birthday, I've become aware that I love you. And before you say how much you love me and send us safely back into the friend zone, I mean I love you as much more than a friend."

As he searched my expression and then locked his gaze with mine, his eyes darkened further with barely a hint of the blue specks. It was like a storm cloud blocking out the sky.

My heart skittered to a stop and then, as if to try to catch the beats it missed, it pounded with increased intensity as I stared back at him, trying to understand his words.

"And while I have you rendered speechless, there's more." Slowly he shifted his eyes from mine, straightening beside me and clasping my hand. "Carleigh, squeeze my hand to let me know you can hear me. I don't have the courage to say this twice."

As directed, I tightened my grasp. *Was this really happening?*

"I know you don't want to move, but Carleigh, a deal on one of the Colonial Village Garden Apartments popped up in my email, and it was too good to pass up. So I made an offer. It's been completely renovated, move-in ready. I know your opinion of the suburbs, but this is basically still in the city. I thought it was a nice compromise if you thought we might have a future. Anyway, the reason it was such a good deal was because the owners needed to sell quickly, and since I've been saving for years, we negotiated with the bank for a faster than normal closing. In fact, I'm closing next week."

"Next week?" I managed to whisper.

"Yes, but you don't need to make any decisions right away. I talked to Dan about renewing your lease when I told him I'd be moving out. He said you could go month-to-month."

"Month-to-month?"

"Carleigh, I know this is coming a little out of left field for you, but we've been together so long, and lately, I've been sensing that your feelings for me have also changed. At least, we're sure of one thing." He bounced his brows, grinning.

I certainly wasn't, and what was his weird face supposed to mean? "What?"

"We know we're compatible, although I'd say when it comes to kissing, we're perfection." His gaze dropped to my lips which buzzed with the memory.

But one kiss didn't prove anything, did it? Although it had with Lawson. Then again, we'd been teenagers. Surely, our skills had improved, but in my time alone with Lawson, we'd never tried another kiss, and thinking about it didn't make me shiver like I did when Spencer merely glanced at my lips.

I clenched my molars, desperate to steady myself. I needed to focus on the more practical parts of Spencer's confession. "What exactly are you saying? You want me to live with you in Arlington?"

"No, you know I'm old-fashioned. I don't believe in co-habitation before marriage. Okay, wow, that kind of made it sound like I was proposing, but I'm not, at least not yet. Obviously we need to date first."

"Obviously? But you're moving." My voice rose slightly as unease mounted, agitating my emotions like the river during a storm.

"I can't afford the mortgage and the rent."

"And you chose this condo with me in mind?"

"It didn't feel like I chose it. More like it chose me. You're going to love it."

"You're making a lot of decisions for me."

"I'm sorry, but you were here, and I didn't want to have this discussion over the phone. It feels so right to me, and the more I think about a future with you, the more certain I am of it. Please tell me if I'm completely off base."

"Being apart from you has been so hard. I can't imagine a life without you in it, and more recently, I have felt things that seem like more than friendship, but I chalked them up to our separation. I haven't considered anything else." As I heard the words I was saying, my skin prickled with awareness. What were my instincts telling me?

"I understand what you're saying, and I know you've been thinking a lot about your life goals." He released my hand and clasped his together. "To be honest, I'm glad we've never crossed this line before. It's given us the opportunity to have this deep relationship without any of the other stuff. We weren't ready until now. I have this sense of rightness that God chose these random circumstances to force us to acknowledge we're meant to be together."

"Now, you sound like Willa which truly scares me."

"Maybe she's right. When it comes to what matters most, she seems wise beyond her years."

"Her priorities are definitely different than mine were at the same age."

"What matters is what your priorities are now. But I get that this is all a lot, and I understand we have more to discuss. I'm simply asking that you give me, us, a chance."

"When you say it like that, it sounds like we're just putting a toe in the water to test the temperature. But when you tell me that you've bought a condo, are moving, and have discussed my rental agreement with our landlord, it's like we're diving into the deep end."

"I'd hoped you'd be more on board."

"Spencer, I've been questioning everything, even whether I should stop Lawson from marrying Willa. And not to pass blame, but then you asked me if I wanted to marry him."

"And?" Worry etched his forehead.

"It's not like that. We're just friends."

"I've heard that the best spouses were friends first, and I'm your closest friend, right?"

"Yes, but does that mean we should pursue a romantic relationship that will be for the long-term? Because if we're wrong, we won't remain friends."

"I'm willing to take that step of faith."

"But what if there's someone out there that you haven't met, and you're settling with me because I'm convenient?"

"Trust me. You're not convenient. If I wanted a low-maintenance girlfriend, I'd still be in DC on a date with Jordan's cousin." He rubbed his neck. "But I don't want you to wonder if you're settling either. If you believe being with me would be giving up something more special, I don't want you to do it. But I don't think it'll take you long to come around." He stood.

"Are you leaving?"

"I have two days of work to catch up on, and you need some time to think."

"Shouldn't I just know if it's right? I'm so tired of thinking." I trusted my intuition, but now, it wasn't telling me anything. All the zips, zings, knots, and clenches were absent, replaced by an odd sense of peace.

Spencer chuckled but then turned serious. "I want to be the person you tell all those crazy thoughts to, who you trust enough to fail in front of, who you won't hesitate to show every emotion to, and I think that I'm him. But if everything you feel for me doesn't amount to more than friendship, I'll understand. The last thing I want is for you to accept my offer because you don't want to upset me or our friendship. Take your time." He bent and kissed my forehead. "I'm sure you'll be busy tomorrow, so let's just plan to meet for the rehearsal."

"Okay," I murmured. As he crossed the lawn, I fell back on the swing and stared at the fluffy white clouds sailing over the bright blue sky. Why couldn't I drift away on one of them? A sensation of loneliness hollowed me out as I considered my life without Spencer. It was hard enough letting Lawson go.

Major life decisions shouldn't be decided on a whim, and Spencer had been pondering all of this for weeks. Did I want to consider all the pros and cons? Should I need to? I shook my head and rose from the swing. The clouds were providing no clarity, and I needed to meet Lawson for our last dance lesson.

While I strolled to the clubhouse, I tried to put Spencer's proposition out of my mind and concentrate on a combination of dance moves to teach Lawson. Of course, that just brought up memories of Spencer and me dancing together.

There'd been so many wedding receptions and charity galas where we'd delighted in our ballroom partnership. But there'd also been random weeknights, when we'd turned on a playlist and danced barefoot in one of our apartments. Those dance therapy sessions started because one of us read something about the activity reducing stress, but it wasn't always about dealing with life. Sometimes it was just because it was our thing, and it felt right.

We had good chemistry on the dance floor, which was interesting for me because I always let him take the lead. In Spencer's arms, I let myself be vulnerable. I trusted his guidance, not that he had to do much anymore. We'd learned to sense each other's next steps, and we moved together in an effortless union. But that was only dancing.

Something I could learn to do with anyone, right?

As I entered the ballroom, I rubbed my head as if I could massage the answer from my brain.

Wyatt emerged from the kitchen with a plate of food. "Hey, Lawson had to run out to the golf course. He said to tell you he'll be back soon and to eat lunch on him." He passed me the plate. "You okay?"

"Yes, I'm terrific." As I offered the necessary smile, Spencer's statements flashed through my thoughts like a cable new's ticker. *I love you. I bought a condo.*

"If you say so." Wyatt headed for the kitchen, but heaving a sigh, he turned and stalked back to the spot he'd just left. "I'm sure whatever's bothering you is none of my business, and I'm not going to pry. But I wanted to thank you for throwing Willa a bachelorette party. She loved it."

"It was the least I could do. I'm glad she liked it." I focused my attention on the grilled chicken salad, hoping he'd take the hint and let me eat in peace.

"I'm sorry we got off on the wrong foot."

"Okay." I glanced to the French doors that led to the porch and a table calling my name.

Unfortunately, Wyatt still stood in front of me, thumbs in his pocket. "It's just that when you rolled up unannounced, I didn't know what to think. I do remember you from school, and you were never the fly-by-the-seat-of-your-pants kind of girl. Which made me think that you might have ulterior motives. But you also were always responsible and dependable. Two traits that I've only recently developed. Still, something felt off."

"But you quickly realized I was the same old reliable Carleigh, and while I'm highly skeptical of people claiming to have made one-eighties, you seem to have made some positive changes."

"Actually I was still skeptical of you because Willa told me about your marriage pact with Lawson, and I believed you'd come down here with every intention of breaking up this wedding. It didn't seem too farfetched that a single woman in her mid-thirties might decide that if she wanted to get married, her best friend was her best chance to make it happen. But my little sister insisted that we trust Lawson, so I let it all play out, and I came to see that you aren't the monster I made you out to be. I'm sorry I doubted you. Only a desperate, lonely, not to mention selfish person would come between two people so totally in love."

My gut knotted even though his characterization was completely inaccurate. I'd been motivated by friendship. Not that I had any plans to explain myself. I was sick of his self-righteous attitude and wanted this conversation over. Where did he get off judging me? He was the one with a history.

"Wyatt, I appreciate your confession and apology, but it's unnecessary." I pursed my lips, and that's when I should've given him a curt nod and walked outside to enjoy my lunch.

But I hate nothing more than a tie score. It's one of the best things about tennis. You have to keep playing until someone wins—and not just wins, but wins by two games. So I continued. "Lawson and I have been friends for a long time. We've been through a lot together, and I'll always support him, even if he wants to throw away his career working in this backwards place with zero chance of advancement. And from what I've gathered, Willa is making some compromises as well. I'm surprised *you* aren't more concerned." With that pair of aces, I strode by him.

But at the sound of clapping, I stopped and peered over my shoulder. "Do you have a problem?"

Wyatt paused his applause, clasping his hands. "Not anymore, but you sure do."

"Excuse me?"

"Carleigh, we're not that different. At least, the person I used to be and the person you've become aren't that different." He smirked.

"How did you pass your last drug test?"

"I'm perfectly sober." Exhaling audibly, he crossed his arms and tilted his head back, his attention on the ceiling. While he stared skyward,

I considered making an escape, but curiosity got the best of me as he continued gazing upward.

"Are you looking for a leak?" I asked.

"For reasons that escape me, I'm praying for patience. I should just let you continue wrecking your life, but apparently, I've had one visit too many with the therapist and the preacher to not share what I know to be true." He lowered his gaze to me. "In high school, we both faced rejection. I mean, unless you're one of our extremely likable siblings, it's often a part of growing up." He paused, raising his brows. "Come on, you want to agree with me."

But I pursed my lips tighter, glaring at him. He had no idea who he was dealing with. Although he'd made a fair point, agreement to small points could be a slippery slope in a negotiation. I preferred to hold my comments or arguments until I heard the whole story. On the other hand, I didn't know how much more of his psychobabble I could take.

"Anyway, some of us get it worse than others, and some of us are hurt by it more than others. I chose to rebel and prove to everyone that I didn't need them, but apparently, you chose to prove to everyone how great you are at everything."

"While I'm sure you'll eventually make a point, I'm having a hard time following your logic." Because being successful would never be viewed in a negative light.

"You might not be able to grasp it for a while, but I'm almost finished. Through a lot of mistakes that unfortunately carried a lot of terrible consequences, I figured out that everything I thought I wanted and even needed to be fulfilled was wrong. Sure, my issues were often of the illegal variety and yours aren't, at least I don't think they are. Although you do work in politics, where the lines between right and wrong often get smudged in a city that isn't exactly known for its high moral standards."

"I'll have you know I stay within the lines, and my advocacy has helped bring jobs to tens of thousands of people along the coast. Not to mention my charity projects. We have nothing in common other than Lawson, and I can't understand why he gave you a second—or was it a third—chance."

"Because Lawson understands there are more important things in life than winning and going after what society considers important. Believe it or not, I've become a bit of a Bible nerd, and this verse from Matthew sixteen comes to mind. 'What good will it be for someone to gain the whole world, yet forfeit their soul?'"

"My soul is just fine. Spencer and I go to church almost every Sunday."

"Great, but I'm guessing you feel like you're missing something. You don't have to admit it, but you might be surprised that even if you do achieve the American dream of *having it all*"—he put air quotes around the words—"you'll still feel like something is missing. If you're going to church, it should make it easier to find the answer. But just in case, consider Romans twelve. 'Don't conform to the pattern of this world, but be transformed by the renewing of your mind. Then you'll be able to test and approve what God's will is, His good, pleasing, and perfect will.'"

"Thanks for the Sunday school lesson. If Lawson ever decides to show up, please tell him I'm on the veranda eating my lunch." Determined to put Wyatt Ramsay and his weird psychoanalysis behind me, I strode through the doors.

From birth, I'd been a Christian, and not the CEO type—Christmas and Easter only—but the every-Sunday-morning-and-youth-group-president type. While I'd been questioning a lot about life, my faith was not at issue. To prove the point, I sat and said a blessing over my salad.

Chapter 19

Over the years, Spencer and I'd happily filled the *and guest* role for each other at many weddings and the occasional rehearsal dinner when one of us had found ourselves in the wedding party, him more than me, since I lacked the requisite girlfriends to achieve bridesmaid status often. But Willa and Lawson's rehearsal registered differently. As I made my way up the aisle, each step felt heavy, like the click of my heels should be echoing through the church. Meanwhile, my nerves hummed with anticipation for something yet to be determined.

Friends first had been my mantra all day to remind myself of the steadiness of our relationship, but it was taking a lot of effort, and it was all because of that kiss that should have meant nothing.

While it hadn't been hard to stay busy with the pre-wedding events, kissing Spencer kept invading my thoughts. It was like I was back in his arms, my lips on his, and electricity zipped through me like I was powering up after a blackout. It didn't seem possible that one kiss and one authentic conversation could amp up my attraction overnight, but something was undoubtedly going on with my body. Even as shivers skittered over my skin, my temperature flared. Basically, I'd either contracted the flu, or I was falling for my best friend.

There was so much to worry about, but my mind wouldn't focus on the logistics, it only wanted to bask in the glow of a new romance. But this wasn't a new romance. This was a very old, very good friendship. So while I vacillated between wanting to throw myself at Spencer and wanting to put something immoveable between us, I decided to do whatever was necessary to get through the night as friends, and not friends with benefits.

After the rehearsal, the wedding party and their dates crowded into shuttles for the short drive back to Magnolia Bluff. A few months earlier, Willa had planned Wren and Nathaniel's rehearsal celebration to be held in his rather magical backyard, complete with rose gardens and an iron arbor. Unfortunately, a tropical storm forced them to move the affair indoors. Since they'd made all the arrangements and bought many items for the party, Wren offered to host Willa and Lawson's dinner.

I hadn't met Wren's husband Nathaniel, and Brad said he was a curmudgeon even if he doted on Wren and wrote beautiful love stories. Maybe I needed to read one of his books for some research on love, since I clearly lacked the required knowledge to recognize when it was happening in my life. But to be fair, Spencer *had* said it had only occurred to him recently.

What if he was just worried about me finding someone else? He'd mentioned that seeing the fake kiss was what had sent him south. What if he'd realized that he was ready to have a wife and family, and I seemed like the easiest choice? He might have denied it, but what if his subconscious was masking the truth?

With all these questions that still lacked answers, I needed to keep my lips to myself. As we strolled into the yard, my arm brushed Spencer's, and I wove my fingers together in front of me to keep them from reaching for his hand.

Friends first, Carleigh!

In front of us, the garden opened to the river and a fiery magenta sky accented with wisps of pale pink clouds.

"Wow!" Spencer touched my elbow, sending ripples of goosebumps down my arms and stopping my progress. "I could write a novel if I had this kind of inspiration every night."

"You could write a novel without all this. Whatever happened to that story you used to tell me you wanted to write?"

"I didn't have this landscape."

"Ha ha. Seriously."

"Writing's like a lot of things that I put off. I kept thinking I'd get back to it, but I never did. Maybe I'll pull it back out." Spencer passed me a flute of champagne from the tray of a passing server. "How are you doing? Do you want to find somewhere to sit?"

"I'm okay. Let's walk down to the dock for a better view."

We strolled by beds filled with flowers that mirrored a sunset, with yellow, orange, pink and even purple blossoms. "I can't imagine how much time it takes to care for all these plants."

"It must be a labor of love," he said.

"They're beautiful, but it's not how I'd choose to spend my spare time."

"What would you do if you had endless amounts of time?"

"Good question." I shrugged. "I'm not unhappy with my life. How about you?"

"I'm not unhappy, but I've been thinking about all the things I haven't done because I'm not intentional with my time."

"You mean like writing?"

"Maybe."

As we reached the dock, a gentle wind blew off the river, ruffling the hem of my skirt. Spencer had shipped me one of his favorite dresses. It was a simple ice blue dress with a halter top and an A-line skirt. Behind my neck, a white striped bow secured the collar, leaving the back open.

Apparently, Spencer appreciated this style of dress, since he'd also been a fan of the dress I'd chosen for the wedding.

"Are you cold? Do you want my jacket?" Spencer grazed his fingers down my arm. "You have goosebumps."

"I'm fine. The breeze feels nice after being inside most of the day." Besides it wasn't the wind causing my skin to react, and I absolutely wasn't cold. I leaned against the rail, peering over the side. A hazy version of the sky reflected in the dark waters like an impressionist painting. "I appreciate how you always look out for me, and I don't take it for granted."

"I know." He joined me at the rail. "With you out of town, I've been spoiling Queenie because I have so much time on my hands."

"It seems like you've been pretty busy."

"Actually, I've been trying to slow down and take account of how I'm living. I don't want to be like that reed." He pointed to the river. "It's just floating along without purpose. It only changes course if it bumps into something and only changes direction with the tide."

"You definitely should write a book."

"You're funny." He tapped the tip of my nose. "But do you get what I'm saying? I don't want anything else to sneak up on me and realize too late that I've missed an opportunity for something great."

Warmth spread from my heart to every part of my body, and I wanted to tell him that he hadn't missed me. But what if I was just caught up in the moment? It was rather romantic, and I did love the attention. What if it was just a case of distance making the heart grow fonder?

So I pointed to a bird gliding in lazy circles overhead. "You could take up birdwatching?"

"Okay, I can take a hint. We won't talk about *us* tonight."

"It's so nice to talk to someone who doesn't need subtlety explained."

"Hmm. Is there a specific person who doesn't grasp your cues?"

"Wyatt. He gave me this long speech about the attributes of Magnolia Bluff when all I wanted was to eat lunch. They should hire him to write ad copy. I mean this place is great, but can you imagine me living here?"

"Not at all." He hugged me to his side in a very friendly way, but it didn't stop the heat pooling in my belly. Resisting him all night was going to be hard. But I always liked a good challenge, so I reinforced my defenses, making myself ready to lean into him and enjoy the warmth his body provided.

Dinner consisted of a seafood buffet with cheese grits, hush puppies, and coleslaw. After we filled our plates, we joined Brad and Zoe and my parents at one of the tables on the patio. Mom gushed over Spencer as usual, but also filled us in on all the plans for Brad and Zoe's wedding. She begged me to stay for a few extra days to try on bridesmaids' dresses, but I declined the offer, citing my job.

When Spencer told them about his new condo, surprisingly, Mom's only reaction was to congratulate him and give me a pointed look. I'd expected her to throw out wild assumptions about him settling down and me joining him, and while her grace was appreciated, it was unlikely to last long. Still, I couldn't help but wonder if she'd finally accepted that we were never going to be more than friends at the precise same time that Spencer decided we needed to redefine our relationship. What was Mom up to? She never missed an opportunity to press me about marriage. Maybe she was satisfied with Brad's engagement.

Still something about her reaction, combined with my own doubts, had me questioning the wisdom of us changing our relationship status. Even if I'd uncovered a physical attraction to Spencer that I'd failed to realize before the kiss, there was a legitimate argument that my physical reactions to him were more about the few men I'd dated and even fewer times I'd been kissed. If my dating life was a sport where you tried to score the lowest number like golf, I'd be a champion.

As supper came to an end, I joined the maid of honor at the microphone to give our toasts. Willa's sorority sister recounted how Willa was like a mom to them, coordinating all their get-togethers and counseling them with her wise advice. To her, this was evidence that Willa had found her perfect job, and they were taking credit for preparing Willa to deal with any potential drama. This got a lot of laughs from the bridesmaids. After a few more accolades for the bride, she mentioned how she hoped to find a guy as great as Lawson, and then wished the couple well.

Since I'd only abandoned hope the day before that one of them would call off the wedding, my speech was rather basic. Okay, I *may* have used AI to help write it. I despised being mushy in front of crowds. Not to mention the new risk of bursting into tears when I thought about weddings, especially this one. So erring on the side of boring seemed preferable to devolving into a whimpering fool.

As I concluded the speech, I paused and smiled at the happy couple. "I have to admit I wasn't sure exactly how to end this speech. If you know me, I'm not very sentimental."

"That's the understatement of the year!" Lawson shouted, and everyone laughed.

"But I did find this quote from one of the all-time best rom-coms, *When Harry met Sally*, and it describes Lawson and Willa's engagement perfectly. 'When you realize you want to spend the rest of your life with somebody, you want the rest of your life to start as soon as possible.'" Smiling, I lifted my glass. "To the bride and groom."

Everyone chorused their agreement, and I hurried away from the spotlight, relieved that I'd made it through tear-free. With the speeches completed, people rose and mingled. A dessert table had been set up inside, complete with the groom's cake that was made to look like a stack of balls from all the sports Lawson loved.

As I navigated around the guests, Zoe stopped me. "Great toast. That quote was perfect. I can't believe they're getting married tomorrow."

"Me either. It all seemed so fast."

"Willa did have that whole unrequited love thing simmering for over a decade, so though they only dated a few weeks and their engagement was short, their relationship has been long. You read stories about people being reunited with their soulmates. It's so amazing to see it happen in real life."

"I'm not surprised that Willa gave into her crush, but it's still surprising that Lawson fell for her so quickly."

Zoe shrugged. "Like the quote implied, when you know, you know, and with Brad, although we both tried to deny our feelings, we were basically a love-at-first-hug kind of romance. Although, I admit, I'd been crushing on him from the moment he appeared in our first video call. To be honest, I don't understand how people date for years and don't know if they're in love, but I guess relationships come in all shapes and sizes, like you and Spencer." She wrinkled her nose.

"Right, of course, like Spencer and me." I tacked on a smile that I hoped appeared confident because the way my guts were tangling together did not shout confidence. Spencer and I weren't a love at first sight or an unrequited love thing. Did we fall in another category? I never liked the *none of the above* option on tests. It always made me worry I'd missed something. I wanted to see the correct answer and select it.

"It's so exciting, but I haven't told anyone about you and Spencer, not even Brad or your mom." She pressed her finger over sealed lips.

"Thanks." My lungs quivered, but Zoe didn't seem to notice my mounting anxiety. Was there really anything to tell? Should there be? We'd been together for years, and only now, when he'd decided to make intentional decisions about his life, did he want to be with me romantically. It seemed more likely that I was available and compatible, and he was settling for a good relationship. I'd already failed to protect Lawson from an ill-advised situation. I wouldn't fail Spencer too.

"Of course, I wouldn't want to break your trust with the first secret you've shared. That being said, it isn't easy, so if you wanted to announce your relationship sooner rather than later, it'd be terrific. But no rush, seriously, whenever you're ready."

"Got it." I glanced over my shoulder, spotting Spencer chatting with the elusive author. "If it's okay with you, I'm going to join him." I gestured to where they stood at the intersection of the brick paths. "And meet Nathaniel. Hopefully, he won't judge me based on my little brother."

"Ha ha. I'm pretty sure you're the only one describing him as little, but I like it. Keeps him humble."

"What else are *big* sisters for?"

"Truth, and by the way, Nathaniel's pretty nice, but don't tell Brad I said so. I don't think they dislike each other as much as they pretend. They just like giving each other a hard time."

"I'll keep that in mind." I turned around and eased toward them. Spencer and I needed to talk, but once we did, things would change between us. Hopefully, not forever, but certainly for a while. Which meant more time without my best friend. But I was doing what was best for him, and I'd survive.

"Nice toast." Our host extended his hand. "I'm Nathaniel Sullivan, Wren's husband."

"Nice to meet you." I shook his hand. "Thanks for the compliment, but as a successful author, I'm sure you can spot a canned speech when you hear one."

He chuckled. "Guilty, but I do appreciate your honesty."

"Your home is fantastic. It was really gracious of you to host this party."

"Hmm. Since we're being honest, I'll let you know I was against the idea, but Wren wanted to do it, so here we are. I'm sure eventually I'll learn to tell her no, but it doesn't look like it'll be anytime soon."

"She doesn't seem like the type to ask for much." I switched my focus to Spencer. "You met Wren the other morning."

"Right, and she insisted on leaving early with breakfast for you."

"She does spoil me." Something caught Nathaniel's attention, and he waved. "It appears that I'm being summoned by my wife"—he winced—"and my housekeeper. I better go see what's the matter. Nice meeting y'all." He hurried away.

"Did you get some writing tips?" I asked.

"Not really, but he did tell me that he wrote his first books at the Kensley Inn, where I'm staying, so that was interesting."

"Are you thinking about forgoing Arlington and moving to Haslemere to be the next great American author?"

"Depends."

"On what?"

Sighing, he dropped his shoulders and raised his brows at me, and I wished I hadn't brought up Arlington, but it was fun to banter with Spencer. It was one of my favorite parts of our friendship.

"Since the toasts are finished, are your duties for the night complete?" His hand slipped down my palm and interlocked with my fingers.

"Don't you want cake?"

"Only if you do."

Friendly chatter flowed from the porch, where people milled about with dessert plates in the warm glow of the house lights. Did I really need to talk to Spencer tonight? Cake meant we could remain in the status quo a little longer, but then what? No, we needed to have this conversation and waiting would only make it harder.

"I'm good to go if you want to go."

"I absolutely want." He tugged on my hand.

Too much emotion thickened my throat, so I nodded and let him guide me out of the garden and to the gazebo behind Linda's house. Instrumental music floated from the party through the quiet night.

"Do you want to dance?" Spencer lifted our hands into position, while pressing a palm to my back, his thumb resting just above the waist band of my dress.

"Okay." I placed my hand on his shoulder. One last chaste dance wasn't going to hurt anything.

"You look stunning, if I haven't already told you. I like it when you pull your hair up. Not that I don't like it down."

Mostly because of the wind and the humidity, I'd opted to spool my hair into a low chignon. "Thank you. I didn't think you noticed my hair." I tucked a tendril that'd fallen loose behind my ear before placing my hand back on his shoulder.

"That makes me feel terrible."

"No, it's fine. It's not important."

"It is, and I should've told you more often. Not that it's an excuse but I don't know exactly what it is that catches my eye more one day than the next. Although when your hair is up, it exposes this area along your neck." Suddenly, his hand was no longer holding mine, and his fingers were tracing the edge of my collarbone as he drew me closer.

My breath caught, and I gripped his lapel, shivers taking over my body, leaving me at his mercy. Without the fortitude to think or speak, I couldn't stop him, and I didn't want to. The only thing I wanted was his lips on that spot.

I lifted my gaze to his, but his eyes were fixed on my neck. He lowered his head, stopping just above the area. "Would it be okay if I test it out?" His warm breath tickled my skin, making my knees wobble.

"Yes," I murmured, tilting my head to give him ample space to test out anything he wanted on my neck, collarbone, or shoulder.

After he explored the area, his lips trailed up my neck, finding my lips. Tenderly, he pressed his mouth to mine, and I dissolved into his kiss. It was so wrong and so right all at the same time. As we lingered together, our mouths surging and receding but never parting, I wanted to stop time. I wanted this to be our reality—to be more than a kiss, but as we parted for oxygen, reality stopped me, and I shifted out of his embrace.

"What's wrong?" He caught my hands as they slipped from his chest. But when I pulled back, he released them.

"Spencer, we shouldn't have done that." I stepped further away, creating more space between us, but it didn't seem like it would be enough.

"You cannot be serious. That was amazing, inspiring, exhilarating. Why did we wait so long to do it?"

"Because we're friends, and friends that do *that* don't last long."

"Or forever."

"Not for us, or at least not for me. I'm not sure I feel the same way about you."

"If your lips are any indication, you're wrong."

"Kisses are nice, and maybe, they're another thing we do well together, like dancing and playing tennis."

"Carleigh, there's nothing similar about hitting a ball on a court and kissing you under the stars."

"So we're wrapped up in this romantic night, but since you told me how you felt, my gut's been tied up worse than traffic on the beltway, and you know I trust my gut. If I were in love with you, I should know. It'd be something I don't need to think about. Surely, by now, I'd have known I was *in love* if it's the love you're supposed to have to marry someone."

"Whoa. I suggested we date." He grabbed the back of his neck. "No one said anything about marriage."

"Spencer, you bought a condo in Courthouse. That's where newly-weds go to start their lives. As much as it pains me, I don't think you love me in that way either. If we did this thing, we'd be making a mistake. I don't want you to settle for anything less than your soulmate."

"And you aren't her?"

"Correct, and I only want what's best for you just like I did for Lawson. It's why I felt so strongly about stopping him from marrying Willa."

"You what?" Brad stepped out of the darkness. "I knew it. Sis, you are a piece of work."

"Brad, what are you doing here?"

"Mom asked me to find you for a family picture, but I stopped when I heard what sounded like an argument. I didn't want to interrupt, but your confession was too much."

"Brad, it's none of your business, and I was unsuccessful, so just pretend you didn't hear anything." I stepped to the edge of the gazebo. "Please tell Mom I'm on the way."

"Fine." He stormed across the lawn.

With the base of my palm, I rubbed my breastbone and turned back to the man I only ever wanted the best for. "Spencer, I'm sorry. Please don't be mad at me. I'm doing this for you."

"Your gut might be telling you something, but your interpretation is incorrect. It's not all your fault. You're conflicted, but that doesn't mean this thing that's happening between us is wrong." He dropped onto the bench and gripped its edge. "I—I lied." He fixed his gaze on me.

"What?"

"I lied," he repeated the words with certainty. "I've loved you for a long time, maybe since we first met. I tried to be content with friendship, hoping you'd come around, but you didn't."

"You dated other women."

"I hoped I could find someone else, but it always failed because no one was you. I thought it was the same for you because of your lack of relationships. But then you were also so focused on your career, and it never seemed like the right time. I believed it would happen eventually, and I could wait." He scrubbed his cheek. "Then you said you were ready to get married, and I finally thought it was our time. But then you came down here to chase after Lawson or at least that's what I believed."

He swallowed. "Some of what I said was true. After the video, it seemed like my last shot, and then you seemed like you were considering me." He shook his head. "I promised myself I'd move slowly, and I should have, but I didn't. Carleigh, I won't be settling with you, but the same goes for you. I don't want you to settle for me either." He stood, crossed the gazebo, and stopped in front of me. "I'm going back to the inn. I'll see you at the wedding."

"Okay." My insides shivered as he walked away, disappearing into the shadows of the live oak canopy.

All I wanted to do was smother my face in a pillow. Instead, I squared my shoulders and hurried to the party. The last thing I needed was Brad turning on me again, telling everyone my secret, and ruining my friendship with Lawson.

Chapter 20

Without knowing how it'd happened, I found myself moving toward the door on the side of the historic white clapboard church. These would be my last moments with Lawson before the ceremony, and I needed to focus on him. But I couldn't manage much more than putting one foot in front of the other and not snagging a heel on the cracked walk.

Everything that'd happened after Spencer left was like a dream that you can only remember glimpses of when you awake. Following the family picture, I'd returned to the cottage. I must've slept some because in the morning, Zoe woke me and drove me to Haslemere for hair and makeup. She didn't say much, which meant Brad had told her what I'd said about Lawson. If I'd talked to anyone, I don't remember, but at some point, I'd slipped on my emerald dress and made my way to the church.

Kara waited outside and pinned an orchid on my dress before ushering me into a small windowless room. All the while threatening my life if I messed up her event with any shenanigans.

Wyatt held the door as I entered. "I'll keep an eye on her."

I wanted to respond with a witty retort, but I lacked the mental energy. Every part of my body felt heavy, like my dress was made of chain mail. It was a good thing that I wasn't carrying a bouquet because I'm not sure I had the strength to hold it.

My every movement, word, and even thoughts took an extraordinary amount of effort. I felt like I was swaying on the edge of a cliff, and any wrong move would send me tumbling through the air into a ravine. I wanted to step back to safety, but at the same time, I wanted to peer over the side.

When Brad and I were still in elementary school, we went on a family vacation to North Georgia and spent a day hiking in Tallulah Gorge. As we'd crossed the suspension bridge, we watched a waterfall crash onto the rocky bottom. And while we couldn't see the droplets of water, a thick mist hung like a curtain sheer around us, making everything appear hazy. It was magnificent and scary. My vision seemed to be narrowing, like I was trying to see the other side. But instead I was focusing so hard that it was more like looking through a peephole in a door.

"Carleigh." Lawson waved his hand in front of my face. "Carleigh." He snapped.

I blinked twice, abandoning my incoherent and overwhelming thoughts. "Is it time?"

"We have a few minutes. Are you okay? You seem out of it."

"I just have a lot on my mind. It's an emotional day, giving your best friend away." Especially when you were losing the other one at the same time.

Wyatt shook his head. "Why don't you look at it as gaining a new friend?"

"I'll try." I sighed.

"Y'all, play nice, please." Lawson paced the short length of the room.

Wyatt cut me a side eye. "Sure, man."

"Of course." I backed out of Lawson's way, pressing my palms against the cool wall.

Wyatt stepped in front of Lawson and grasped his shoulders. "Relax. Everything's going to be perfect."

"You're right. Why am I so nervous? Nothing in my life has ever felt more right."

"Would you like me to pray?" Wyatt dropped his hands.

Lawson chuckled. "Who'd have ever imagined you'd be asking me if *you* could pray for *me*?"

Wyatt slung an arm around Lawson's shoulders. "We've come a long way from you and my little sister dragging my drunk butt into the house, but God does work all things for good."

"Well, let's do this then. I could use some of that peace that surpasses all understanding," Lawson said.

"You got it, man." Wyatt glanced at me. "Carleigh, do you want to say anything?"

I shook my head. "It seems like you've got this." I clasped my hands and closed my eyes.

"Dear Heavenly Father, we don't always understand your ways or your timing, but in moments like these, we can see how perfect and good you are. You are a way maker, and I thank you for bringing Lawson and Willa together in this seemingly impossible way. Thank you for blessing them with a love that they will celebrate in good times and cling to in hard times. I pray you will be the center of their marriage, guiding them daily. Please be with Willa and calm any worries she has about things being less than perfect and help her instead focus on her joy. Please also give Lawson peace as he waits to take this huge step, knowing that you're always with us. Lord, help the rest of us support Willa and Lawson in the years to come. We love them and pray your blessings on them. Amen."

"Amen." I opened my eyes. Not that I'd tell Wyatt or start taking his advice, but he was fairly good at praying. Even my strength was returning.

"Thanks, man." Lawson rolled his shoulders back and dropped his head from side to side like he was preparing for an athletic competition. "I'm ready."

At that moment, one of Kara's assistants opened the chapel door and indicated we should enter.

"Perfect timing," Wyatt whispered as he moved behind me.

I nodded as the hairs on my arms stood up like his words were prophetic. Perhaps my instincts were failing me because while Wyatt might have changed for the better, prophet status remained beyond his gifts.

As we walked to the altar, a violinist accompanied the piano with a classical song I recognized but couldn't name. It was a simple, calming piece that filled the room with a sense of wonder and gave me the space I needed to breathe. The church was small, with less than twenty rows of pews and an aisle down the middle. Through the simple paned windows, the early evening sun splashed light over the dark wood floors. Occasionally, a ray would reflect off a watch face or piece of jewelry, catching my eye as I surveyed the congregation.

Although Spencer had said he'd see me at the wedding, I wouldn't have blamed him if he'd packed his car and left town. I'd tried to re-call everything he'd said, but only one word was clear—settle. Before I'd scanned every pew, the heavy wooden doors at the end of the aisle opened, and beside her father, Willa stood, beaming. When I checked Lawson's expression, his eyes shimmered with tears as his lips turned up in an almost shy smile, and I saw between them something I'd failed to notice or maybe I'd actively ignored. Without saying a word or touching a finger, they were connecting, communicating with each other in this intimate way that none of the people in the room, including me, could infringe upon.

My pulse increased, and as the blood rushed through my veins, everything in the space became more vibrant. In an instant, it turned from gray scale to full color, but it was more than that, like it glowed. And not just visually. The music sounded richer, fuller, and the scent of the altar arrangement sweeter but also more complex. I inhaled deeply, filling my body with the energy that radiated through the moment.

By the time Willa reached the altar and her father passed her hand to Lawson, my body no longer felt heavy but light, and while I'd never admit it, bubbly. I checked the church again, and when my gaze landed on Spencer in his dark gray suit, I held his attention for a second before unwanted tears pooled at the corners of my eyes. As I blinked them away, I returned my focus to the preacher, but I couldn't concentrate on his words.

What had I done?

Spencer loved me. He'd always loved me. He'd waited and waited, and I'd never considered the possibility, while everyone else saw it. Why hadn't I?

I glanced to the back of the church.

Spencer stared forward, but he didn't meet my gaze. I tried to send him a message, but clearly, I didn't have the gift of telepathy. When he didn't respond, I returned my focus to the preacher who was directing Lawson to put the wedding band on Willa's finger while reciting words of devotion. As Willa took her turn, her eyes glistened with joy.

My emotions grew too big for me. The tears overflowed. I wanted this kind of love, and I wanted it with Spencer. Sniffling, I swiped under my eyes, and swallowed down the lump in my throat. He'd been right—my instincts had been telling me something was wrong, but it wasn't this marriage that I was witnessing. It was my feelings for Spencer, and I needed to tell him. My fingers tapped against the sides of my legs with unspent energy.

"Relax. You've almost made it to the end." Wyatt dropped a firm hand on my shoulder, and when my heels hit the floor, I realized I'd been bouncing on my toes.

As I nodded, he slowly removed his hand, and I pressed my palms together and focused on regulating my heartbeat and not rising again onto the balls of my feet.

Finally, the preacher said, "You may kiss the bride."

As Lawson kissed Willa, everyone applauded. Including me, ready to get to my own encore. When the instrumentalist started playing an upbeat march, I took the opportunity to check in with Spencer. When my eyes found his, I beamed at him, dabbing the moisture away at the corners of my eyes.

He spared me a half-hearted smile before he switched his gaze to the door. But he wouldn't just leave. Surely, he wouldn't give up so easily. Couldn't he see that I was hopeful, bordering on expectant, and looking at him?

After an inordinately long kiss, Lawson released Willa's lips and took her hand as they retreated up the aisle. Following Kara's directions from the rehearsal, I waited until they were passing the third row and then fell in step with the maid of honor. As we proceeded out of the church, one of Kara's minions directed us around the side of the church for pictures.

When I turned to go and find Spencer, Kara herself stepped in front of me. "You'll have plenty of time to visit with the guests when we're finished. I'm sure you don't want to cause any distress for the happy couple." She handed me a tissue. "You look like you could use this."

"Thanks." I blotted my face as I followed the wedding party into the choir room.

"Were you crying?" Lawson drew me into a side hug. "I haven't seen you moved to tears since you lost the presidential election in high school."

"It's a new thing for me. It's all this fresh air." I sniffled. "I'm thrilled for you and Willa."

"Congratulations, brother." Wyatt clapped Lawson on the shoulder before pulling him away from me and into a hug, while also keeping an eye on me.

I waved my hands in defense. I'd never go after a married man. No, I had only one man in my sights, and no one was going to stop me from finding him and telling him that I loved him.

Well, no one except a very feisty event coordinator with a clipboard and a headset. It was fine. Spencer had waited this long for me to realize he was more to me than a friend. What was another hour? The reception would be the perfect time.

An hour and twenty-eight minutes later, after no less than a thousand snaps and flashes of the photographer's camera, I took a glass of champagne from Kara as I boarded the shuttle. I slid into the window seat on an empty row, only to look outside and see the photographer positioning Willa and Lawson for more pictures as they paused in front of the van.

Seriously? Who wanted a visual reminder of the dusty black van that played a very minor role on their wedding day? Although it'd begun to register as rather integral for my own happiness. Perhaps I'd take a selfie with the modern-day carriage if we ever left and arrived at the reception.

Defeated, my chin slumped to my chest. Now would be a good time for a fairy godmother to appear and help me escape my current reality.

But instead, Wyatt claimed the seat beside me. "You'll be happy to know they've decided to only stop at every other pine tree we pass to take a picture."

"What?" I snapped my head up with what was surely crazy eyes.

"Sorry." He winced. "I was just joking. You looked like you could use a laugh but I guess my timing was off."

"Reading the room has never been one of your strengths."

He grinned. "And she's back. Good, I was starting to worry about you, especially with all those alligator tears."

"It's crocodile tears, and if you're implying that I wasn't being sincere, you're wrong. The last thing I'd fake is crying, especially in front of an audience." I shifted my focus out of the window of the now-moving van, watching the aforementioned pine trees zip by in a blur.

"It did seem out of character for you, but you've seemed sort of frazzled all day."

"Why do you find it necessary to point out all my flaws?"

"That wasn't my intent. Besides, I'm sure you have many flaws that I'm unaware of, so I couldn't bring them to light."

"Was that supposed to help?" I tapped the side of the plastic flute.

"Simply keeping the record straight. For what it's worth, if you want to talk, I'm here. But I'm guessing that's something you don't do either."

"I talk." Confident that we weren't stopping for more pictures, I turned to face my unwanted therapist.

He raised his brows. "But not about yourself."

Do not engage with terrorists or wannabe therapists. I pressed my lips together and stared back at him.

Wyatt chuckled. "You do realize that you're proving my point."

I took a sip of my champagne, enjoying the bubbles bursting in my mouth and refusing to let him goad me into saying anything else. He may have thought he'd won the battle, but my silence would continue to attack him. It was my version of guerilla warfare. Besides, my mission didn't need any interference from an unknown and likely unreliable ally.

Chapter 21

As the shuttle parked in front of the clubhouse, Kara gave us directions for our entry. We were going to be introduced and then there'd be the first dances. The entire reception was on a tight schedule so that Lawson and Willa wouldn't miss their flight.

Wyatt stood and held out his hand. "It's been lovely chatting with you."

Ignoring him and his hand, I rose and followed the bridesmaids off the shuttle. As we paraded into the ballroom, I glanced around but didn't spot Spencer. While I didn't want to remain in the circle around the dance floor, swaying with the rest of the wedding party, I also wanted to be present for these moments with Lawson. No matter what had happened, he was still one of my closest friends, and he'd supported me through so much. Hopefully, this would be his one and only wedding, and I couldn't abandon him now. Spencer would understand because we'd been there for each other over the years in all kinds of situations. And as soon as the music ended, I'd find him.

While Willa might have known about Lawson's private dance lessons, she seemed genuinely surprised at how well he executed the steps. After he'd passed her off to her father for their first dance, Lawson joined me. "Willa said to thank you."

"Y'all looked great out there," I said.

"Not half as good as I'm sure you and Spencer will later." Lawson took a quick survey of the room. "Where is he?"

"I'm not sure, but you better find your mom for your dance."

"Right. Everything is happening so fast, and I'm trying to savor each moment, but I'm afraid it's a lost cause." He gave me a quick hug. "Thanks again."

Willa's dad twirled her around the circle one last time before yielding the floor to Lawson and his mom. With her eyes overflowing with tears, they danced simply, not bothering with any fancy moves. It was so sweet that it left everyone teary-eyed. As the song came to an end, they hugged before exiting the floor, freeing me to find Spencer.

I pivoted and hurried through the crowd, but people kept stopping me and complementing my dress and my toast from the night before. Trying to be gracious, I thanked each of them and wished them well but made sure not to engage in conversation. While I'd mastered the fine art of small talk for my job, I wasn't interested in showing off my skill. The only discussion I wanted was the pivotal one I needed to have with Spencer.

But where was he? As I reached the hall, a heavy hand landed on my arm.

"Spencer, I've been looking—" I turned around to find my brother, glaring down at me. I wasn't short, especially in three-inch heels, but Brad still towered over me.

"We need to talk." He tugged on my arm.

"This isn't the best time." I snatched free from his grasp, not that he was holding on particularly tight. It'd been a long time since I'd bested him in a wrestling match, and he obviously could've stopped me with his strength, but after another look at his strained expression, I paused to make sure he wasn't going to use what he'd overheard the night before against me.

"I tried to have this conversation last night before you slipped away. I'm not taking the chance you'll disappear again, and the next thing I know you'll be on a jet headed for DC."

"Fine, but can we make this fast? I need to talk to Spencer."

"Right this way." He led me into the offices, and before I could say anything, he held up his finger. "I'm sure you have some great explanation for what I overheard. I'm fully aware you can convince people of almost anything. I'm also aware that you're smarter than me. That being said, I told Zoe what you said, and she said that I must be wrong because you're with Spencer. Now, I did kind of get the impression that I was interrupting more than a disagreement between friends, but I also know what I heard, so what gives?"

"Is it relevant given that we're at Willa and Lawson's wedding reception, and we both witnessed them get married only a little while ago?"

Brad fisted the back of a chair, his knuckles losing color. "It's important to me if you're going to be standing at the altar beside the woman I'm exchanging vows with before God and our family and friends."

A sinking sense of regret anchored me. Did he think so poorly of me? But based on what he'd heard, why wouldn't he? I swallowed away the thickness forming in my throat, ready to reassure him with my explanation. "Okay, fair point, but Zoe and you are great together. However, I didn't believe Lawson and Willa should get married for both their sakes. I was worried he wasn't thinking logically and acting too fast. Did you know Lawson and I had a marriage pact that expired on our birthday, the same day he proposed to Willa?"

"No. A marriage pact doesn't sound like something that you'd be a part of."

"At the time, I was twenty-two years old. It didn't seem like it'd matter, but when Lawson called, I don't know . . . I started doubting a lot, and worrying about the future, his and mine. But Zoe is right. I want to be with Spencer, and I need to tell him, which was what I was trying to do when you stopped me."

"I get that, but Carleigh, you could've ruined two people's lives. Don't you feel an ounce of guilt?"

"I believed I was doing what was best for them. They seemed to be rushing into a big decision with permanent consequences."

"As I've already said, you're intellectually superior, but you're missing so much about life. I get that you believe you've got something to prove to the world, but give the rest of us the benefit of the doubt that we can make decisions for ourselves without your input."

"You haven't asked for my advice in years, not like when we were kids, and you thought I knew everything. I was thinking earlier about our trip to Tallulah Gorge. You followed behind me like I knew where to go." But I'd only been following the path. I'd loved hiking, trekking aimlessly down a trail, going where it took me, trusting it knew the way. I smiled. "Remember?"

"Yeah, I wouldn't walk across the suspension bridge until you held my hand. I looked up to you back then. I just wish you'd stop seeing me as that scared little kid or worse, that idiot teenager."

"It's been hard to see you as little for a long time," I said, hoping to lighten the mood and detour this conversation, but he just stared back at me, for once his blue eyes not sparkling like he'd stuck his finger in an electrical socket. "Also, I'm sure you're not helpless and definitely not an idiot. You're doing great. We just see things differently."

"After my apology, I'd hoped we'd be able to improve our relationship or at least have one. High school was tough for you, I know, but I hadn't realized how much it'd changed you. I miss the girl you were." He released his hold on the chair, flexing his fingers. "And now, I hate to say it but it's going to be hard for me to trust you. I get that you and

Lawson are tight, but he's one of my closest friends too, and I'm having a hard time accepting your rationale."

I matched his glare. "Well, now you know how I've felt for the last fifteen years." Brad and I were never going to be best friends, and the person I'd been as a child was naïve and too trusting. He might want her back, but I did not.

Thankfully, before either of us could utter another word, the door swung open and Zoe rushed inside. "Carleigh, thank goodness I found you." She grabbed my hand. "Willa is about to throw her bouquet." Pulling me to the door, she glanced over her shoulder at Brad. "I'm sorry, I had to tell him about you and Spencer. He thought you wanted to be with Lawson, but now you don't have to hide your relationship, and if you catch the bouquet . . ." She squeezed my hand.

If I caught the bouquet, I could show it to Spencer as a sign of my feelings. As we increased our speed, a ribbon of hope twirled through me.

Zoe hurried me through the ballroom and out the French doors. "I found her!"

Everyone turned in our direction, sending heat dashing over my skin as I gave a little wave to the crowd and joined Willa's sorority sisters, all of whom I also could've babysat. But with age came experience, and where normally, I'd have scooted to the back of the group, this time I strode to the center. I may have spent years perfecting my technique for avoiding the bouquet, but with that same skill set came the ability to know the best place and way to catch one.

I rubbed my hands together and checked the girls to either side. They were young and pretty, but they'd be no match for me.

Laughing, Willa shook the flowers at us and then turned around, holding them over her head. After a glance over her shoulder, she tossed the bouquet in the air, and as it soared toward the hopeful women, I flipped my arms wide to the sides, giving my competition a slight shove.

Then I channeled my middle school basketball skills and bounced off my toes, lifting my hands into the air and reaching with my fingers until they snagged the flowers.

"Yes!" I held up a hand to high-five the girls around me, but they regarded me with sour expressions, so I flipped my hand over and shrugged smugly. "Sorry, girls. Better luck next time."

"You caught it!" Zoe clapped as I strode toward her.

"That was really something," Kara said sarcastically as she joined us with the dreaded photographer. "After the garter toss, we'll need to get a quick picture with you and Willa."

"Oh, okay." I slumped.

"Don't look so disappointed. This will provide you with a visual reminder of how you put it all out there and captured the prize." Kara chuckled. "I didn't have you pegged as the type to fight for a bouquet but good for you. I hope it pays off."

Beside me, Zoe clasped her hands under her chin. "Me too."

"Speaking of it paying off, have you seen Spencer since we left the church?" I asked.

"I haven't, but I'm sure he's here somewhere."

Chapter 22

But he wasn't. After the photo shoot, which involved a lot of teasing from Lawson over my exuberant performance, which hopefully no one caught on video, I scoured every square inch of the clubhouse, including waiting outside the men's restroom until it was vacant and taking a peek inside. Don't judge. In my line of work, sometimes you have to take extreme measures to close a deal. You'd be surprised how many powerful men will hide from confrontation in a restroom. Although I usually just waited them out . . . usually.

Anyway, the point is Spencer was nowhere to be found, and he wasn't answering my calls or texts. The only explanation was that he'd returned to the bed-and-breakfast in Haslemere, but I didn't have a car, and it was too far to walk or take a golf cart. And while it should come as no surprise, not that I didn't check, my rideshare service didn't have a driver in the area.

Pacing along the front porch of the clubhouse, I searched for a solution to get me to town that didn't involve asking my family for a ride. The last thing I wanted to endure were the inevitable questions from my mom about why my date had vanished. Where was that fairy godmother and her horse and carriage when a girl needed rescuing?

Instead, the person I couldn't seem to stop encountering, no matter how hard I tried, appeared, swinging a motorcycle helmet in lieu of a wand. "You look like you need a ride." Wyatt smirked.

Why me? I looked to heaven, not sure if I wanted God's input. From where I stood, miles away from Spencer, my choices seemed rather limited. For better or worse, and it certainly seemed to be the latter, Wyatt was my best and only hope.

I lowered my gaze, smiling. "I need a ride to Haslemere. Are you available?"

"Don't do that." He circled a finger in front of my face. "I'll give you a ride because for whatever reason, I believe it's the right thing to do, but don't think for a second that I'm buying your little act."

"Then why are you willing to help me?"

"It'd be hypocritical of me to tell you to show grace and give people second chances if I won't show you the same courtesy, but if I'm being completely transparent, it's fun to prove you wrong."

"Seriously?"

"Also, Zoe decided we should decorate Lawson's car, and I was nominated to run to the hardware store for supplies." As he put on his helmet, he glanced at me. "You coming?"

"Yes." I hurried after him.

From a compartment at the rear, he retrieved another helmet and passed it to me. "If I'm correct and Spencer's been MIA since the church, I'm assuming you want to go to the Kensley House."

I secured my helmet. "Are you going to ask me a lot of questions?"

"Nope. I think we've established that you don't want to talk to me." He grabbed the handlebars and swung onto the bike. "You can consider me a means, albeit a very chivalrous one, to an end." Wyatt patted the seat.

"Thanks." Still holding the bouquet, with one hand I hiked my skirt to my knees and climbed on behind him.

Was it awkward? Yes. Did I care? Not at all.

"By the way, once the engine starts, you'll notice that conversation is fairly difficult, so asking you questions was never a possibility." He chuckled.

"I'm glad you're getting a kick out of my predicament."

With nothing more than a smirk, he fired up the engine, and much to my dismay, I grabbed onto his waist. Never in my worst nightmares had I envisioned any scenario where I'd end up on the back of Wyatt Ramsay's motorcycle, barreling down a country road. I realized millions of people found this wind in the face thing exhilarating. I, however, could only think about the tort case I'd studied in law school involving the defective brakes on a motorcycle that lost control and crashed into a school bus.

Squeezing my eyes shut, I held onto Wyatt with renewed strength. Spencer better appreciate the risk I was taking to chase him down. Adrenaline zipped through me as Wyatt sped into town. Finally, when we came to a stop, he disengaged my hands from his waist, and I became aware of just how aggressively I'd been clinging to him.

With fire spreading over my skin, I jerked loose. "Thanks for the ride."

"Not a problem." He climbed off the bike.

I swiveled around, trying to regain a modicum of decency as I dismounted, while Wyatt, to his credit, averted his eyes.

"Do you have my number if you need a ride back?"

"Even if I need a ride back, I won't be calling you." I removed my helmet. "Don't get me wrong. I do appreciate your help, but I'll never take another ride on a motorcycle."

Laughing, Wyatt mounted the bike. "Never say never." Waving with one hand, he coasted slowly down the street toward the square.

I gaped, staring at him. He couldn't have been going faster than one of the golf carts.

"Carleigh?" Spencer's voice stole my attention, and I turned to face him.

"Hi."

His gaze drifted over my shoulder. "Did you just get off that motorcycle?"

"Yep." I adjusted my skirt. "I'm trying all kinds of new things these days."

He knit his brow, studying me. "Okay."

"You weren't at the reception."

"Nope."

"It wasn't easy, but I caught the bouquet." I held up what was left of it after Wyatt's wild ride.

"I see. Congratulations." He stared at me with cold gray eyes, making my heart clench.

Then I noticed the roller bag beside his feet. My heart dipped, but I wasn't too late. Everything would be okay. "Are you leaving?"

"I wanted to get a few hours in tonight."

"Can we talk?"

He took a deep breath. "I don't have much more to say."

"I totally get that, but could you just listen, please?"

"Fine." He aimed his key fob at his car, and the trunk popped open. "Just give me a second to pack this." After he stowed his luggage, we walked to the front porch and sat in the wooden rockers.

"The ceremony was beautiful, inspirational. It made me think about us, and everything you said last night. It all seemed so sudden, and because I wasn't sure of my feelings or like you said, I was misinterpreting my gut, I believed you were wrong about us. I thought you might have felt pressure because of your uncertain future, especially with the condo. That's such a huge step."

"Carleigh, I'm fully aware of all the reasons you think I'm wrong."

"That's just it. You're not wrong. You're right. When I saw you tonight in the back of the church, it all became clear to me. My world suddenly came into focus like never before, and I wanted to tell you, but

I couldn't get to you at the church, and then you weren't at the reception. Then I rode on the back of a motorcycle to get here. I want to be more than friends with you, to have a future with you, to absolutely kiss you more. I'm ready to settle down with you in Arlington, if that's what you want."

Spencer covered his mouth for a moment and then slid his hand to the back of his head, his gray eyes landing on me, and then the ground, before he shifted his gaze to stare into the distance. "After all these years of wanting nothing more than to hear those words from you, I can't believe I'm going to say this."

"Don't say it then."

"Carleigh, I do love you, and it's taking every ounce of resolve not to pull you into my arms and kiss you senseless. That's part of our problem—my fixation with us, with you, especially lately. I'm trying to change our relationship too fast, but it didn't seem quick to me because I've wanted it for so long."

"And I want it now too. So what's the problem?"

"The problem is that I don't know if you do want it, want us, want all of it with me. Your tears at the wedding . . . were they for something lost or something gained? Or just because you're afraid of being alone?"

"All the above, if that's a choice, but it doesn't change how I feel about you."

"It kind of does. I don't want you to settle for a relationship with me for any other reason than you love me and want to spend your life with me. I don't want you to agree to be with me because it'll make me happy. I won't be your compromise. You deserve to be with someone you want as much as he wants you."

"Why can't that be you?"

"Because you just came to this solution when you didn't have any other choices. I won't be your last choice." He stood. "I want to be your first choice."

"What are you doing?" I rocked to my feet. My brain spun from the quick movement and I teetered on my heels.

Spencer clasped my arm and settled me back in the chair. "I'm going home. On Wednesday, I'll close on the condo, but the seller is letting me move in on Monday. While you'll likely always be a part of my life, I'm going to need some time before we reconnect."

"How much?"

He shrugged. "Let's take it one day at a time."

As he jogged down the stairs and across the lawn, tears blurred my vision, but not enough for me to miss his taillights drifting further and further away until they disappeared completely. My heart withered like the flowers in the bouquet. Was this really the end for us?

Once Spencer left, I stared through the tree canopy and my tears, trying to focus on each star in the onyx sky. It seemed like a way to force myself to connect with something concrete and constant. After a while, I ran out of tears, and I knocked on the door of the Inn. A sweet woman answered and offered me a ride back to Magnolia Bluff. She seemed to know who I was and what had happened, and blessedly, didn't ask for any explanation. A definite benefit of the small-town rumor mill.

At the cottage, I found a note from Willa and her car keys. She said I could drive her car to the airport, and they'd pick it up when they returned. Guilt settled in my stomach. I'd missed their send off. I'd planned to make it back with Spencer, ready to celebrate.

After I changed out of my dress and into my pajamas and booked a flight back to DC for Monday afternoon—I couldn't bear to watch Spencer move out—I texted Lawson.

Lawson: I don't believe you.

Me: Enjoy your honeymoon. We can talk when you get back. Tell Willa I said hi and to take away your phone.

Lawson: Love you and praying for you.

Me: <3

Queenie hopped on the bed and snuggled under my arms. Although I doubted I'd be able to rest, I still turned off the light, closed my eyes, and then miraculously fell asleep.

Chapter 23

Evidently, two days of emotional highs and lows will exhaust a person, but after my body rested enough to recharge my brain, I awoke on Sunday morning. It was light outside, but still early. If it hadn't been for Queenie, I might have wallowed in bed all day. Instead, I shuffled to the kitchen and made her breakfast and coffee for me. After so many days with so much chaos, the silence I hated pressed in on me. I yearned to go somewhere I didn't have to listen to nothing—or worse, myself.

With what felt like purpose, I downed my coffee and a protein bar, while I texted Wren for the service time at the church were the wedding had taken place. Then I took a quick shower, applied mascara and lip gloss, and slipped on my sandals with a simple sage sundress. After I gave Queenie a scratch behind the ears, I scooped up Willa's keys and headed to the church.

When I arrived, the dirt parking lot was packed, though I had ten minutes to spare. A wave of nerves swirled through me, but I shoved them away and got out of the car before I could change my mind. I'm not sure what was driving me, but I didn't want to reflect on the events of the last few days or ponder what my future held. I'd never viewed church as a distraction, but if that was its best purpose today, I was fine with it.

Surely, God would rather me be in His house a little scattered than in bed bingeing World War II movies. Although in all likelihood, that was how I'd fill the rest of the day.

An elderly man greeted me at the door and handed me a bulletin. "Good morning, I'm Chester. We're so happy to have you worship with us this morning. Be sure to sign the attendance pad. There's a special treat for first-time visitors."

"Um, okay, but that's not necessary. I'm from out of town."

"Sweetheart, you don't want to pass up on the treat. It's one of Bonnie's lemon pound cakes."

"Yes, sir." I smiled as warmth filled me. If they wanted to give me a cake, I'd take it. Furthermore, I'd add comfort food to my plans for the afternoon. Hopefully, the General's Diner took to-go orders. As I slid into an empty spot on the back pew, my mouth watered for the mostly fried dinner. But before I could start planning the menu, my smartwatch buzzed.

Spencer?

I flipped my wrist over, but it was only a text from my mom inviting me to supper. So much for wallowing in grease and movies, but I didn't want to discuss Spencer either. Why couldn't there be an easy option?

When the chords from the piano interrupted my thoughts, I decided to text her later. After I checked the bulletin for the number of the hymn, I pulled a hymnal from the pocket on the back of the pew and flipped to the right song as I stood. The small choir led the congregation through three hymns. Everyone seemed to know the tunes and sang with ardor, and I enjoyed the challenge of keeping up with the lyrics and the melody. While I couldn't tell you the name of the songs or the subjects they covered, there was something cathartic about blending my voice with everyone else's and not worrying about anything but the next line of verse. When the worship music ended, I lowered onto the pew and checked the bulletin. The order of the service was traditional and predictable, exactly what I needed.

The preacher's message focused on rest from our busy lives with ties into Labor Day. I'd almost forgotten that it was the next day. I'd be flying home, and happily, going back to the safety of my routine. My heart squeezed, but I clenched my molars. I was done crying. Spencer might be living somewhere else, so I'd have to make some adjustments, but work would still be busy, and my office would still be my happy place.

For the rest of the sermon, I focused on not thinking about Spencer, which of course meant I only thought about how different my days were going to be without him. Finally, we were again standing with our hymnals and singing. At the end of the song, the preacher gave a benediction from the back of the church, and people started chatting as they moved to the doors. I appreciated that my anonymity protected me from much more than friendly smiles and nods. Since I didn't need a whole pound cake, I folded my bulletin in half and reached for my purse to leave without notice.

"Carleigh?" asked a voice both familiar and unwelcome.

Straightening, I pressed my lips into a polite smile. "Good morning, Wyatt."

"What are you doing here?"

"I told you I go to church most weeks."

"I guess you did, but I didn't expect to see you this morning." His eyes got big. "Oh, no, did things not go well with Spencer?"

Before I could respond, the usher I'd met when I arrived reached around Wyatt. "Here's your cake. I hope you enjoy it. And don't feel like you have to share it with this young man. He already got one and didn't even offer me a taste."

"Thank you." I took the foil-wrapped loaf. "If I had a knife, I'd cut you a piece."

"Not at all, not at all. God bless you." He cocked his head to a woman bustling up the aisle. "You're sweet to offer, but I wouldn't dare."

The woman stopped at his side and looped her arm with his. "Let's go, Chester. You know the doctor said you need to limit your carbohydrates."

"Yes, dear." Chester tossed me a pleading look over his shoulder as they exited the church.

Wyatt chuckled. "Chester's a character, but he'd give you the shirt off his back if you needed it."

"That's nice." I shifted to move by Wyatt.

"The offer still stands if you want to talk." He retreated down the aisle, giving me space. "But don't get any ideas. I'm not auditioning to be the third member of your boy band."

"Ha ha. You must've missed the announcement—the band broke up." I tried to play off his quip, but my voice lost power, ending in a whisper.

"I'm sorry, Carleigh, truly. Even though all this change has been hard, I believed you'd be better for it."

"Hmph. I guess you were wrong about me after all."

"Oh, I wasn't wrong. I'm just surprised how blind you are when it comes to evaluating your life." He spun his key on his finger.

"My life is fine. I was just thinking how glad I'll be to get back to the office."

"I'm sure. It'll keep you busy, and you won't have to deal with the stuff that's really bothering you. Have you ever considered that you might be afraid to be still?"

"I'm still all the time."

"I don't mean physically. You have so much crowding for space in your brain, you don't notice the things that you're missing, like taking deep breaths."

"If you mean yoga, I tried it once and I'll agree with you, it was too slow for me."

"I didn't mean yoga. Just consider that the pace of your life is too hurried to fully appreciate God's blessings. You've been so busy chasing the next accolade that you aren't present in the moment."

"If I stop, I'll fall behind. Just look what happened with Spencer and probably my only hope of having a successful marriage and family." I cringed. Those were truths I hadn't meant to let slip out.

"I think that's the first honest thing you've said, and I'm guessing it wasn't intentional. Being vulnerable is hard, but it's also freeing to admit your brokenness. We all have our stuff that we need to deal with. You've been über-successful, and from what I can see, you have a life most people would be envious of, but you still want more."

"I wanted it all, but I'm not sure what that means anymore."

Wyatt nodded. "What if it simply means accepting God's love and resting in His grace? Jesus calls to all who are weary and burdened and tells us that He will provide rest. He says to learn from Him because He is gentle and humble in heart. His yoke is easy and His burden is light."

"I hear you, but I'm not sure how that's supposed to help me. Unless you're suggesting I swap out my stilettos and tailored suits for overalls and a plow."

He grinned. "Not exactly. The yoke is a metaphor, and Jesus is on the other side, helping you hold it up. If you surrendered to his will, his direction, his timing, and his pace, I guess everything else would fall into place."

"You guess?"

"Carleigh, I'm a rather new Bible nerd, so you should do your own research. I'm pretty sure you will, anyway."

"Fair point." I twisted my lips, studying him.. Wyatt had definitely gained some wisdom over the years.

He raised his brows in question.

"So, you're a man."

"Last time I checked."

"You know, occasionally, you could just answer me without all the sass. I'm trying to have a serious conversation with you."

"Carleigh, I—" He shook his head and then he started laughing, and I don't mean a little chuckle. Oh no, he grabbed his belly and threw back his head like I'd just delivered the funniest joke he'd ever heard.

"Never mind." I took a step toward the door.

"No, wait." His fingers touched my arm, but he was still snickering like a middle school girl. The mean kind.

I glowered at him and yanked my arm to my side, squaring my shoulders.

Wyatt swallowed. "Sorry. I'm sorry. It's just that, wow, when it comes to hurling verbal zingers, you are so far out of my league. I'm just trying to keep the score close with my weak returns."

"Was that a compliment?"

"I suppose it was." He shrugged. "Let's get back to your original question. I'm assuming it has to do with me being a man."

"Yes. While my two best friends have been men, I don't have a lot of experience with dating. In your scenario with the yoke, how do I make that all apply to getting Spencer to give me another chance? He thinks I'm settling for a relationship with him."

"You aren't going to like the answer." Wyatt pulled a face, one eyebrow inching up.

"It's fine. I can take it. Do I need to cut my hair? Learn to bake like Zoe? Believe it or not, I'm rather adept at groveling if it means I win in the end." I lowered my shoulders and pushed my lips into a pout, so he could get the idea.

"I believe you." He covered his eyes with his hand. "No need to demonstrate, and it's none of those things."

"What then?"

"It goes back to what you said about wanting it all. Spencer can't feel like he's just another tally mark in your win column. He needs to know that you're invested in the relationship. He's going to need to know the changes you're making aren't just for him. You're going to have to talk to him a lot more about your stuff, like all your stuff. And it might take some time."

"I can be patient if I'm sure I'll get what I want in the end."

"Carleigh, bless your heart. You've got a long way to go, but it's not all your fault. In this world, we're told to go faster, get more, time's running out. The truth is that life is short, so wouldn't it be better to be present for each moment and soak them in, instead of letting them skip by like a movie montage with you seeing just the highlights?" He pointed at me. "You're going to have to slow down, way down, and relish what you'll think are insignificant moments. But I'm betting that after a few more days without Spencer, you'll be better able to cherish the time you have together. Hopefully, as you focus more on pleasing, praising, and glorifying God, Spencer will see that the changes you're making are more about you growing in your faith, and hopefully, that will be true. You do know you can't do anything to earn God's love? He gives it to you freely."

"Knowing it and fully embracing it are two different things, especially when you've lived most of your life believing that with determination you could achieve whatever you put your mind to. This marriage stuff and my relationship with Spencer are the first things in my life I couldn't achieve with only my grit and ingenuity." I smoothed my thumb along the wrinkles of the aluminum foil protecting the poundcake.

"Then I'd view this as an opportunity to grow closer to God. After all, he is a miracle worker."

"Do you really think I'm going to need a miracle?"

"We're already witnessing a miracle."

"We are?"

"Carleigh, you're asking *my* advice, and I'm giving a Sunday school lesson. If that doesn't scream miracle, I don't know what does."

By the time I rolled up to the cottage, I knew the first thing I needed to do, so I texted my mom that I'd be at supper and asked her to invite Brad and Zoe. Then I bowed my head and thanked God for his grace and prayed he'd help me fix the relationships that I'd neglected. With my amen, the regret gripping my chest loosened its hold a little.

A few hours later, I parked in front of my parents' house for the first time in years. Mom had updated me on the upgrades, as she called them, but I hadn't fully appreciated how much would be different. They'd changed the paint color, replaced the front door, and installed brick pavers for a new circular drive. The landscaping might have been the same, but it was all larger and fuller. I climbed out of the car with my church pound cake and walked up the short path that was lined with red and yellow gerbera daisies. When I got to the door, I pressed the bell and waited.

A few seconds later, Brad opened it. "Did you really ring the bell?"

I shrugged. "Was I not supposed to?"

Shaking his head, he stepped outside and closed the door behind him. "Mom said you asked her to invite us, but if you're going to try to defend your actions, I'm not here for it. I'm done playing the comparison game with you, and I don't want a relationship with you if it's based on anything other than the truth."

"I hear you, and I'm sorry. No more comparison game. Besides, while I was steadily making base hits and slowly driving up the score, in the last couple of years, you've rallied for the win. I mean how many grand slams are you capable of? It's rather impressive."

"Thank you?" He narrowed his eyes, watching me like I was holding a water gun behind my back and I was about to soak him.

"Don't look so scared." I held out my empty hand as if to demonstrate that my words weren't loaded with anything but sincerity. "Something you said last night has been needling me and making me think about our childhood. I usually disregard any negative thoughts, but, well, I'm trying something new. Anyway, there was a time when I loved playing games. I mean, I've always been competitive. We have that in common. But I used to love the competition almost as much as the win."

"Okay, what does any of this have to do with your attempt to break up Lawson's wedding?" Brad asked.

"I wasn't lying when I told you I believed I was looking out for Lawson's best interests. But once I knew they'd given their future a lot of thought, and they believed they were making the best decision for them, my instincts kept telling me that something was wrong."

"And now what?"

"Good question. I don't have a solid answer. I'm still getting used to the idea of evaluating myself, and I'm not ready to go on a deep dive into my personal stuff with you."

"I get that. We weren't exactly brought up to admit defeat or talk about things that weren't pretty. I think it's one reason Dad and Mom were so upset when I failed out of college. They couldn't pretend to their friends that our family was perfect. Not that they didn't gloat about your successes all the time to cover up my failures."

"It didn't help that I felt like I needed to prove to everyone here how great I was, so I fueled their tank with my achievements."

"Don't downplay your success. You earned it." He gave me a playful jab to my ribs.

It wasn't enough to make me giggle, but something about the gesture released the tension I'd been harboring and made me want to continue working on this relationship.

"You didn't need my accomplishments constantly rubbed in your face. Something I learned when the tables were suddenly turned."

"Makes sense. And just so you know, I've also struck out a lot in the last two years. I doubt Mom or Dad would've told you anything but the good stuff. If you want all the ugly details, Zoe would be happy to tell you the story. She thinks it shows how we grow through adversity and should inspire others."

"Zoe is kind of wonderful."

"She is, isn't she?" Brad's lips morphed into a goofy grin. "The best part is she loves everything about me, even my flaws."

"I'm glad y'all found each other."

"I'm sorry about Spencer." Brad pulled me into one of his signature hugs. "Word is, he didn't leave on the best of terms."

"How did you hear that?" My body tensed as I stepped back.

"Carleigh, Haslemere is really small, and Magnolia Bluff is even smaller. We have no secrets, especially when it comes to romance. You are aware that Nathaniel Sullivan sets all his books there, and from what I hear, they're very romantic."

"Noted." I laughed, relieved that I wouldn't have to give all the details to my family.

"I love the work that we're doing over there, but Zoe and I agree that we aren't ready for small town life." Brad moved to the door. "I'm assuming if you don't want to talk about yourself, you also don't want to talk about your relationship."

"You'd be correct."

Before he opened the door, he placed an arm around my shoulders and drew me to his side. "I'm glad we're on the same team, so we can win together."

"Me too." I hugged him back as we walked inside. "And I'd appreciate it if you'd help divert Mom's attention from any inquiries about Spencer."

"Sure, and I'll tell Zoe to help."

"It's nice to have a third member of the team."

"Oh, she's going to love that you said that." He gave me a squeeze before hurrying away to find his fiancée.

But our scheming was unwarranted because Mom didn't even drop a hint about my relationship status, much less Spencer's abrupt departure. I don't know if it was Zoe's presence or everyone's collective exhaustion from the weekend's festivities, but supper lacked any angst. Mom seemed so subdued that I started to worry something was wrong. She didn't even try to guilt-trip me about not going shopping with Zoe and her for bridesmaids' dresses.

After supper, while I helped Mom with the dishes, she told me about a fundraiser she was helping with to raise money for Wren's charity that was supporting mural projects with local students. It sounded great, and I appreciated the reprieve from her nagging, but it wasn't our normal. Guilt was Mom's go-to tool for manipulation, but she left it in the toolbox. As I fixated on her seemingly innocent words, my pulse picked up until I couldn't stand the politeness any longer.

"Mom, what's going on?"

"I'm sorry. I don't know what you mean."

"You haven't said one word about Spencer or the wedding or my lack of marriage plans, and at the rehearsal dinner, you acted like you were totally cool with Spencer and my friendship just the way it was." I scrubbed the dried grits off the bottom of a pot. "Is something wrong? You're making me nervous."

"Honey, there's nothing to worry about. I know you get defensive when I bring up marriage, and I guess watching your interactions with Spencer in person, I realized that you weren't ready for marriage. After being around Brad and Zoe so much, I saw something different in you."

"You did?" And what made her think I wasn't ready for marriage?

But before I could decide if I wanted to hear Mom's response to my follow-up question, she patted my shoulder and said, "But just to be clear, Spencer is crazy in love with you."

"Thank goodness. I was starting to think you'd hit your head on something, and you were suffering from a concussion."

"I'm fine, but I don't want you to interpret my behavior the wrong way because I'm concerned about you. I just don't want you to pull away anymore. You're finally here, and I like having you around." Normally, I'd have taken her words to be a jab of guilt, but there was a sincerity and longing in her eyes that hit me in the gut.

When had avoiding my family become so natural to me? While my parents might not be great at accepting setbacks, they'd always supported my dreams. If sometimes they were a little excessive with their cheers, it was okay. I always knew they were proud of me, but it made it hard when I felt like I was failing. Had I felt like I was failing? Was that what my instincts were trying to get me to acknowledge?

"Carleigh . . . honey . . ." Mom brushed a loose strand of hair behind my ear.

"Sorry, Mom. I'll try to be more available."

"My intention is never to burden you. Your career is important." Okay, those were the passive-aggressive statements I was used to hearing from her. I wanted to call her out, and one day, I'd tell her how irritating her comments were to me, but it wouldn't be today.

Still, I wasn't so full of grace that I was going to indulge her with a response either. Hey, no judgment. I learned from the best—my dad.

So ignoring her comment, I passed her the clean pot and sacrificed my brother. What can I say? Old habits die hard. "So are Brad and Zoe thinking about starting a family soon?"

And my question worked like a match to dry wood. Mom needed to vent about how busy they were going to be with their construction and design projects and traveling to California. She barely paused for more than an *oh* or a *mm-hmm* from me. Soon we'd finished the dishes, and I was hugging everyone goodbye. Unlike in the past, I didn't feel the need to run to my car and avoid their calls. I wasn't planning to move home, but I had a desire to keep in touch, and I was looking forward to the wedding.

And for about five minutes, I was content, but then I started to make plans and was hit again with the realization that Spencer wouldn't be my date if I didn't fix things between us. Wyatt said it might take time, but I had less than two months. Unlike Willa, Brad had checked the college football schedule before picking a date, so the wedding was the third weekend in October when the Georgia Bulldogs always had a bye week. Which meant I needed to figure out this whole slow-down-to-find-God's-peace thing in a hurry.

Yes, I realized the paradox within my plan, but when you've been going after it your whole life, changing course is about as fast as moving legislation through Congress. Still, if I fully committed to changing, the transformation could be like one of those unicorn bills that everyone agrees on and passes without debate.

After I parked at the house, I purposely slowed my pace, taking in the star-filled sky and listening to the sounds of the night. When I got back to the city, there'd be the lights on the monuments and the Capitol to admire and the sounds of traffic and people. Neither was better than the other, just different, but the problem was that I didn't stop to notice. I leaned against the cottage door and took several slow, deep breaths. But my efforts didn't result in peace. Instead, anxiety tightened my chest, and my breathing shallowed.

Fantastic. It was almost like I was worried about not worrying. Knowledge had always helped me control my anxiety, and I'd even read a couple self-help books on the topic. However, given Wyatt's lecture, the Bible seemed like the best book to study. I knew that verse about not being anxious about anything, so I'd start there.

Giving Wyatt even an ounce of credit annoyed me, but he was right. I hadn't studied scripture in a long time, and I'd avoided thinking too deeply about my life. Undoubtedly, I'd be wretched for a while as I took on the big questions, struggled through the answers, and considered how to implement the changes into my life. Like when you try a new physical activity. After those first few sessions, muscles you didn't know you had ached, but if you keep doing it, keep trying, keep learning the technique, the post-workout pain subsides.

It didn't take a deep dive into my conscience to grasp that my focus on having it all would bring me a happiness that was fleeting and based solely on my current circumstances. If I wanted lasting joy, I needed to go to another source for it. My faith seemed like the best place to start.

Chapter 24

When I arrived home on Monday afternoon, I slugged past Spencer's door. It wasn't Spencer's anymore, and I'd have to stop thinking of it like that. It'd been a long day, and Queenie had been very vocal about being caged during our flight. After I freed her, I pulled out my notebook and continued researching what the Bible had to say about obtaining peace. Most of it had to do with focusing on God, which seemed obvious, but also on being grateful for his blessings and understanding that when we struggle, he is with us. It still felt like theory.

Reluctance weighed heavy within me as I considered my two choices. Ask myself the hard questions—the ones I'd been avoiding by reading every verse of scripture having to do with peace, anxiety, or worry—or dwell on the empty apartment across the hall. According to Wyatt—why I was giving his advice so much attention, I don't know—I needed to deal with my stuff before approaching Spencer.

So I took a deep breath, read over my notes, and bowed my head. "God, I'm trying to take an authentic assessment of my life, and I realize that I haven't checked with you to ascertain what my priorities should be. What's my purpose? Am I doing the right things? My success used to be enough, but I'm not satisfied. I want to live with purpose, your purpose. I can even be okay with losing occasionally. Trophies tarnish and collect dust. I want to focus my life on the things that are important to you. Show me what to do next."

I opened my eyes and scanned the room, then I checked my phone for messages, but evidently, God wasn't going to answer right away. So, after journaling about the verses I'd read, I prepared for the next day and the dreaded new morning routine. I set out my clothes and decided to eat breakfast at the diner down the street, so that obtaining coffee wouldn't be a thing. All the while, I tried to pause and look for a way to be grateful or a way I could grow from the adversity.

And yes, I'm perfectly aware that going to a diner for breakfast and coffee is not what most people consider a difficult morning, but when your heart is crumbling because everything about the new routine represents your personal loss, you should get a little grace.

To my relief, breakfast wasn't devastating. Mostly because my new friend, George, poured a tasty cup of coffee and served breakfast to me like I was one of his children. As I left the diner, I moderated my steps, walking as slowly as possible. It seemed pointless, but also like a challenge, and I rarely turned my back on a challenge, which might not have been the right perspective. Still, if I kept doing it, surely I'd understand why it mattered so much. With my new unhurried attitude still mostly intact, I strolled into my office as if I was on a garden path.

"Good morning." Jordan approached, carrying a wrapped box. "Someone asked me to give this to you, but I'm not supposed to say who."

"Thank you." I took the gift and placed it on my desk. "How have you been?" I asked and waited for her reply. Although I, one, wanted to rip into the box, and two, wanted to ask her about a bill I'd been alerted might be getting some traction. Instead, I practiced being present—or at least pretending I was present. The new me was leaning heavily into the idea of fake-it-till-you-make-it being a legitimate path to change.

"Life's been pretty great." She eyed the box. "Don't you want to open it?"

"Yes, but I'm trying to be more present and unhurried in my relationships."

"If it helps, you're doing a great job, and I'm totally here if you want to practice *later*." She emphasized the word while fingering the bow on top. "But please open this. I've had it all night and all morning, and I'm about to go crazy with curiosity."

Laughing, I slipped a finger under the fold of the wrapping paper. "I don't want to imagine what you were like as a child on Christmas morning."

"It wasn't pretty. I may have spent some time rewrapping gifts that'd been left under the tree. My favorite presents came in bags. Tissue paper is so much easier to remove and replace."

"You've given this a lot of thought." I pulled the rest of the paper back to reveal a single-serve coffee maker. *Single-serve.* My throat thickened as I inhaled a sharp breath.

Jordan turned the box, reading the description. "This one is super high-end. I saw it when I registered but didn't think anyone would spring for it. I guess I should've left it for Spence—" She covered her mouth, stopping her words. "Oops."

I swallowed, regaining my composure. "Don't worry about it. I guessed who it was from. How is he?"

"Okay-ish." She shrugged. "He didn't say much when he gave me the gift, but his expression was pretty downcast for a person sending a surprise present. I'd hoped it was a make-up gift."

"I wish."

"What happened between you two in Georgia?"

"It's a long story, but maybe this gift is an olive branch." It really was sweet, and maybe Spencer didn't mean to send any messages other than that it would be easy to use. I should be grateful that he hadn't cut off all communication.

Shivers skipped up my arms as an idea started to form. What if I sent him something in return? Surprises were our thing. But this gift would need to be equally thoughtful, showing that I'd heard and understood him—we could be friends. If it bloomed into something more, I'd be very grateful, but for now, I'd follow Wyatt's advice and take things slow while I continued to explore my faith.

Should I pray about my response? It would take longer, but as my emotions leveled, I knew I'd turned an important corner.

"Carleigh, are you okay?" Jordan asked, pulling me from my musings.

"Yes. Just give me a few minutes, and I'll meet you and Ashton in the conference room."

"Got it." She moved into the hall.

After I closed the door, I sent Spencer a text.

> **Me:** Thanks for the coffee maker.

> **Spencer:** Jordan wasn't supposed to say it was me, but you're welcome.

I started to type a response about how it wasn't a mystery, but I stopped. I didn't want to fall back into our text banter and pretend nothing had changed. If I truly meant to reorder my priorities, I needed to give this slower pace more than one morning.

By the time I paused for lunch, my fingers itched to message Spencer, but he hadn't reached out, and he'd said he needed space. Instead, I prayed. "Lord, I'm so thankful that Spencer hasn't completely cut me off. I think I need to respond with more than a text. Help me find something that won't scare him off."

Hoping for inspiration or at least a distraction, I scrolled social media while I ate my grilled salmon salad. When my feed only presented post after post of edited versions of my friends' perfect lives, I started to close the app. Then a post about Nathaniel Sullivan's new book popped up. Apparently God could use all things for good, especially if he was employing social media.

Time to go shopping for a surprise. I opened my web browser and searched for books on writing. After reading several reviews, I selected one and sent it to Spencer's office since I didn't have his new address. At the thought, I expected to experience that horrible sinking sensation, but it didn't come. It didn't amount to a huge victory either. More like a steady step in the right direction.

If only the rest of my afternoon could've been so carefree. Instead, we'd discovered a potential initiative by a few Congress members that would result in some of our clients losing control of large parts of their property to burdensome regulations. We'd immediately convened in the conference room to strategize the best way forward for our clients.

A few hours later, when I finally exited my office building, my watch buzzed with a notification. All the alerts weren't helpful for keeping my calm, but I'd never noticed before. It just seemed like a part of life, but it didn't have to be. I didn't need to be reachable every second of the day. No wonder I rarely evaluated my life. I was too busy responding to messages. Then again, I hadn't wanted to think about all this stuff before.

By the time I glanced at my watch screen, the message had been replaced by the clock. When I got home, I'd respond to whoever it was and change my notification settings. For now, I slipped off the watch and put it in my bag.

Then I squared my shoulders, but that felt wrong. This wasn't supposed to be about power or determination. Although, not reading that message had my fingers twitching, so I took a deep breath, relaxed my shoulders, and strolled at as slow a pace as I could manage. I've always been a fast walker. It's just the way God made me, so I settled into a comfortable stride for me.

As the last rays of the sun bounced off the white buildings, a cool breeze feathered my hair and a peace enveloped me. In the middle of everything with Spencer, not to mention the chaos that often surrounded my job, I knew I wasn't alone. I only needed to do my part, and while the results and the process might not be what I believed was best, it'd be okay.

As I turned onto my street, I glanced over my shoulder. The views had been nice, and letting my brain wander hadn't ended with me on the verge of a panic attack. I should consider starting my day with a morning jog. Spencer always said that his runs helped him prepare for the day.

While I prepared Queenie's meal, I allowed myself to check the message.

> **Spencer: Thanks for the book.**

So I chose same-day delivery. It was only a little more, and it seemed like a blessing that it was offered. What if Spencer wanted to start his writing journey after work and didn't know how?

> **Me: You're welcome. I hope it helps. I didn't think you'd want to worry over a potted plant.**

> **Spencer: Just don't expect me to produce a book right away. I'm just considering the idea.**

> **Me: No pressure. You can donate it if you change your mind.**

> **Spencer: Thanks. BTW, I ordered your favorite coffee to be delivered monthly to the apartment.**

> **Me: Wow. Thanks. You didn't need to do that.**

Spencer: I considered it a service to the community.

Me: In other news, I've decided to go for a jog in the morning. Any advice?

Spencer: Don't try to race anyone.

Me: I'm serious.

Spencer: Me too. Don't try to race anyone.

Me: Any other advice?

Spencer: You might need a jacket. The mornings are getting cooler. The mall will always be one of my favorite places to run.

Me: Thanks. I'll let you know how it goes.

Spencer: <thumbs up emoji>

I stared at the tiny picture. Was he telling me he'd had enough of this conversation? I didn't want to overshare, but I couldn't stay silent and have him think I was making changes for him and not myself.

Me: Since we're in a kind of weird place, I want you to know I'm doing some self-evaluation through scripture. Jogging is part of that.

Spencer: Okay. Hope it helps.

"Me too." I lowered my phone before I could type a response. Healing our relationship might start through texts, but I couldn't share everything I wanted without talking to him in person. And I couldn't rush it if I wanted to succeed.

Chapter 25

When I first started thinking about my purpose, I'd worried I'd discover that I needed to change my job, and I loved my job. Most people think being a lobbyist is just short of taking a position in Satan's army. Thankfully, I'd learned that I shouldn't be considering the opinions of the masses. God's approval was the only one I needed to seek, and with each day I spent helping our clients, my sense of purpose grew. However, what also came as a rather shocking revelation as I jogged along the reflection pool Saturday morning was that I'd been willing to give up my job if it wasn't compatible with my future. Somehow that realization provided the insight that my priorities had found a new and improved order, and it couldn't have come at a better time.

It'd been five long days, and the time at the office had been the best part of it. Coming home and remembering Spencer would not be there—bringing me mail or suggesting a takeout option for supper or asking me about my day—had me taking stock of how well he took care of me, and how I took his friendship for granted. If we were going to have a healthy relationship, it needed to be different and a lot more balanced. Not that we should keep score because, with my tendencies, I'd make it into a competition.

I'd texted a little with Spencer, mostly about my observations while jogging, from the scenery to the people, to an occasional insight, but nothing too deep. I wanted to save the pivotal revelations for a time when we were both ready to have a conversation about our future. A future I prayed for every day and believed would be my reality. I may have done some daydreaming too. Hey, just because I was moving slowly in real life didn't mean I couldn't let my imagination take me on adventures where Spencer and I would recreate that kiss from the gazebo in new locations—under palm trees, on mountaintops, in our kitchen.

Saturday afternoon, hope bubbled up in me as I strolled the short distance from the metro stop to Jordan and Cooper's new condo. They'd planned a cookout to go along with the college football games of the day. When Jordan told me that Spencer would be there, I'd started to decline, but she assured me that Cooper had asked him, and he was fine with it. Still, knowing Jordan wasn't above matchmaking, I texted Spencer to be sure it was okay if I attended. I didn't want some awkward encounter to ruin the get-together.

At the row of red brick condo buildings, I paused. Large trees shaded the sidewalk, while friends chatted on benches. It wasn't so bad. Each unit had a variation on a colonial white-columned entry. I proceeded down the sidewalk, and at the bottom of the stairs leading to Jordan and Cooper's front door, I double-checked the address and re-read Spencer's response.

Spencer: It's fine.

Not exactly encouraging words, but also not a no. Hopefully, he wasn't just being polite and once again sacrificing for my happiness. Gone were the bubbles of hope, popped by the nerves compressing them.

Before I could rethink my choice, the front door opened and Jordan waved. "Happy Saturday. Come on in. I was just running to the bakery for the cookies I forgot to pick up this morning."

"Okay." I stopped on the first stair. "Do you want me to come with you?"

"No, no. I'll be quick. Get Cooper to give you a tour." She skipped past me.

"Okay." I took the last few stairs and walked through the front door. People sat watching the game on a television mounted above the mantel. Others gathered in clusters, chatting and munching on appetizers. The sliding glass doors were open to a small balcony that overlooked a park area carpeted in dark green grass. I had a weird desire to walk outside and lie down so I could watch the clouds travel across the sky.

"Not so bad, huh?" Spencer appeared at my side.

"Oh, hey." I shifted, wrapping my arms around my middle. "Um, yeah, I mean, no, I mean it's lovely. Objectively speaking, I mean. Would anyone consider a well-landscaped park ugly? Well, perhaps some industrialists might find it too soft." I snapped my lips closed and clenched my molars. What was I talking about?

"So we're going to do the awkward thing?"

I cringed. "Sorry, you just startled me, and I was trying to be conciliatory."

"So we're totally cool?"

"I wouldn't go that far, but we don't need to be awkward." I smiled, trying to convey something along the lines of harmony, even if my pulse was pounding like I'd just finished a sprint.

"You seemed to be deep in thought. I almost didn't interrupt you."

"Right, well, that's my new thing, deep thinking. I've discovered some very interesting things inside my brain."

"Really?" He eyed me thoughtfully, but not like I was an old friend who might be struggling with some personal stuff. No, his expression was more like he was observing a strange electric blue frog at the zoo who, while very tiny, could kill a grown man.

Since he didn't seem ready to hear my deep revelations, I decided to start with a personal discovery that wasn't as serious but would give him a hint of the internal work I was doing.

"Yes." I flipped a hand in front of me like I was giving a presentation. "Turns out that I only have a problem with one particular blonde girl from high school, not all of them. And she doesn't even know it, so I've forgiven Bree Flanders once and for all. Best part, I'm now able to prepare a charcuterie plate with brie cheese and not simmer with bitterness."

"That is progress." The corner of his lips twitched, but he didn't give into the smile, acting disinterested and refusing to give me credit for my wit. I wouldn't give up that easily.

"Yes, I started slowly, just passing by the cheese case at the grocery store. But yesterday, I reached in and grabbed a wedge. I ate part of it for supper with crackers and a green salad. Delicious."

"So you've forgiven Bree, huh?"

"I think all my angst with her was fueling a lot of the issues I had with my family, especially Brad. We also realized that our parents, while well-meaning with all their gloating about our accomplishments, just pitted us against each other. We're both so competitive that we've spent a lot of time playing a game of comparison, but we're not doing it anymore."

Spencer nodded. "I'm glad. I didn't want to tell you, but I thought Brad was a decent guy, and Zoe, she's—"

"Like a fairy godmother. She's so sweet and she bakes and she only sees the best in everyone."

"Don't forget the glitter."

"Impossible. I'm still finding it on my clothes." I laughed and the tension binding my guts loosened. We were doing this. He still seemed a little standoffish, but we were making progress.

Jordan paused in front of us with a pastry box. "Glad you kissed and made up."

"What? No we didn't." I palmed my burning cheeks.

"Relax, Carleigh, it's just an expression. I didn't think you'd literally been sucking face." She chuckled.

"I know," I said, forcing a polite laugh that would never fool Spencer, but what else could I do?

"We're good," Spencer said flatly.

"I'm glad. I just want my friends to be friends." Jordan continued to the table.

Before we dealt with the tension that her *expression* had resurrected, a pretty and, of course, blonde woman joined us. She seemed familiar but I couldn't place her.

She beamed at Spencer. "There you are."

"Here I am." He gave her a quick one-armed hug.

Then she extended her hand to me. "You must be the famous Carleigh that I've heard so much about. We never got to meet at Jordan and Cooper's wedding, I'm Mary Katherine, but my friends just call me MK."

"Nice to meet you." Although the disappointment sinking within me disagreed. I smiled and shook her hand. "I'm hardly famous."

Before Mary Katherine, because I wasn't ready to be her friend and use her initials, could respond, Spencer interjected, "This is Carleigh's first visit to Courthouse."

"Oh, that's right you live on the Hill in Spencer's old building." She gestured to the room. "Isn't this place superb? I love all the charm of the Colonial Garden homes. It's no wonder they don't stay on the market long."

"MK is an interior designer."

"I've been giving Spencer some advice. His unit has been recently updated and is exquisite. Have you seen it?"

"Not yet." I scanned the room, seeking an escape.

"Spencer, you have to give Carleigh a tour."

"That's okay. It looks like the game is kicking off. I'm sure Spencer doesn't want to miss it."

"I could take you," she offered.

"No," Spencer and I both said at the same time.

She switched her gaze between us. "Okay."

"It's just we missed all the games last weekend because of the wedding, so I don't want to miss a play." I turned, focusing my attention on the television, hoping she'd let it go. While I was curious about Spencer's apartment, I didn't want my first time in it to be with his new friend. But why didn't Spencer want Mary Katherine to show me his place?

"We can walk over during halftime," Spencer said.

"Oh, sure. That's a much better plan. I'm going to get a bottle of water. Can I bring either of you anything?" Mary Katherine asked.

"No thanks," we both responded, keeping our attention on the game.

For most of the first half, I prayed for God's peace and that Mary Katherine might find something else to do during halftime. With each second that the clock counted down, the idea of touring Spencer's new home weighed heavier on me. I wasn't anxious, but contemplative about my future, especially with Spencer. This step into his new space would give me a glimpse into what our life together might be and how I might be joining him on his journey . . . our journey.

But as the station cut to commercial, Mary Katherine looped her arm with mine. "Finally. I like football, but I have to admit I prefer the social aspects of the game."

Social aspects? What was she talking about? I rubbed the area between my brows and tried to appreciate her nonsensical perspective.

"Right." Spencer jangled his keys. "We better get going, so we don't miss the start of the second half." He led the way with Mary Katherine clinging to my arm while she gave a history of the area and gushed over how smart Spencer had been to snatch up the condo when he did.

"You should consider selling houses instead of interior design," I said.

"One of my clients is a real estate company that I do some staging for. That's how I heard about this amazing deal, so I told Spencer since he was looking. I like to help out friends if I spot a good deal."

Why had I insisted that Spencer meet and date this woman? Regret surged through me, alerting my fight-or-flight reflexes, but I swallowed down my emotions and pressed the corners of my lips up into a smile. "I'm surprised you didn't claim it for yourself," I said as evenly as I could.

"Here we are." Spencer jogged up the stairs, unlocked the door, and held it open.

"Wait until you see the floors." Mary Katherine finally released me as she backed up the stairs. "They're the originals and have been refinished."

Taking slow steadying breaths, I followed her into Spencer's home. Although the building was historic, the interior appeared fresh and bright. The wood floors were as beautiful as described, and the walls were painted a creamy white with bright white trim.

Mary Katherine gestured to the windows in the living room. "I've been sending Spencer fabric ideas for window treatments for weeks, but he can't make up his mind."

For weeks? I clamped my mouth shut, trying not to read too much into her words, but seriously, hadn't Spencer been professing his love for me only seven days ago?

"I just want to make the right choice, and I'm okay with living here awhile, getting used to the place. It still feels surreal that I own a condo."

"It does seem kind of empty with only the furniture from your apartment," I said.

Mary Katherine mimed a small box with her hands. "It's the scale."

"I see."

"This way to the kitchen." Spencer indicated.

The kitchen was a part of the great room because of the open floor plan, and it included a small nook for his bistro table. The appliances were all on the opposing wall and all appeared to be brand new. Although I wasn't much of a cook, I could envision preparing a simple weeknight supper with Spencer. With warm fuzzies filling me, I resisted the urge to express my raw emotions.

Spencer certainly didn't seem ready to broach the topic of us being more than friends—if we'd even reached friends status. There'd be moments when everything felt normal or better than normal, but then he'd turn indifferent, and I wondered if he was building a wall. Or worse, had already built a wall that I wouldn't be able to overcome. Not to mention whatever was going on with Mary Katherine. Hadn't they only gone on that one date?

The rest of the tour consisted of the primary bedroom with Spencer's old furniture that I agreed with Mary Katherine needed to be replaced, and then an empty guest room where he'd piled broken down boxes.

Spencer moved to the other side of the room where he stopped in front of a large window. "I'm thinking about making this an office." He met my gaze. "It would help me with a project I'm considering."

"The light in here is magnificent." Mary Katherine tilted her head, studying the room. "You might want to include a sleeper sofa for guests until you complete the renovation on the third room." She switched her attention to me. "Spencer was so lucky to score a three-bedroom. There are only a handful in the complex because people had to combine units to get them."

"Unfortunately, they ran out of funds for the reno, so I only have the shell of a bedroom and bathroom."

"I see."

Mary Katherine held up a finger. "But it meant you got a great deal. You were so smart to act fast."

"Sounds like it." I pressed a palm to my middle, refusing to feel anything but happiness for Spencer and maybe me. My heart squeezed as I fixed my eyes on his. "I'm so glad you took a step of faith and now own this special place. You may have some work to do, but it already feels like a home you're going to love."

"Thanks. It means a lot to hear you say that." He stared back at me, creating an invisible chain between us, each link a part of our history that bonded us together in a way that didn't seem like it could be broken.

"Aww. That's so sweet, especially since Jordan said you'd never think anywhere was better than your apartment on the Hill," Mary Katherine said.

Spencer and I blinked, shifting our attention to the person who could interrupt our moment but not break our bond.

"Hmm. I do love the location of my apartment, but I doubt I'll live there forever." Tapping my finger against my chin, I lifted a brow. "Experiencing something in person has a way of altering a person's opinion." I loved living on the Hill . . . I just loved Spencer more. I could and would compromise. It wasn't settling, but would he believe me?

"I totally agree." Mary Katherine peered out the window. "And the view of the courtyard is so nice."

Spencer crossed the room. "We better head back or we'll miss the whole third quarter."

"Right behind you." I glanced at Mary Katherine, who he'd been pleasant, but not overly attentive, to and had abandoned by the window. She didn't seem fazed by his indifference as she gave the room another once-over like she was picturing it decorated.

Without interrupting her thoughts, I stepped into the hall and hurried to catch up with Spencer. I'd done a little research that I still needed to share with him, and I absolutely didn't want to include Mary Katherine in my plans. I wasn't taking any chances with their relationship, even if I didn't believe Spencer would move on so quickly. While he wanted to find a wife and start a family, he'd proven that he wouldn't settle for anything less than love. I just needed to make sure he knew I wouldn't either. He was the man I wanted to love for the rest of my life.

Unfortunately, in addition to all her other attributes, Mary Katherine was quick on her feet, and before I could utter a word, she'd joined us. Once we arrived back at the party, a lot more people had arrived. Cooper carried a platter of burgers and hot dogs in from the porch, and we all made plates of food. While we ate and watched the end of the game, I tried to find a moment to talk to Spencer, but it was too crowded.

As the second game started, I decided to head home and settle for texting Spencer my invitation.

But as I thanked Jordan and Cooper for their hospitality, Spencer held open the door. "I'll walk you to the station."

If nothing else, he was always a gentleman. In the past, I'd have waved him off and told him it was unnecessary, but never again. If this man wanted to be close to me, I was here for it.

"Thanks." As I stepped into the cool night, I slipped on my jacket. "I know you want to see that game, so I really do appreciate it."

"Not a problem. Although most of those people are likely my new neighbors, they're currently strangers, and it was getting crowded. I'll be able to watch the game better on my own."

"Oh." My heart dipped with disappointment.

"Sorry, that came out wrong. It's not that I didn't want to walk with you. It was more like a bonus."

"Okay." *Bonus* at least sounded positive, and since it really was a short distance to the metro, I didn't have time to ponder his words if I wanted to say the things I'd planned. "So, I did a little research on this area, and I found what seems like a great church. I listened to several of the pastor's sermons and thought you might want to check out a service. They're at nine and eleven. I guess that's normal, but anyway, are you interested? If not, it's totally fine. I just thought we could try something new, and there are some great brunch restaurants out here. But if you already have plans or you don't want to go with me, there's no pressure—"

"Carleigh." Spencer touched my arm, pausing my speech and my breathing. "Slow down."

Registering that my pace had increased as rapidly as my words, I regulated myself as we crossed the street. "Sorry, is this better?"

The last thing I wanted was for him to think I was rushing to the station. It was unnerving that even while I was making great efforts to slow down, my natural inclination was to move quickly.

"Yes." His fingers left my arm. "It just didn't seem like you were paying attention to where you were going, and I didn't want you to trip on the curb."

"Thanks. I got a little excited. Or if I'm being completely real, nervous." Pulling my jacket tighter, I methodically secured the buttons.

"I thought we weren't doing the awkward thing."

"Agreed, but I'm not sure where I stand with you. I hoped we could try the church and brunch thing or just church. Really, whatever you want." I stopped at the road as cars passed us.

He pressed the button for the crossing signal. "Thank you for your candor and for taking the time to research the area for churches and restaurants."

"You do that sort of thing for me all the time, and I want to support you the same way. But if it's too much right now or if I'm overstepping by invading your new neighborhood, just tell me to lay off."

"It's not too much. I'm just a little surprised that you want to come back out here tomorrow. What about our usual places?" Spencer asked as the signal changed and we proceeded into the square.

"If that's what you want, it's fine with me, but maybe it's time to make some changes and explore some new spots."

"A fresh start sounds kind of nice, and I'd hate for all your research to go to waste. But I don't want you to be inconvenienced." He stopped a short way from the entry to the metro.

"Oh, no you don't." I turned to face him. "I won't let you give me credit for making some kind of sacrifice. If we're going to have any kind of relationship, I need to do my part, and I can and want to meet you where you are, which it seems is here."

"That's fair." He smiled. "I'll see you in the morning?"

"Really?"

"I'm not going to lie. This was not how I expected this night to go. You've surprised me, and I'm just curious enough to want to see more of this version of you, so I'm willing to take a chance. Besides, it's church, so my decision seems safe."

Not wanting to give him a chance to change his mind, I didn't dare ask for more assurances. "I'll send you the address for the church. We can meet there."

"Sounds good."

"Thanks for walking with me." My heart began pounding as I shifted to leave him. Normally we'd hug before we parted, but very little about the night had been our normal. I wrapped my arms around my waist and began retreating slowly.

"Let me know you got home safely?" He closed the distance between us in two steps.

I stopped moving and lifted my gaze to his. "Of course."

"Okay. Well, good night." Then he gave me a quick hug, turned, and strode away.

"Good night." I covered my mouth to keep from squealing. After our passionate kisses, it seemed crazy to be so overcome by a friendly embrace, but I wouldn't take for granted the progress we'd made in only one week.

Chapter 26

The next morning as I strolled from the metro, I shivered as a cool breeze rustled the green leaves on the trees along the street. In a few weeks, the area would be a fiery display of red, yellow, and orange. The change of seasons demonstrated such a beautiful transformation, but the old remained a part of the new. We couldn't have one without the other.

Outside the church, Spencer waited, wearing a light blue button-down shirt with khaki pants and a navy fleece vest. "Good morning," he said with hands tucked in his pockets, making it unlikely that a hug would accompany his greeting.

"Good morning. I know it's cold, but I love how it feels like autumn."

"And you got to wear your favorite boots." He smirked.

But the familiarity of his teasing made my insides turn to mush. "There can be more than one way to appreciate God's creation."

"For sure." He gestured to the church doors. "Shall we?"

Inside we chose seats, and I pulled out my Bible, journal, and pen from my bag, determined to focus on worshipping God and not on Spencer's nearness. During the opening songs, I closed my eyes and listened more than sang. Peace and hope spread through me, and I prayed for courage to trust Spencer and for me to be vulnerable. I'd texted Wyatt about my plans, and he'd said he'd be praying for us and reminded me not to hold back my personal baggage from Spencer. In so many ways, I wanted to open up to him because it would bring us closer, but it wasn't natural or easy for me.

To my relief, the pastor didn't leave a lot of space to worry. His sermon was packed with too many thought-provoking points. But what I appreciated most was how he brought it all back to the Gospel, and when we stood to leave, my heart filled with strength fueled by love.

As we walked the short distance to the restaurant where I'd made a reservation for brunch, I said little. Instead, I listened to Spencer's takeaways from the sermon. He mentioned that he felt challenged to study scripture on a deeper level and that he might consider joining one of the Bible studies that had begun with the new school year.

In law school, we'd participated in a prayer group that included a short scripture passage. It was a nice change from all the reading for our classes, but neither of us could bring ourselves to read much else. I already went to bed every night with blurred vision, but that was nothing more than an excuse—and a poor one. I could've listened to scripture and devotions on my phone. Unfortunately, we both fell into the habit of attending church and then putting away our Bibles, and for the most part our faith, until the next Sunday. Clearly, it hadn't been enough, and thankfully, Spencer had come to the same conclusion.

After a short walk, we entered the café. Amongst the friendly chatter, mismatched painted chairs circled tables, and large canvases of original artwork hung on the sky-blue walls. There's something cheery about spaces where people share brunch. The room could have been decorated in gray scale and the environment would still have thrived with the hum of bright colors. If I weren't already bubbling over with bliss, this place would have done it.

After we were seated, Spencer studied his menu. "What are you going to order?"

"I haven't looked at the menu. I've been so busy taking this all in."

He shifted his attention to me. "You seem more observant and, I don't know, pensive these days."

"I'm just trying to be present and appreciate all that's around me."

"How'd that go on the metro? You appreciate all the aromas?"

"Ha ha." I lifted my menu and scanned the specials.

Spencer's finger dropped on the top, lowering it enough to see my eyes. "They offer a brunch for two with quiche Lorraine, blueberry coffee cake, seasonal fruit, and croissants. What do you think?"

"I'll need to pick up my mileage this week."

"I'll take that as a yes." He grasped my menu and stacked it with his as a server approached with pitchers of water and coffee. Once the server filled our cups, Spencer gave our order, and I sipped my coffee.

It'd be easy to keep our conversation light, simply discuss the café's paintings or the results of football games. It was how I usually communicated. But we weren't going to get anywhere chatting about the upsets in college football.

Spencer eyed me skeptically. "So, what's going on?"

"As you know, I've been making some changes, and I don't want you to think it's a ploy to get you to change your mind about us. Please just hear me out, and we can figure out our stuff later. Mostly, I'm just glad you agreed to meet me."

"Remember, curiosity." He tapped his temple.

"Right. So last Sunday I went to church where the wedding was held, and afterward, I ran into Wyatt, who, it turns out, has become quite the Bible nerd."

"Interesting. I thought he was really frustrating to you."

"Oh, he was still frustrating, but my defenses were down, so I found myself listening rather than arguing. On another note, I'm starting to accept that people can change, and I should give them a chance before I discount them as being the same as they were in high school."

Spencer's brows inched up. "I agree, but I feel like you're burying the lede."

"I have so much to tell you, so the order might seem jumbled. Wyatt told me about the passage where Jesus invites all who are weary and heavy burdened to take up his yoke for a better way to live. When I got home, I started studying that passage and then all the verses on anxiety and worry. There are a lot, by the way. Most of them direct us to go to God first and always, but also, we need to surrender our ways for His. That's what I've been focusing on as I evaluate my life."

"I see." Spencer made room in the center of the table for the server who'd returned with our brunch. The display was impressive, and moreover, an excellent distraction, giving me the chance to gather my thoughts.

On the bottom of a three-tiered tea stand was the quiche in a tart pan. The next level held squares of coffee cake, and on top, a cut glass bowl held a variety of berries. In the last space on the table, the waiter placed a basket filled with mini croissants.

After our drinks had been topped off, Spencer served each of us a slice of quiche. For a moment, I waffled on whether I needed to tell him everything, but if I wanted a healthy relationship, I had to show him I trusted him with the raw truth.

"I'm aware this is kind of heavy conversation for brunch, so I appreciate you not asking for a box and making a run for it." I pinched off the end of a croissant.

"Not at all. I'm trying to understand how we've avoided these kinds of discussions for so many years."

"For my part, I was doing a pretty remarkable job of burying my stuff under busyness, so I wasn't dealing with it on my own, much less with you. But all that peace and quiet at Magnolia Bluff left way too much space for me to think, and then I got back here and you were gone and Wyatt's words kept berating me, and then I started running without earbuds. I couldn't help but deal with my stuff. And the Holy Spirit was at work on me too, and it has been work . . . hard work."

"I'm sure. I wish I'd been there for you to talk to. I feel like a terrible friend."

I shook my head. "This was work I needed to do on my own. You're the best friend for speaking the truth to me and forcing me to see how I was misinterpreting my instincts. What seemed problematic had very little to do with Lawson and Willa and way more to do with me." I patted my chest.

"What I've come to understand is that with everything that happened in high school, I developed a strong desire to prove that I was important, and somehow being successful on every account became my goal. I wanted to have it all and show everyone. Honestly, I'm not even sure who everyone is anymore. But I started to ponder these kinds of questions as I read verse after verse on anxiety. Why did I care what anyone from my past thought? Why did I let it shape me? Sure, I'm objectively successful, so why don't I feel satisfied? And while everything with Lawson and you highlighted my inability to find contentment, my problem stems more from my failure to understand who I am as a child of God. With that in mind, I'm starting to reorder my priorities." I popped a bite of the croissant into my mouth.

"Wow, that's a lot. I knew the stuff with Bree and your brother had messed with your perspective, but I didn't realize to what extent."

"All the stuff from high school wasn't bad. In some ways, my strength and self-reliance are good traits, but not at the expense of not trusting anyone with my fears and worries."

"You didn't trust me?"

"I didn't trust myself to consider not winning at the game of life. Seeing everything through the lens of what society says success looks like led me to believe that I was achieving it all. Now, I see my motives were selfish and all about prestige. What you said on the dock about being more intentional made me think that I needed to do the same thing and allow my faith to direct my decisions."

"We all could stand to do more of that," he said.

"Well, that just about covers it." I scooped a bite of quiche. "Let's eat this delicious meal."

"While I'm all for eating, I don't think this conversation is over. We're just scraping the surface of a lot of issues. But I'm glad that you confided in me and started the dialogue. While our friendship is no doubt in a precarious place, it's not hopeless. We can't go back to the way things were, and that's a good thing. In the meantime, can we take some time to process where we've been and where we are now, before we decide how we'll move on?"

"Does that mean we can be friends while we figure it out?"

"I think so, but you've given me a lot to ponder, so you're going to have to bear with me."

"Not a problem." I ate a bite of quiche, and Spencer broke off a piece of the coffee cake. From that point, we chatted mostly about the food and a little about the art. When it was time to part, our hug wasn't awkward. Not that my heart didn't flutter at his nearness, but I managed my emotions. We were connecting on a deeper, better level, and we'd be stronger for it. I could be patient.

Following my new morning routine of coffee and prayer, I braided my hair and tugged on my running shoes. When I was in high school, I went on a three-day retreat, and my counselor encouraged us to start each day with a quiet time. Since then, I'd gone through periods where I'd faithfully followed through, but there were far more times when I'd found excuses to skip it. However, this time felt different. Making my faith my first priority every morning, of course with coffee, reminded me what mattered most in my life. Like Wyatt said, everything else seemed to find its proper place at the proper time.

And while my faith in God's timing had grown, finding Spencer stretching in the rays of the rising sun was not the miracle I'd expected. Blinking, I paused in the doorway and rubbed my eyes.

When the door clicked shut behind me, he glanced over, grinning. "Surprise."

"Good morning." I joined him. "What are you doing here?"

"I had to see if it was true with my own eyes." He gave me a brief hug.

I shoved him playfully. "You doubted me?"

"Of course not." Blue specks twinkled in his gray eyes, teasing me with my favorite version of my best friend. "I thought you might want a little company to help with all the peace and quiet that's been plaguing you."

I laughed. "How can I thank you enough?"

"It's just what friends do." He stepped into a lunge. "Also, as your friend, I suggest you stretch."

"Yeah, you've mentioned that before." I pulled my foot behind me, loosening my quad. "By the way, I'm more of a jogger, so don't feel like you have to hang with me."

"If I wanted to run alone, I could've done that in Arlington."

I switched legs. "Got it, but if this is going to be a thing, I should come out there sometimes."

"Why don't we take it one day at a time?"

"Okay." I crossed my ankles and bent at the waist. "Change of subject?"

"Fine, but nothing too serious. I did have to get up early, so I might be a little foggy-brained until the endorphins kick in."

Without standing, I recrossed my ankles. "I was just wondering if you've had time to check out the book I sent you."

"Yes, and it was helpful. I have a lot to learn if I want to write fiction."

"Ready?" I stood, rolling my shoulders a few times.

"Sure."

We jogged to the corner and crossed the street, heading toward the mall.

"What kind of books would you write?"

"For years, I've had this idea, percolating of an adventure, mystery-type story for middle school boys."

"You've never mentioned it."

"Because I wasn't sure how you or anyone else would react. It sounds a little silly even to me. What if I'm not good at writing anything other than legal memos? Still, since you're putting yourself out there, I'm trying to do the same. You know my parents were overprotective, so my greatest adventure was going on a class field trip without one of them as a chaperone, and it only happened twice. Not to mention my gated neighborhood in the Maryland suburbs wasn't exactly rife with chances to take risks or solve mysteries. Anyway, when I was a kid, I devoured this type of book. I've got notebooks filled with story ideas."

"I'd love to hear them or read them. You know I love a good spy novel."

"We'll see. You may have noticed that I'm not great with rejection."

"I'm not sure how I should respond to your implication because I do care about what happened between us. But I also want to support your dream, and since I know nothing about books for middle school-aged boys, I wouldn't be anything more than a person to bounce ideas off. And if you want to talk about the other stuff, that's up to you."

"Maybe later. Topic change?"

"Okay." My heart pinched, but I pressed my nails into my palms and kept running. While being patient was rarely easy, I hadn't predicted how much it'd hurt when he shut me down.

"We haven't played doubles in forever. How about setting up a game with Ashton and Brock?"

"That sounds fun." I unzipped my jacket. "I'll check with her at work."

"How is work? You aren't thinking about trying something crazy like writing novels?"

"Work is good. I enjoy my job, but I did pray about giving it up.. For now, I think it's where I belong. And for the record, I don't think you're crazy."

"Thanks, and I like my job most of the time too. I guess when people asked me what I wanted to be when I grew up, I never saw myself as a regulatory lawyer. What about you?"

"I didn't know what a lobbyist was until I was in high school. As a kid, I told people that I wanted to be President, but I'd settle for a cabinet position."

Spencer chuckled. "I can totally envision ten-year-old Carleigh in a navy power suit."

"For your information, I didn't get my first power suit until I was fourteen when I served as a congressional page."

"So what about now? Do you still dream of running for office?" Spencer asked.

"Not really. I mean if the opportunity presented itself, and it was right for me and my family, and I felt a strong call, I'd do it, but I'm afraid I'd get consumed by the job. I see it in some politicians I deal with. They start with a noble pursuit to serve their constituents and make the country a better place, but then their title and position become their entire identity, and they believe if they lose an election, they'll lose their worth."

"That's sad, but I see how it happens. I imagine it's hard to keep the right perspective."

"Don't get me wrong. Some find a way to stay grounded and humble, but it isn't easy. They're the ones who spend a lot more time at home than in DC. They stay connected to their friends and families and churches. I know one Senator who's been teaching a Sunday school class to seventh grade boys for over twenty years."

"That's bound to keep anyone's ego in check."

"Right?" I tapped my foot on the bottom step of the Lincoln memorial before we turned to head back toward the Capitol building.

"Speaking of small groups. I sent an email last night about joining one at the church we visited."

"I'm glad you're getting involved."

"Will you come with me again next Sunday?" He glanced at me, a bolt of energy zipping between us.

"I'd like that." I tucked my bottom lip between my teeth to keep my mouth from morphing into a goofy grin.

As we jogged, sunlight painted the buildings with swaths of yellow as it rose higher in the sky and warmed the earth. I loved these early fall days with brisk mornings and cool nights, signaling the end of one season and the beginning of the next. Similarly, our lives seemed on the brink of change, and like the trees, we might need to lose our leaves before we were ready to grow new ones.

Chapter 27

That night when I arrived home, I snuggled onto the couch with Queenie, restraining the urge to hop on the metro and go visit Spencer. Our time together had been wonderful, but it made me crave more. All day, I considered texting him, but I didn't want to overwhelm him and stall our progress toward the place I hoped we were going. It was killing me to move slowly, but it seemed to be what he—correction, *we*—needed.

Thankfully, as I prepared Queenie's dinner and ordered takeout, my phone buzzed.

> **Spencer:** I hope you had a great day, Madame President.

> **Me:** Ha ha. Pretty average. How about you?

> **Spencer:** I found out I can work remote a couple of days a week, so it might give me a little spare time to write without the commute and lunch break.

> **Me:** Great timing.

Spencer: Now I have to get my office set up ASAP.

Ughhh! I didn't want to hear where this might be going. I'm sure Mary Katherine was a fantastic resource, but couldn't he just order office furniture online? Then I had a brilliant idea.

Me: Zoe could help you.

Spencer: I'm sure she could, but I've got help.

Yuck, yuck, yuck!

Me: Okay. Well, let me know if you change your mind.

Spencer: BTW, the run was fun this morning.

Me: Yeah, we should do it again, but I can't make it out to you this week. I've got early meetings every day.

Spencer: Same, and I'm going to be moving to a shared office space.

Me: If you need help moving, let me know.

Spencer: Will do. I'll text later, but I've got dinner plans.

Me: Sure. Good night.

"Not dinner plans." I folded my body over the kitchen counter, smacking my palms against it. While his plans could be with anyone, I could only picture Mary Katherine stretching her tape measure around Spencer's office, and it made me want to puke. It was wrong and showed a lack of faith, but I felt like Spencer was slipping away even though he'd given me no reason to think Mary Katherine was anything more than his friendly interior decorator.

A couple of hours later as I prepared for bed, my phone vibrated on the vanity, and I snatched it up.

> Spencer: I just want to thank you for the church rec. I met with a great group of guys tonight.

I slapped my palm to my forehead. "You don't deserve this man."

The next couple of days went much the same way. I'd worry about Mary Katherine for no reason, chastise myself, and then Spencer would give me some nugget of information about his life, and I'd share something I hadn't told him about my hopes or worries. Our friendship seemed to be growing in a healthy way.

Moreover, he hadn't mentioned her since he originally told me about his home office, but somehow that made it worse. Still if she was helping him, surely Spencer didn't see her as more than a friend. Right? *They're just friends* had become my mantra, and I needed to trust God, but old habits die hard, and the doubts would occasionally break through the wall I'd constructed to keep them out. The mature thing to do would've been to simply ask him. We were talking about everything, and this was the only topic I avoided. But he wasn't bringing it up either, which meant there was nothing to bring up—or he didn't want to hurt me.

I sighed as I tried to focus on the legal brief Ashton had prepared about a new regulation from the EPA that would affect our new client, King's Grantees of Georgia. They feared the agency would essentially commit a taking in the name of environmental protection. While the government wouldn't actually acquire the property through eminent domain, the burdensome regulations would have the same result. All members of our client's group had owned their property for generations and were superior stewards of the environment. They didn't want the federal government interfering with their property rights. Lately, we spent a lot of our time fighting these regulations that became more like laws in practice. We were entering the comment period for the new rules, so I needed to understand every aspect to protect our client.

Unfortunately, my mind kept drifting to daydreams of a life with Spencer. I'd created one for each season. In the autumn, we were having coffee on the balcony overlooking the park as the red, yellow, and orange leaves fluttered to the ground. In the winter, we cuddled in front of a smoldering fire, sharing the highlights of our days. When spring arrived, we'd stroll to the square and enjoy a late lunch at a sidewalk café. During the summer, we'd host cookouts and visit with our neighbors. Perhaps my plans leaned to the idyllic, but that's why they're called daydreams.

Today when Spencer and I'd met for a quick lunch, I'd implied—okay, I'd admitted with glaring clarity—how much I liked the Courthouse neighborhood, but Spencer didn't even joke with me about my change of heart. I couldn't tell if he was trying to manage his own response so he wouldn't get his hopes up or to protect me from his plan to keep me in the friend zone.

I pushed off my desk and collapsed against the back of my chair, staring at the ceiling. Something needed to change soon, or I'd start falling behind on my tasks. Maybe it wasn't all bad that I hadn't fallen in love before now or I'd never have been named partner. I'd probably have been fired. Another tally mark in the God column for His perfect timing. These days, I could delegate and rely on the associates, and it was nice to have the support of a team I trusted.

Exhaling a long breath, I straightened, rolled my shoulders, and popped the cap off a highlighter. Then I hunched back over the document.

But before I knew it, I was on my phone, checking the movie schedule for the theatre in Courthouse. On Friday night, I could plan a friend-date with Spencer, and then he'd come to my place for football on Saturday, and then we'd have church on Sunday. Once the plans for Friday were made, I'd be able to focus. I closed the browser and texted Spencer.

> Me: Movie and pizza Friday? I can get tickets for that new WWII movie for 8. We could get pizza at Fire Works or whatever you want.

After hitting send, I watched for a response, aimlessly drumming my nails on my desk. Once several minutes passed with no answer, I forced myself to turn my phone display-side down and focus on the brief. As I read, I made notes in the margin and highlighted areas of concern that I wanted to discuss or needed more research on. Spencer's delayed response didn't leave my mind, but it wasn't interfering with my concentration anymore. When I finished reviewing the document, I glanced at the screen of my smartwatch which hadn't buzzed for too long.

What would I do if Spencer said no? Not just no to the movies, but no to taking the relationship to the next level. What if I'd missed my chance? Could I be okay with friendship?

"Hey, have you got a minute?" Jordan stood in my doorway.

"Sure. What's up?"

She took a seat across from me. "We need to get with the Georgia Ports Authority and be sure we're all on the same page with funding. Do you want me to set up a meeting?"

"Good idea. Thanks for taking the initiative."

My watch vibrated, and I glanced down to read the text.

> Spencer: Sounds fun, but I can't Friday. I have plans.

Chills skittered over my arms as dread settled inside me. *Stop it, Carleigh! It could be anything.* His brother could be in town. Although it seemed like that'd be something Spencer would've mentioned.

"Everything okay?" Jordan asked.

"Absolutely." I snapped my focus back to her, tapping my nails on my watch screen. "I was just trying to make plans with Spencer for Friday night, but he's busy. We'll just do it another time."

"Oh, right. MK mentioned they're going to the symphony at the Kennedy Center. I'm glad she found someone who likes to go to those kinds of things. Before Spencer, I was her go-to partner for all things cultural. Occasionally, we'd drag Cooper along, but he's not a fan."

"Oh. Yeah. Spencer's great like that." I swallowed. Not because he liked art and classical music. It was something he endured to be a good friend, which might be all this was. Although all the evidence pointed to it being a date. *A date!*

"So, I'll check the calendar and schedule the meeting." Jordan stood.

"Fantastic." As disappointment tugged at my resolve, I feigned indifference, shifting my attention to the computer screen like I was starting a project. That's what I needed to do—focus on my job. With renewed determination, I typed a lengthy email to Ashton, outlining our next steps on the King's Grant matter. But as soon as I hit send, my fingers quivered over the keyboard. I snatched my hands to my lap, interlocking my fingers with intensity.

"Lord, please help me know what to do." I threaded my fingers through my hair and massaged my scalp as my eyes watered. Sitting here, wallowing, while Spencer went out with Mary Katherine did not seem like my best yes. I crossed my office and closed the door, then walked to the window, rubbing away the tears. *My old ways of doing things were wrong, but what was the right thing to do?* I paced to my desk and back to the windows a few times. Then I spotted my phone and peace spread through me. God had given me *two* best friends, and the other one had become an expert in resolving unrequited love, so why not ask him for advice?

I dashed around the desk and grabbed my phone. I dropped in my chair, sending it rolling across the plastic mat. As I made the call, a flutter of anticipation tickled my chest. Was it hope?

"Hey," Lawson answered.

"I want to hear all about your honeymoon and married life, but right now, I need help." I gripped the phone.

"Carleigh, you sound a little scary. Calm down and tell me what's wrong?" Lawson asked.

"Don't tell her to calm down. That never helps. Sorry, Carleigh," Willa said.

"It's Spencer. He has a date on Friday with Mary Katherine, and I don't know what to do." Even as the words left my mouth, the familiarity of my situation made my head ache. With my spare hand, I rubbed my temple.

"Are you sure it's a date? From what I've gathered, things with y'all might have encountered a slack tide, but I'm surprised he gave up so easily."

"They're going to the symphony, and please, for all that is good in the world, no more metaphors." My nose started running, so I wiped it with the scratchy napkin still on my desk from my takeout dinner the night before.

"Ignoring your sass because you sound unhinged, but unfortunately, that does sound like—" He paused. "Willa wants to know if it'd be okay if we put you on a video call, so we can all help."

"Who's there?" I squeezed my eyes shut, pretty sure of the answer but also happy to get all the advice I could get, and Willa had proven she knew how to get an old friend to become a husband.

"Just Wyatt and Willa."

"Okay." I opened my eyes and ended the call, waiting for them to connect on video. I propped up my phone on a framed picture of Spencer and me from the White House tree lighting the year it snowed.

The phone signaled an incoming call, and I tapped the button to connect.

"Wow, you don't look so good." Wyatt frowned. "Are you sure you aren't sick?"

"You aren't making my aching head hurt any less." I cupped my cheeks in my hands, taking in my appearance on the screen. Puffy eyes, red nose, splotchy skin—I did look terrible.

"Nope, she's fine, brimming with grace and patience as always. " Wyatt winked. "Have you been doing what we talked about?"

Lawson wrinkled his brow. "Y'all had a productive conversation?"

"Yes, and Wyatt can fill in the details later. And to answer your question, I've been reading my Bible and praying every morning. I'm even running to give myself extra time to think. I've confided in Spencer about a lot of personal stuff. We've been spending some nice quality time together, and we seemed to be making progress. But what if he still just wants to be friends? And what if he's decided Mary Katherine is better for him than me?"

"Have you talked to him about any of this stuff?" Wyatt asked.

"You told me to work on my faith and be patient, so that's what I've been doing. We were supposed to find our way back together and be better after this time of growth, but now, I'm worried." I raked my fingers through my disheveled hair. "I don't want to rush things either and not wait for God's timing. It hasn't even been two weeks."

Willa tilted her head. "But you've been together for over a decade."

"Yeah, y'all have practically been living together since law school," Lawson added.

"I have to agree." Wyatt shrugged. "It won't be rushing to tell Spencer that your feelings haven't changed since y'all talked the night of the wedding. I understand that you're trying to be faithful to God's timing, but maybe this is the moment He's selected."

"I wish you could be more certain." *Like a hundred percent.* I picked up a pen and clicked the end. "He said he didn't want me to settle for him because I didn't have any other options."

Willa waved her hand. "Then you're going to need a grand gesture."

"A what?" Both guys eyed her suspiciously.

"A grand gesture, like when Lawson came to my apartment with the flowers and begged for my forgiveness. But it needs to be grander. No offense, honey." She patted Lawson's cheek. "But as far as grand gestures go, it was rather lackluster. It needs to be on the scale of the one Nathaniel concocted to win Wren back. There was an actual Ferris wheel and fireworks in the shape of hearts."

"Seriously?" Lawson asked.

"Yes, honey, but I love how we made up, so don't worry about it. Besides, Nathaniel had the entire town of Haslemere helping him."

"Anyway, not that I don't have a lot of questions about Nathaniel's resources, but could we focus on me? Fireworks and carnival rides aren't in the budget or my style."

"What's something that will show Spencer you're seriously in love with him and want to spend the rest of your life with him?" She narrowed her eyes. "We are talking about marriage here, right? Because if you suggest y'all date to see if it's the real thing or just taste a cake sample or anything that isn't the whole white dress, gold bands, vows, and merging your investment accounts kind of proposal, your gesture will fail."

"I mean, of course that's what I want, but I don't want to scare him off. Will he think I'm coming on too strong?"

"No," they answered in unison.

"Got it. So, I mean other than showing up in wedding attire with a preacher and a wedding certificate, how do I do it?"

At that moment, I noticed how Lawson and Willa's skin was so tan from their tropical honeymoon. Then an idea started to form, and my lips spread into a wide smile. "Never mind. I know exactly what to do. Thanks so much for your help." I reached for the phone, ready to put my plan into action.

"Wait, what is it?" Willa tilted her head to the side, attempting to see around my palm.

"No time. I'll let y'all know how it goes. Bye." I tapped the screen to end the call and then turned to my computer, sliding my mouse to the internet browser. With amazing clarity, I typed in the words *Kokomo Resort Fiji*. "Lord, if this is wrong, please stop me, but if it's right, please make Spencer's heart ready."

Chapter 28

The next afternoon, I left the office early to make final preparations. Specifically, I wanted to put my hair up the way Spencer liked it. If this was going to be my grand gesture, nothing could be considered insignificant. And so far every part of my plan had fallen into place. Details that I hadn't considered were resolved with ease and better than expected. As I exited the Court House metro station, my chest filled with confidence.

I shivered and wiggled my numb toes exposed to the dropping temperatures, but the strappy high-heeled sandals completed my ensemble. A little discomfort would be worth it when Spencer saw me. Besides, the ivory halter dress I'd spotted in a boutique was perfect for the mission, and it also seemed like the final sign of assurance that I was doing the right thing. Seriously, who puts a sundress in the window display in September, especially one in a shade of white, two weeks after Labor Day?

Dressed more for a summer evening than an autumn one, I tightened my parka around myself as I hurried down the sidewalk to Spencer's condo. At the top of his stairs, I paused and took a deep breath before I shed my coat and rang the bell. Thankfully, the adrenaline pumping through my veins warmed me. Instead of feeling nervous or afraid of Spencer's reaction, my body hummed with excitement and expectation.

As the door opened, I smiled brightly.

"Oh, wow!" Spencer's eyes grew wide as his gaze skimmed over me, from coral-painted toenails to twisted-up hair, then settled on my eyes. "Carleigh, you look beautiful." Attraction surged between us, before a cool breeze interrupted the moment and Spencer registered the temperature outside. "But you must be freezing. Come in here."

As he stepped to the side, I grabbed my coat from the railing and entered. "I promise I'm fine."

"Trust me, fine is not nearly adequate to describe your appearance. I'm pretty sure beautiful isn't either. I guess if I'm going to be a writer, I'll need a thesaurus." He closed the door and proceeded into the living room. "Anyway, if your aim with that dress was to get my attention and take my breath away, you more than succeeded."

I fluttered the skirt. "It just seemed like the appropriate thing to wear for my presentation."

"Are you on the way somewhere and thought you'd stop by to jump-start my pulse?" Folding his arms over his chest, he leaned against the sofa. He didn't seem mad, but he did seem wary.

"I'm not going anywhere else, and I have to say that I'm glad you're being honest about your attraction to me. It makes what I need to say easier."

"Carleigh, you'd catch the attention of most men in that dress. I don't like thinking about other men ogling you, and I'm relieved that you wore that long parka on the metro."

"I'm not interested in other men's attention. You're the only one I care about, and while you apparently find me objectively attractive, I hope you feel something more." I held up my hand to stop him from responding. "Please let me finish. If you still just want to be friends at the end, then I'll accept your answer."

I pressed a palm to my chest. "I love you. I didn't know how much until you left me sitting on that porch rocker in Georgia. But I'm glad you did. It turns out that I had a lot of stuff I needed to deal with before we could have the relationship that I hope we will. Don't get me wrong, I still have work to do, but I don't want to do it without you. Over the last week, it's been so nice to open up to you so you could really know me, and my love for you has grown deeper with your willingness to forgive me and share this intimate friendship. But I want more, and I think you do too. Picturing you on a date with Mary Katherine makes me want to vomit. However, if she's who you choose, I won't stand in your way. Mostly because I'll be tossing up my cookies. Regardless, I've learned my lesson, and my greatest desire is for you to be in a loving relationship. I just hope it's with me." I reached in my clutch for my visual aids.

"Carleigh, I—"

"Hold on, I'm not through." I passed him the color brochure and airline tickets I'd printed.

He studied the items and then me with his brows pinched in confusion. "What's this?"

"Your dream honeymoon to the private resort island of Kokomo in Fiji. I've booked everything. Obviously, we'll start with a wedding on the beach. Then we'll spend a week doing whatever you want." As the gravity of my words occurred to me, heat rushed over my cheeks.

"But the date on these tickets is only two weeks away."

"Correct. I tried to get it earlier, but this was the best I could do. And you don't need to worry about your job. I checked with your secretary, and she said that your schedule could be adjusted."

"You told Janice about this?"

"Not specifically. I only told her that I was planning to surprise you with a vacation. Is that your only question?"

"Oh, no. I have lots of questions. Or at least I think I should."

"While you ponder that, I have one question for you and it will make the rest less important."

"Okay."

"Do you love me?"

His shoulders dropped. "I've tried to change my feelings, but the answer is still yes. I love you. And by the way, I told MK that I wasn't ready to date, so she said we could just hang out as friends. To soften the blow, I bought some office furniture, but now I'm not too sure about it."

Tears pooled in my eyes as I laughed. "I'm so happy and relieved to hear you say that."

"But Carleigh—" He pushed off the couch, closing the space between us, then brushed his finger gently over my damp cheekbones. "I'm not sure I'll ever get used to seeing you cry, even if it is tears of joy. I do love you, but isn't this happening a little fast?"

"A wise woman once said in a particularly lame toast that 'when you realize you want to spend the rest of your life with somebody, you want the rest of your life to start as soon as possible.'" Meeting his gaze, I slid my hand over his heart. "You're that person for me. I love you."

I barely got the words out before Spencer's mouth was on mine, answering me with an urgency that I hadn't expected. I melted into him as hope shoved away any lingering doubt.

But then Spencer jerked back. He caught my shoulders, staring at me, and then frowned. "I need to get something." He dropped his hands to his sides and backed away from me, watching me like I might disappear.

"Okay." As my nerves realized the source of warmth had departed, I shivered and rubbed my arms.

"Don't go anywhere. I'll be right back." Spencer turned and hurried down the hall toward his bedroom.

Had he said yes to my proposal? He'd said he loved me. That's what was important. And he hadn't said no. What could he possibly need? I heard a drawer slam and then Spencer rushed into the room. Without a word, he draped a sweatshirt around my shoulders, tying the sleeves in a knot under my chin.

"Thank you." Was he really that concerned about me being cold?

Then he dropped to one knee and lifted up a diamond-and-emerald ring. "Carleigh, I love you. You are so much more than my friend. Leaving you in Georgia was the hardest thing I've ever done, but you're right that we are so much better for it. In that moment, I wasn't sure of your feelings, and I needed to know that you weren't just reacting to everything going on with Lawson and even me. I never wanted you to doubt your decision to be with me."

He shook his head. "If there'd been a different way, trust me, I'd have chosen it. I hated seeing you hurt. I hated thinking of you alone at your apartment. I hated moving into this place without your support or input. I wanted this to be our first home together, and it felt so lonely without you." He glanced around the space before settling his gaze on me, the corners of his lips easing up into a smile. "Obviously, I couldn't stay away from you for long. Your friendship is nourishment for me, and I'm so beyond grateful that you love me and want to share your life with me. But I still want to be the one to ask the question. Carleigh, will you marry me?"

"Yes." I reached out and traced the side of his face.

He took my hand and slipped the ring on my finger. "It fits perfectly."

"It's gorgeous." Two small dark green emeralds flanked a large emerald cut diamond on a gold band. "When . . . how did you . . .?"

"It was my grandmother's." He stood, holding my hand, rubbing his thumb over the precious stones. "I've had it for a while. Before everything went wrong, I'd planned to propose to you when we returned from Magnolia Bluff, and I showed you the condo."

"So I'm not the only one who didn't want to delay our wedding?"

"Well, I was only planning an engagement, but I can't wait to marry you, and I'm so glad I don't have to wait." Chuckling, he enveloped me in his arms before he pressed his lips to mine with careful attention, lingering and exploring, yielding and surging. We lost track of time that no longer mattered.

Epilogue

Five Weeks Later

Spencer

I parked our rental car in front of Carleigh's parents' house and squeezed my wife's hand for a much-needed boost of confidence. "Do you think your mom's forgiven us for eloping?"

"No. The best we can hope for is that she'll be so distracted and overjoyed with Brad and Zoe's wedding that she'll forget to be mad." Carleigh spun her rings around her finger. We'd been married nearly a month, and every day was like a dream that I'd never dared to imagine. Maybe Nathaniel had the right idea with writing romance, although my adventure story was taking shape.

"At least your dad's on our side since he didn't have to pay for the wedding." I kissed the back of her hand. "We can't stay out here much longer. I'm sure they're watching from the windows."

"You're right." She opened the door, and I hurried around the car and caught her hand, lacing our fingers together.

Carleigh paused on the porch. "Last time I was here, Brad chastised me for ringing the bell, but it feels weird just barging in."

"I kind of knock and holler when we go to my parents' house."

"Good idea." She rapped on the door as she opened it. "Hello."

"Surprise!" people shouted.

"What's happening?" I leaned in close to her.

"We're having a party to celebrate you guys!" Zoe approached Carleigh with a DIY glitter-covered veil and placed it on her head.

"This weekend is supposed to be about y'all. I don't want to take anything away from your special day," Carleigh said.

"Nonsense. We'll have plenty of time for us tomorrow and Saturday." Zoe pecked me on the cheek. "I'm so looking forward to having you as a brother-in-law."

"We're going to have to stick together."

Wren gave Carleigh a bouquet of cut flowers. "Congratulations. Nathaniel and I are so happy for you. These are from our garden."

"They're beautiful."

Brad held out his arms, shaking his head. "Congratulations on another win! You just couldn't let me beat you." He engulfed Carleigh in his arms.

"Ha ha. Thanks for everything y'all did at the house." She squirmed out of his embrace. "It's fantastic. We'd still be choosing tiles and paint colors if it hadn't been for you."

While we'd been getting married and enjoying our honeymoon, Zoe and Brad had flown to DC to surprise us. When we arrived home, we discovered they'd moved Carleigh's things into my—our—condo, and as part of their television show, they'd completed the renovation and given the rest of the rooms a 'freshen up,' as Zoe called it. She'd insisted that the home needed to merge our styles into one, like marriage unites two people. It was the best wedding present to walk into our home, and have it not look like my stuff and her stuff, but instead our place.

"You're welcome. It was all Zoe. I just do what I'm told." Brad turned his attention to me.

"Somehow I doubt that," Carleigh said as her brother gave me a big hug and a firm pat on the back. "Welcome to the family." Carleigh laughed.

"Thanks for being patient with my big sis." Brad released me, chuckling. "But seriously, I'm glad y'all finally figured out what we've all known for years."

"Absolutely." Lawson joined our circle, holding Willa's hand.

She beamed at Carleigh. "When you said you had an idea for the grand gesture, I didn't think it'd involve Fiji and getting married. You have to tell me all about the resort. I found it online. It looks gorgeous."

"The pictures don't capture it adequately. The people were so friendly, and the pace of life was so unhurried." My wife gave me a knowing look that warmed my heart.

"It was perfect." I put my arm around her shoulders.

And it had been. As soon as we'd arrived on Kokomo, the staff had whisked us away to the spa where they'd more than pampered us. We'd dressed for the ceremony—Carleigh in the dress she'd worn for her/my/our proposal, and me in a relaxed linen shirt and pants. At sunset, we met under an arbor of tropical flowers and said our vows. The moment my lips met hers, sealing our covenant, everything and nothing changed. We would always be best friends, but now we'd live as one, united by God.

Carleigh nestled into the place where she fit perfectly at my side as her parents approached. "Mom, Dad, this is so nice."

"It'll do. Zoe and Willa worked hard to coordinate the food and decorations." Mrs. Chastain hugged her daughter. "And we already had the rentals for the rehearsal supper, so we just had them deliver everything a day early."

"I know it's not the wedding you dreamed about, but it's perfect for me."

"At this point, I'm just grateful you're married and aren't too old to have babies." As my new mother-in-law hugged me, my cheeks burned.

"Leave her alone, Laura." Carleigh's dad shook my hand. "Congratulations, son."

"Thank you, Mr. and Mrs. Chastain. This is so thoughtful." I gestured to the guests who mingled inside the house and outside on the patio under a white tent.

"We were happy to do it, and Spencer, please call us Jim and Laura. It's not every day your little girl gets married," Laura said. "I'm sorry your parents couldn't make it on such short notice, but since we still have most of the wedding budget, we'll throw the most amazing baby shower, and I'll be sure to give them plenty of notice. You might be able to get married in under two weeks, but babies generally take a minimum of forty."

"Mom, again with the babies."

"Honey, you may not want to admit it, but biology is biology, and your time is now."

"Okay, I'm going to introduce Spencer to a few people." Thankfully, Carleigh looped her arm through mine and guided us away from the unfiltered wannabe-grandma. "Sorry about my mom. Brad mentioned that she's been dropping hints about grandchildren, but I didn't expect her to be so blatant."

"It's okay. It's not like she's far off from our plans." We'd agreed before we left for Fiji that we wanted to start a family right away. I squeezed her hand. "But I'm not ready to discuss our sex life with your mom. Actually, I won't ever be."

"Me either." She grimaced.

As we visited with friends and extended family, Wyatt joined us. "I'm glad everything worked out for y'all." He wore the servers' uniform of a white button-down shirt and black pants. "I'd have come over earlier, but I've been busy helping Chef in the kitchen."

"No worries," Carleigh said.

"I owe you big, man. If you're ever in the DC area, I'll buy you dinner. Not that it would be enough for helping us find our way back together." I shook Wyatt's hand.

"I'll take you up on the dinner because DC has a great food scene, but I'm not taking the credit for what God meant to be." Wyatt clapped me on the shoulder. "Congratulations, y'all. I better get to the kitchen." He hurried away.

"I can't believe you had a problem with that guy. He seems all right." I slipped my arm around Carleigh's waist, holding her close. Desire buzzed in my veins. How I'd been able to make my body okay with only mere hugs and dance holds for so many years still amazed me. I could not get enough of her nestled in my arms. Touching this woman and knowing she was mine would never get old.

"That's because he isn't challenging everything about you and forcing you to see how messed up you are. Not that he was wrong, but it still didn't feel great," Carleigh responded, still unaware of how her nearness affected me.

"Time for your first dance." Willa escorted us to a small area in front of the DJ. He played Kokomo by the Beach Boys, and we laughed as we danced. Then he played My Girl, and Carleigh danced with her dad.

Zoe presented a two-tiered wedding cake. "Willa had the pastry chef who is making our cakes create this one for you."

We shared the first bites carefully because Carleigh and I both hated when brides or grooms shoved cake in the other's face. When Jim and Lawson gave toasts, Carleigh took the tiniest sip of champagne which made my pulse race. What if she was already pregnant?

Zoe arched a curious brow, but thankfully, chose discretion, instead focusing on the bouquet toss. She directed Carleigh to a spot and corralled all the single women and a couple of girls, who I think were Zoe's nieces, to the center of the patio.

Before Carleigh turned around, she faced the group, probably pondering her bouquet toss history. Then she said, "Ladies. And guys, for that matter. Over the last few months, I've learned how important it is to slow down and make sure your priorities are in the right order, especially with your faith. While it might have looked like I had it all, I was hurrying so quickly through life, accumulating accomplishments, that I was missing what was important: my faith, the love of my best friend, and the grace that comes in family relationships. I believed if I caught the bouquet, I'd be poised to win all the pieces for an abundant life, but I nearly lost everything important. I just want to say thank you to my husband, Spencer, for calling me out and then still loving me when I showed him who I really was." She lifted her glass to me, and I air-tapped hers as my emotions threatened to result in tears. As they pooled at the corners of my eyes, Carleigh continued.

"I also want to thank my family for loving and supporting me, even when I ghosted you with an amazing fortitude. And I want to thank God for blessing me with this life that I don't deserve. Sorry if that was a little heavy. I'm just so grateful that I learned what having it all truly means. Okay, now, I hope that one of you still wants to catch this bouquet. The one I caught did change my life for the better, so I hope it might for you, too." She turned around and tossed the flowers over her head.

But not one woman in the group caught it. Instead it landed on the platter of sliders that a woman in a chef's uniform was carrying from the kitchen. Laughing, she lifted it in the air and strode on to the buffet tables.

My beautiful wife crossed the room, took my hands, and gazed into my eyes. "I feel like we're living in a miracle. I'm glad that I learned to appreciate these moments being surrounded by the people I love and who love me. We truly are blessed beyond measure."

And while I might have scripted a much faster timeline for our relationship, my wife was right. We might not have it all by the world's standards, but we had all that mattered.

S ome days just start out right—sunshine and a light jacket kind of days. You almost feel like singing with the blue birds. That's how my morning began, but friends, that's not how it ended.

Pleasantly unaware of what was to come, I breathed in the fresh morning air as I strolled down the tree-lined street on a perfect spring day. But as I rounded the corner, the flashing lights of an ambulance ended my serenity.

I picked up my pace. As paramedics rolled a gurney out of my office building with my very pregnant boss on board, my bliss evaporated like the dew on the azalea petals.

When Kara caught sight of me, she yanked off her oxygen mask and held up her hand. "Stop!"

Not surprisingly, they halted. Not too many people ignored Kara Monroe's directives. It's why she was such a great event planner. She knew what she wanted and she made it happen. I loved working for her and hoped to be as successful, but this wasn't how I'd expected to be promoted.

"Willa." She waved me over. "Thank goodness you're early."

Even as a self-proclaimed perfectionist, I don't believe in arriving right on time. I'd decided years ago that on time meant precisely eight minutes early which is exactly what time it would've been if I'd continued walking at my earlier pace. Instead, I was likely ten minutes early.

Without checking my watch, I rushed to Kara's side. "What happened? Is it the twins?"

"I'm fine. The babies are fine."

"Should I call Jamey?"

"He's the one who called the ambulance. He was on his way to Atlanta when I called and told him I was cramping a little. He totally overreacted. I told him I could wait for him to get here or take a rideshare, but he insisted on calling an ambulance. He's meeting me at the hospital."

Given the serious looks on the paramedics' faces and the IV attached to her arm, it seemed unlikely that everything was fine or that her adoring husband had overreacted, but I didn't want to upset her further, so I remained silent. In my experience, I'd found if I remained calm, people tended to trust my plans.

"This is all"—Kara twirled her hand in the air—"just a precaution, but it does mean that you'll have to handle the meeting at Magnolia Bluff on your own. I have complete faith in you, and I'll only be a phone call away. I'm sure I'll be cleared and back on my feet by tomorrow. Tell the clients not to worry, and take the van. The keys are on the hook."

"Of course. I've got everything under control. Just take care of yourself and the babies."

Gasping, Kara pressed a hand to her belly as her face contorted.

One of the paramedics replaced the oxygen mask over her mouth and nose. "We need to go," he whispered. "Excuse us."

I stepped aside, but Kara grabbed my arm with one hand while she slid the mask back down with the other. "Willa, this is a high-profile client, and this wedding could lead to lots of business."

As the paramedics moved her to the ambulance, I strode beside her, nodding with what I meant to be a reassuring smile even as I ground my molars. I knew well the importance of the event. But it didn't seem like the best time to remind my boss that it'd been an unexpected tip from *my* vagabond brother that had led to us being hired by the groom. Not only would the wedding help the firm, but I'd gain invaluable experience working for a high-profile client. Every new event helped me grow my portfolio and moved me closer to running my own business.

Kara raised her brows, fixing her gaze on me. "Don't forget the samples for the linens and the portfolio of pastry chefs for the cakes. We are on a tight turnaround, especially with the photographer." As the paramedics lifted the gurney, she released her grip on me, but continued with her instructions. "There're only a couple left with openings. They need to decide today who they want us to book."

"Got it. I'll call with an update as soon as I get back to the office." I clasped my hands just as the paramedics prepared Kara for transport.

Magnolia Bluff was nearly an hour away from our offices in Savannah, so the plan had been for Kara and me to drive together. This would be our first meeting with the groom and his fiancée. The bride had been reluctant been reluctant to hire a wedding coordinator, so in addition to choosing a photographer, a pastry chef, and a million other details, I needed to reassure her that I would make her day perfect.

"Willa, call me before you leave Magnolia Bluff in case you forget something," Kara shouted from the ambulance.

"Yes ma'am." I touched my fingers to the edge of my tight smile and stepped onto the sidewalk out of her line of sight. While I understood that she was in the middle of what must have been a more serious medical situation than she wanted to admit, and while I'm sure she didn't mean to imply that I was incompetent and irresponsible, her words still stung. However, one of my strongest qualities was holding my tongue while pressing my lips into a pleasant smile. Besides actions spoke louder than words, and I would prove my abilities to our clients and to Kara.

To read the rest of the story, join Leslie's newsletter. This novella will be offered exclusively to newsletter members in July, 2026. Be sure to subscribe on my website. https://lesliedevooght.com/contact/

Discussion Questions

1. Carleigh is best friends with two men. Do you believe men and women can be friends without romance? Why or why not?

2. How did Carleigh's experiences in high school shape who she became as an adult. What about you?

3. How does Carleigh feel about people's ability to change? How does that affect her own transformation?

4. In what ways did Carleigh and Brad's parents contribute to their relationship issues? How do you interact with your own siblings?

5. Carleigh's attitude toward the bridal bouquet toss evolves. What do you think about the tradition?

6. The story takes place in Washington DC and Magnolia Bluff. Which place would you rather live and why?

7. Spencer and Carleigh both learn to live more intentionally. Have you ever considered how your lifestyle is affecting your

emotional and spiritual health? What did you discover?

8. Spencer and Carleigh love to surprise each other. How do you feel about surprises? What's the best surprise you've either planned or received?

9. Did you know Kokomo Island is a real place? Where's your dream destination?

10. Romans 12:2 says "Do not be conformed to this age, but be transformed by the renewing of your mind, so that you may discern what is the good, pleasing, and perfect will of God." How did the themes in this verse play out in the story and in your own life?

Acknowledgments

Wow, publishing four books in twelve months didn't happen without a lot of help. Thank you to my writing buddies for brainstorming, encouragement, and a lot of honest critiques. Hopefully, y'all all like Carleigh now or at least don't hate her. Big thanks to Laura Debow, Jordan Millsaps, Kristi Ann Hunter, and Lindsey Brackett for reading this story early.

Thank you to my editor and friend Laurie Sibley. You make my writing sparkle.

As I'm navigating marketing books, I've made some great new friends who are helping me get my stories in front of a much larger audience. Thank you to my launch team members and ARC readers. Your posts and reviews mean so much to me.

Y'all, I have had the best time meeting with readers this year. Thank you to all the people who have invited me to their groups to share my stories and my faith.

A super special thank you to my AXO pledge sister, Amanda Abraham, who polled her younger co-workers about residential life in the DC area. Old friends are the best friends!!

Thank you to my children who keep me relevant and make fantastic reels that get so many views, and big thanks to my parents, who are always sharing my books and cheering me on. Also, thank you to Libby for proofreading while on your choir tour. At least, I didn't ask you to help me write a cover letter.

Without my generous and thoughtful husband, there would be no books. Thank you Carlton for continuing to support me and reminding me that my work is a ministry.

Finally, thank you Jesus for always being near and teaching me new lessons in life, like how to slow down and realize how good God is. I feel so blessed to know that even the painful parts of my life can be used for His good, especially when it comes to my writing.

About the Author

Award-winning and Publisher's Weekly Bestselling author Leslie Kirby DeVooght writes women's fiction with faith, love, laughter, and a lot of Southern charm. Her stories are inspired by romcoms, coastal Georgia, and fried okra! When Leslie isn't writing, she's cheering on her three children and enjoying date nights with her husband.

In addition to writing her own stories, Leslie co-owns *Spark Flash Fiction*, an online magazine that publishes romance collections of short, short stories. Check out Leslie's flash fiction stories on her website h ttps://lesliedevooght.com/contact/and join her newsletter for updates, giveaways, and early release opportunities. Keep in touch on Instagram and Facebook @lesliedevooght.

Stealing Magnolias
Book 1 - Magnolia Bluff

When Wren Frazier heads south to honor her grandmother's final wish, she finds five unexpected challenges, one grumpy (but handsome) neighbor, and maybe—herself.

Although an artist, Wren packed away her brushes and paints and sought a practical career as an interior designer in Chicago. She's always put herself last, happy to please everyone around her. But with a team of dedicated co-workers and a small town of quirky characters supporting her, she's forced to give herself a little attention. As her artistic heart starts to awaken, Wren finds herself rediscovering the joy of creation and living authentically.

But while she's exploring the enchanting Georgia Low Country, creating beautiful paintings, and taking a chance on love, she uncovers a secret that shakes the foundation of her newfound happiness. With the revelation threatening to ruin the delicate balance Wren has only begun to realize, will she give up her fairytale and return to her reality?